SHAME *the* STARS

SHAME *the* STARS

Guadalupe García McCall

Tu Books
An imprint of Lee & Low Books, Inc.
New York

This is a work of fiction. Names, characters, places, and incidents are either the product of the author's imagination or are used fictitiously, and any resemblance to actual persons, living or dead, business establishments, events, or locales is entirely coincidental.

TU BOOKS, an imprint of LEE & LOW BOOKS Inc.,
95 Madison Avenue, New York, NY 10016
leeandlow.com

Manufactured in the United States of America by Worzalla Publishing, September 2016

Book design by Neil Swaab
Book production by The Kids at Our House
The text is set in Espinosa Nova
10 9 8 7 6 5 4 3 2 1
First Edition

Cataloging-in-Publication Data is on file with the Library of Congress

Para mi padre,
el señor Onésimo García,
un hombre de honor, integridad, y mucho valor!
¡Con todo mi corazón!
Lupita

CAST OF CHARACTERS

JOAQUÍN DEL TORO—*eighteen-year-old son of Don Acevedo and Doña Jovita del Toro*

DOÑA JOVITA DEL TORO—*Joaquín's mother*

DON ACEVEDO DEL TORO—*Joaquín's father and owner of Las Moras*

TOMÁS DEL TORO—*Joaquín's brother and priest of Capilla del Sagrado Corazón*

DULCEÑA VILLA—*eighteen-year-old daughter of Don Rodrigo and Doña Serafina Villa*

DOÑA SERAFINA ESTRADA DE VILLA—*mother of Dulceña*

DON RODRIGO VILLA—*Dulceña's father and printer/publisher of* El Sureño

MATEO AND FITO TORRES—*fraternal twin sons of Manuel and Doña Luz Torres*

DOÑA LUZ TORRES—*housekeeper at Las Moras*

MANUEL TORRES—*foreman at Las Moras*

CONCHITA OLIVARES—*Mateo's girlfriend, waitress at Donna's Kitchen*

CAPTAIN ELLIOT MUNRO—*leader of the Texas Rangers in Morado County*

SHERIFF BENJAMIN NOLAN—*sheriff of Monteseco*

MIGUEL CACERES—*deputy sheriff, second in command to Sheriff Nolan*

CARLOS—*tejano rebel leader*

POLLO AND CHAVITO—*tejano rebels*

MADAME JOSETTE—*Dulceña's tutor*

SOFIA AND LAURA—*young maids at Las Moras*

GERARDO GUTIERREZ—*young ranch hand, tejano rebel*

FLORA GUTIERREZ—*Gerardo's mother*

APOLONIA MORALES—*Gerardo's girlfriend*

NACHO—*county-jail clerk*

PAT THOMPSON—*justice of the peace*

SETTINGS

LAS MORAS—*home of the del Toro family*

MONTESECO—*fictional town nearest Las Moras in fictitious Morado County*

ARROYO MORADO—*a creek that separates Las Moras from town*

CAPILLA DEL SAGRADO CORAZÓN—*the town parish in Monteseco*

SHAME *the* STARS

EXCERPT FROM *EL SUREÑO*,
EASTER SUNDAY, MARCH 23, 1913

TEJANO

These are dangerous
times in South Texas,
times of trouble,
times of loss.

Tejano,
Texas Mexican,
laggard field hand, still
your heartbeat, stay
your station, till the earth,
don't you dare look up.

Never mind the injustice.
Your father's land is not your
own anymore. It has been sold,
passed hands, bought and paid
for. It's history. It's gone.

Close your ears,
mind your tongue,
let the Rangers do their job.

Tejano,
suppliant borderman,
vagrant son of Tenochtitlán,
don't you see? Don't you know?
Why can't you understand?

To seed, to plow,
to weed, to tow, to toil
for the Anglo immigrants,
the new Texan, the new boss,
that is now your lot in life.

Close your ears,
mind your tongue,
let the Rangers do their job.

Tejano,
rustic campesino,
sluggish farm worker,
quell your subversive spirit,
quiet your dissident heart,
quit your questions.

Suppress your rage
and silence your thoughts.
Don't let your foolish
mestizo pride defeat you,
the conquistador in you beat you,
the Nahua eat you.

Close your ears,
mind your tongue,
let the Rangers do their job.

Tejano,
peon, ranch hand, Kineño,
let the white man reap and sow.
Let the King nation grow.
Let him disseminate, propagate.
He is keen. He is keeper.
He is kind.

Don't listen to the roar of
your ancestral blood.
To quake, to quiver,
to shake, to shiver, to watch
your rebellious brothers hang,
swing from tall, majestic trees,
sway against the breeze,
that is now your lot in life.

Close your ears,
mind your tongue,
and let the Rangers do their job.

Be safe. Be smart.
Be innocuous.
That is the best
way to shame the stars!

—*Anonymous*

Prologue

The sun was still warm and bright that Easter Sunday afternoon. It bounced off the water in the cement fountain, gleamed off every new blade of grass, and blinded us as Dulceña and I chased each other around the courtyard behind the main house at Las Moras.

My two best friends, Mateo and Fito, the fraternal twin sons of our housekeeper, Doña Luz, and our foreman, Manuel Torres, were too busy to join us. While their mother and father helped Mamá keep the younger children engaged in the day's activities, the twins were huddled together on a nearby bench.

The twins were counting the pennies, nickels, and dimes they had collected after I made seventy-three children very happy by swinging with all my might and busting open the giant piñata dangling from a tall oak tree in our courtyard that morning. The younger kids, sons and daughters of the field workers and ranch hands who resided at Las Moras, had all thrown themselves to the ground and grappled for the pieces of candy. The rest of us, being older and wiser, knew there was money in the tiny floral satchels my mother had stuffed in the piñata.

While we all entertained ourselves in our own different ways, Mamá sat on a nearby bench under a jacaranda tree beside Dulceña's mother, Doña Serafina Estrada de Villa, watching over us. The day's revelry had, for the most part, wound down, and the evening star was growing brighter and brighter on the dusky horizon behind us.

"Gotcha!" I said, cracking a cascarón over Dulceña's head and rubbing it against her scalp to release all the confetti inside. Then, because Dulceña shook her head vigorously and recovered quicker than I'd expected, I started running. Dulceña held her white lace skirt above her shins as she chased after me, up the garden path toward the main house.

She almost caught up to me, but I swooped around the birdbath, cutting across the rosebushes and rounding back toward the house like a jackrabbit. I was about to bound up the porch steps when I overheard Dulceña's father laughing.

Papá was with him. They were sitting in their usual chairs at the table on our back porch, drinking their favorite Madero brandy and smoking cigars. I slowed down to take the stairs one step at a time because Papá didn't approve of me running around like a child anymore. I was, after all, sixteen years old, a man in my father's eyes.

"Ah, here they come. Where's your mother, Joaquín?" Papá asked.

"She's on her way," I said, peeking around the porch and

seeing that Dulceña had stopped to wait for our mothers.

I stood by the stairs, waiting for the women while my father and Don Rodrigo continued their conversation. The two men on the porch couldn't have been more different. My father, Don Acevedo del Toro, was a giant of a man, light-haired and fair-skinned like an Anglo, but he was all mejicano—tejano to the core. In contrast, Don Rodrigo, Dulceña's father, was small, dark, and so wiry you'd think he was a compressed metal coil, wound up and ready to spring into action.

Dulceña came up the steps looking less than dignified with her confetti-ratted hair and her stained white satin dress. It was obvious she'd been playing in the cobbled courtyard all morning, but she smiled demurely and walked slowly up the stairs, because being the same age as me meant she too had to act like a grown-up, a refined lady, befitting her station as the printer's daughter. Let's just say her father would not have approved of all the running around she'd been doing that morning.

"Hola, Papi," she said, going over to Don Rodrigo and leaning in to kiss him on the cheek.

"¡M'ija! You look like you've had a bit too much fun today," he said, tugging on a strand of Dulceña's long, curly black hair. "Did those niños get the better of you?"

"Yes, you know how children are," Dulceña said, lifting her eyebrows as she made eye contact with me. Smiling, she picked several pieces of confetti off her ruffled sleeve and tossed them over the railing, where the wind caught and swept them away.

I pulled out a chair for Dulceña next to her father. When our mothers came onto the porch, I pulled out chairs for them too, seating them next to each other between their husbands. My father began reading the special Easter edition of *El Sureño*, the newspaper Don Rodrigo's family had been printing in Monteseco for more than twenty-five years.

My heart raced when I saw that Papá had just started looking at the front page. He was reading the main story at his leisure, as if he didn't have anything better to do, which was not true because my father always had something better to do. As heir and sole proprietor of Las Moras, six hundred acres of fertile farmland owned by our family since 1775, before Tejas became Texas, Papá was always busy.

I waited quietly, wondering how long it would take him to get to the poem. Because my father was a reserved man who preferred we stay away from politics and public life, I wondered what he would say about a poem with such charged overtones, disparaging the Texas Rangers and everything they stood for.

I didn't have to wait long. My father perused a few more pages and then stopped to read the editorial section, which is where Don Rodrigo had managed to squeeze in the poem, "Tejano."

"Well, what do you think?" Dulceña's father asked when he saw my father read the poem with interest. "It's a nice little verse, don't you think? It came in the mail two weeks ago, but I saved it for today. I wanted it to get into as many hands as possible, and I knew today's edition would sell well. Holiday editions are always sellouts."

"Couldn't you have found something better? If you had to publish poetry at all—certainly you had many more suitable pieces to choose from, especially for the Easter Sunday edition. You should have asked Tomás to submit one of his sermons. He might have written something more appropriate for this edition."

"What do you mean, appropriate?" Don Rodrigo's left eye twitched as he looked directly at my father.

"I mean something less . . . incendiary," Papá answered. My heart sank at the sight of his eyebrows almost touching as he frowned distastefully at the poem.

A dull hotness washed over my face. I picked up the pitcher and a tall glass from the tray sitting in the center of the table and poured myself some lemonade. The tartness made my tongue tingle and my eyes water, but I drank it down without adding more sugar to it. I needed something cold to offset the embarrassing flush taking me over.

"Incendiary!" Don Rodrigo repeated, only, the word coming out of his lips sounded loaded, like a barrel full of gunpowder.

"Yes," Papá said. "This makes you look like an agitator, trying to stir something up between the people of Morado County and the Rangers, as if there isn't enough racial tension between us already. It's the wrong tone for a family-run paper. Don't you think?"

Mamá picked up the paper then. A tiny ghost of a smile

played with the corners of her mouth as she read it over and said, "It's not so bad, Acevedo. Most people in Monteseco know what's going on. They see how tejanos are being treated in this country. This isn't going to offend anyone. At least, I don't think so."

From her spot, standing just within the frame of the back door, our housekeeper, Doña Luz, cleared her throat and asked, "Shall I bring out the capirotada, Doña?"

"Oh, yes, I almost forgot about it. I made my special bread pudding this morning." Mamá pushed back her chair and got up.

"Wait. Let me help you with it," Dulceña's mother said, getting up herself. "Come on, Dulceña. Come help us."

I picked up the paper and pretended to read it. "I think Mamá is right," I said as the women went into the house. "I don't think the poem is meant as an affront to anyone in particular. It's more of a statement about the troubles tejanos are experiencing in this country."

"Tell that to Munro," Papá said, referring to Captain Elliot Munro, the man in charge of the Texas Rangers in our area. He was responsible for upholding the law in Morado County, even more feared than the local authority, Sheriff Benjamin Nolan, in Monteseco. "Now, there's an explanation I wouldn't want to have to give."

Don Rodrigo smirked at my father. "Really? I thought you were friends with him, compadre."

"Munro respects me and my family. He and his men have always taken care of us out here." My father took the newspaper back from me and looked over the poem again. "But I don't know that he would take kindly to what's being implied by this scathing little piece. It's just too—"

"Sardonic?" Don Rodrigo gritted his teeth. "Filled with irony and truth?"

"It's seditious!" Papá said, punctuating the last word by folding the paper and tossing it to the side in Don Rodrigo's direction.

I stared at my poem lying on the porch floor and regretted sending it in.

"It's candid," Dulceña's father said. "That's why I printed it, Acevedo."

Papá smoothed out his mustache. "I wasn't going to say it, but it concerns me, Rodrigo," my father admitted. "The direction you've been taking with *El Sureño* lately. That long article about the Mexican Revolution, the outrageous editorials glorifying insurrection, and now this nonsense about tejanos and injustices and Texas Rangers. Well . . . it's all very dangerous."

"I'm a journalist, Acevedo." Don Rodrigo took the paper and laid it in front of Papá, tapping it directly over my poem. "These things need to be said. They need to be read and talked about, discussed by every member of our community. Your son Tomás certainly understands that. He tends to our people. He sees their struggles, listens to their afflictions."

"Yes, but Tomás doesn't concern himself with politics." My father was suddenly furious. "My son is a good shepherd. He has to listen to these people, but like the rest of us, he knows better than to question the law, especially the Texas Rangers. That's not his job. To listen to confession, *that's* his job. That's all he does, listen. But he knows to keep his mouth shut."

Don Rodrigo glared at Papá. "Then whose job is it to start these conversations, if not yours and mine, Acevedo? As leaders of this community, as landowners and businessmen, we owe it to our friends and neighbors to speak out against such prejudices!"

"He's right," I said from my seat between them. "It's important to print things like this, Papá. To get the people thinking and reacting. It's the only way to wake them up, to make them stand up for their rights, to call attention to their situation."

"You stay out of this, Joaquín," Papá said, pointing a finger in my direction. "This doesn't concern you."

"But it does concern me." I sat forward and planted my forearms firmly on the table. "As an American citizen, as a tejano. It concerns me to watch our people be mistreated and robbed, to have their spirits trampled on."

Ignoring me, Papá got up and paced the length of the porch. Then, coming back to the table, he said, "Do you see what this does? It makes trouble, Rodrigo. Joaquín would never talk to me like this if he hadn't been reading this nonsense in your paper."

"This isn't nonsense," Don Rodrigo said. "This is our plight. Our gente are suffering, and it's our job to help them!"

"The only thing you're going to accomplish by printing these riotous stories is to get yourself killed, Rodrigo," my father warned. "And then, what's your family going to do without you? Go live in Colonia Calaveras like the rest of those poor souls whose husbands cared more about politics than their own families? Thanks to men like you, selfish men chasing rabbits into dark holes, those destitute women and children have no one to protect them, no one to provide for them. Is that what you want? To expose my comadre and goddaughter to that kind of existence?"

"My wife and daughter support me." Don Rodrigo's lips trembled almost as much as his words. "They are fully aware of the situation, and believe me, they are just as concerned as I am about our people."

"Do me a favor," Papá said, leaning over the table and speaking in a low, ominous tone. "Don't bring this into my house. I can't tell you what to believe or even what to print. If you want to endanger your family, that is very much your business. But as long as you keep printing that garbage, keep it off my porch and out of my sight."

"What is going on here? What's all the yelling about?" Mamá asked as she came out of the house holding the casserole dish of capirotada in front of her. Doña Serafina and Dulceña were flanking Mamá. Silently, the women set down dishes and flatware on the table as Mamá put down the dessert and placed the matching yellow potholders beside the steaming hot dish of capirotada. The sweet, spicy scent emanating from the bread pudding mingled with the bitterness in my heart, causing my stomach to twist and churn as I looked into my father's displeased face.

"I'm sure it's nothing, comadre," Doña Serafina whispered. She waved for Mamá to sit next to her. "You know how these men get when they've had too much whiskey. They think they can solve the problems of the world in one afternoon."

"It's brandy." Papá picked up his glass and swirled the amber liquid around before bringing it to his lips and drinking the last of it down. Then, as if disgusted by the taste of it, he went back to pacing, his boots scuffing the wooden planks resentfully. "And it's not nothing. I meant what I said, Rodrigo. If we are to remain friends, if we are to ever sit at my dinner table together again, I don't want to see another one of your incendiary rags in my home."

"Acevedo! Is that any way to speak to our guests?"

Mamá's shock propelled me into action as she stood up at the table. "I'm sorry, Papá," I said. "But you're not being very fair to Don Rodrigo."

Papá pointed at me with his free hand. "Joaquín, I've heard all I need to hear from you today."

"No, you haven't." Then it all came rushing out, everything I hadn't meant to tell him. "This is all my fault, Papá. You're mad about that poem, but the fact is I wrote it. It's the way I feel. It's what I've seen. What I want others to see. Don Rodrigo didn't know anything about it. I mailed it without a return address to the print shop. I'm sorry if it offends you, and I'm sorry it's made you so angry you feel like banning the newspaper it's printed in."

"You did *what?*" My father's voice boomed. His massive frame loomed over the table, over me. His face turned bright red, and he picked up the paper one more time, as if he needed to read it again to believe it.

"¡Ay, Joaquín!" My mother, who was standing beside Papá, took the paper away from him and reread it. "What were you thinking?" Mamá finally asked, putting her right hand over her throat.

"I'm sorry, compadre, if I had known—" Don Rodrigo began, but my father was so enraged that he didn't let him continue.

"What?" Papá asked, gritting his teeth. "What would you have done? Thrown it out? Brought it to me? Do us both a favor, Rodrigo—get out of my sight. Go home. Get off my porch and get off my land!"

"Acevedo!" Mamá's voice trembled with unshed tears. Then, taking Doña Serafina's hand in hers, Mamá continued, "I'm so sorry. I don't know what's gotten into him. Please don't go. I'm sure we can work this out."

"Of course! It's just a misunderstanding." Doña Serafina patted my mother's hands.

Don Rodrigo got up to leave. "I know you're upset right now, Acevedo. But in time, perhaps you'll see."

"In time, you'll understand what *you've* done here." Papá slammed his fist against the table, startling Dulceña and her mother. "If this gets out—If Munro gets wind of it . . ."

"Munro would never hurt you. Your blond hair and green eyes guarantee you that much!" Then, because my father's face turned even redder, Don Rodrigo apologized. "I'm sorry, Acevedo. That's a reflection of him, not you. Listen. As far as my family and I are concerned, this conversation never happened." Don Rodrigo put his hand to his heart. "On my word of honor, neither I nor anyone else in my family will ever repeat the details of it."

"Go home, Rodrigo," my father repeated. "Stay away from Las Moras and take your damned paper with you!"

Excerpt from a handbill for the "Plan de San Diego," 1915

A cry of indignation and rage has sprung up from the very depths of our souls at the sight of the crimes and assaults committed on a daily basis against the defenseless women, old people, and children of our race by the bandits and contemptible Texas Rangers who patrol the banks of the Rio Grande . . . The moment has arrived. It is necessary that . . . we resort to our weapons and the cry of "Long live the Independence of the states of Texas, New Mexico, California, Arizona, and parts of the states of Mississippi and Oklahoma, which from today forward will be called the 'Republic of Texas.'" Join our comrades in arms who are already waging the battle, proving their valor and patriotism.

¡Viva la Independencia!

Tierra y Libertad

First Chief of Operations
Luis de la Rosa

Second Chief of the General Staff
Aniceto Pizaña

Chapter 1

The letter came in the same manner as all the other letters, unexpectedly and without a clue as to the identity of its deliverer. It just simply appeared, slipped under the door while I was getting ready for the day. It was going to be a grueling one, seeing as we were getting the herd ready for the annual cattle drive up to Fort Worth.

While the rest of the men gathered equipment, the wranglers picked the best horses for the remuda, making sure they were healthy and strong enough for the long cattle drive ahead. Doña Luz put together provisions, while Papá, Manuel, and I worked with the cattle and Trueno, the stout steer Papá had chosen to lead the herd. I named him Trueno because of the perfectly shaped lightning-bolt mark on his forehead. So far, he was proving to be a good pick for lead steer. The herd was willing to follow him as they grazed in the morning and were driven down the trail throughout the day, to get them used to the grazing and driving system.

After the cattle drive, Papá would concentrate on digging

a well and setting up an irrigation system in the easternmost part of the property because he was going to expand and plant a hundred more acres of sugarcane next year. But I wouldn't be at Las Moras for that. Like Tomás before me, I was expected to go off to school in the fall. For me that meant MAC, or Michigan Agricultural College, to be precise. The letter of acceptance had arrived in late April, just before graduation, and my parents couldn't have been happier. In their opinion, MAC was the best place I could go because it would provide the knowledge and skills necessary for me to succeed as the future head of Las Moras.

I wished I shared their enthusiasm. But I truly believed they were sending me there to keep me as far away from Dulceña as possible because, whatever else had happened in the last two years, our families had never managed to mend their relationship. If anything, they'd become even more estranged. My parents made it very clear they did not condone my attachment to Dulceña, so they weren't going to make it easy for me to see her after I left Las Moras. I could have gone to Austin, to the University of Texas, like Tomás, but suddenly that wasn't good enough.

"But what's wrong with going to school in Austin?" I had asked when Papá first refused the idea of my going there.

"UT is a decent college, a fine college, even," Papá said, shaking his head and moving papers around on his desk. "But our money would be better spent making sure you have the best agricultural training in the country, and MAC has that. So as far as I'm concerned, you're going to Michigan. It's in your best interest. It's in the best interest of Las Moras, and that's what matters."

He wouldn't listen to me, but if you asked me, Austin was just a bit too close to San Antonio and Our Lady of the Lake College, which is where Dulceña would be enrolling in the fall. But I wasn't about to argue with my father. He could refuse to pay for me to go anywhere else but MAC, but that didn't mean he could make me stop loving Dulceña.

Regardless of it all, to be honest, I just couldn't see myself going off to college anymore, not when it meant leaving my family and the girl I loved behind at such a tumultuous time. What if Las Moras was raided by bandits? What if someone got hurt? Who would get word to me if there was an emergency? Because no matter how fast I could ride, even in an automobile, it would still take days to get back home.

No. It was obvious to me. I couldn't leave just yet. Not until the politics in our world changed. The Plan de San Diego, drafted by revolutionaries in Mexico and brought in by Basilio Ramos through Texas, was discovered by US authorities in January. The manifesto called for a rebellion in Texas, and a rebellion was what US lawmen were getting. Across the southern United States, from California all the way to the Gulf of Mexico, but especially in South Texas, tejanos were raising arms, fighting for their rights. While Mexican bandits caught up in their own civil war were crossing over to the United States, pillaging small Texas towns and blowing up railroads, tejanos dealt with wrongful accusations, unlawful raids, and the hanging of relatives suspected of working with

Mexican revolutionaries. This turbulent time had created the tejano rebel, a new breed of outlaw, a Texas Mexican fighting to keep his land and his dignity in the place he had called home long before it became part of the United States. Until Mexican revolutionaries stopped trampling on American soil and Rangers stopped accosting and killing innocent tejanos, my family wasn't safe and I couldn't leave.

Papá would probably disagree with me, but I couldn't ignore it. It was a conversation we would need to have very soon, before he and Mamá packed my bags and tried shipping me off to college.

With so much on my mind, it was taking longer and longer to get ready in the mornings. When I heard someone stop outside my door that day, I turned and saw the pink envelope sliding quietly across the wooden floor, stopping five feet short of my bed, where I sat pulling on my work boots.

I launched into action, grabbing the letter off the floor as I rushed to the door. But when I peeked outside, there was no one in the hallway.

Standing on the threshold, I felt the weight of the envelope in my palm and traced the single letter on its front with my index finger. The *J* was handwritten in an elaborate script. There was no mistaking it. It was from her.

"Joaquín?" my father called. I jerked, hiding the letter behind my back as he rounded the corner. He caught me standing there half in and half out of my room with only one boot on. He glanced down at my feet and frowned. "Are you almost ready?"

I shook my head, sliding the letter into the deep side pocket of my work pants. "Not just yet."

"Well, come on, Son. We don't have all day."

"I know," I said. "Just give me a second. I'll be down in a minute."

Papá grumbled to himself, like he didn't know what to do with me anymore, and I sighed, closing the door behind me. In the privacy of my room, I fought the urge to tear the envelope open, deciding to read what was surely a long letter when I got back for almuerzo, the second meal of the day, which was usually followed by a short afternoon nap. I would certainly have time to read it carefully then.

The fact was I hadn't seen much of Dulceña since March, when her parents pulled her out of school to finish her education at home under the instruction of a pretentious Parisian tutor, Madame Josette, who had very high standards and only tutored the "best-behaved children"—meaning the wealthiest families in town.

However, Dulceña had not been pulled out of school for the privilege of being tutored by a certain Madame Josette. No, the truth was Don Rodrigo was afraid. With tejano rebels attacking ranches and small businesses all over South Texas, in retaliation for the part Anglo immigrants played in the matanza—advocating, sometimes even demanding the "evaporation" of numerous tejanos—the Texas Rangers practiced their own brand of vigilantism. They deputized anyone willing to fight on their side and summarily killed

Mexicans and tejanos alike without bothering to bring them in to be tried in court for their crimes.

Attempting to shed light on the plight of innocent tejanos who had fallen victim to the Rangers, Don Rodrigo's reporting in *El Sureño* had changed the way he was perceived by the Anglo citizens of Monteseco. The anonymous threats he received almost daily in the mail, coupled with random acts of vandalism to his print shop, made him withdraw Dulceña from school to have her educated at home. I thought for sure Dulceña would object to this turn of events, as I was strongly against it myself. But she wasn't going to fight it.

"I know my father's afraid for me, but it's not fair, keeping me holed up in the house," she had admitted when I brought it up on that last day before she stopped going to school. We had been standing side by side behind the schoolhouse with a handful of classmates milling around, courting each other, while our teachers kept an eye on us from afar as they supervised their younger charges playing on the open field. "My time would be better spent helping my father in the print shop. I'd rather be interviewing victims and writing editorials than sitting around with the women all day waiting for him to come home to let us know what is happening."

"Have you told him how you feel?" I asked.

Dulceña nodded and lowered her voice. "I tried talking to him about it, but he's not having any of it. He says it's better for me to stay home with my mother and Madame Josette—who's a very sweet person by the way—but she and my mother just don't understand what I'm going through. I have so much to offer the world, both as a woman and as a reporter. Things are changing in this country, and our role as women has to change with it if we're to keep up with the times. I think Madame Josette understands, but she doesn't want to anger my parents, so she just nods and agrees with everything they say."

"I wish I could do something," I whispered, taking her hand and squeezing it.

She leaned in and rested her head on my shoulder the way she used to when we were kids and our families were still friends. "It's okay," she whispered. "I'll be fine."

I continued to hold her hand longer than appropriate, but I couldn't help it. "I'm going to miss you," I said. This felt like good-bye.

"Oh, we'll still see each other. I'm sure of it." She smiled up at me even as her eyes welled with tears. "Where there's a will—"

"I'll write to you," I promised.

Dulceña nodded, her dark eyelashes fanning her cheeks as she lowered her gaze and stirred the dirt with the toe of her blue satin shoe. She squeezed my hands between hers. "Private letters?" she teased. "Secret messages? Clandestine notes?"

"Something like that, yeah." I rubbed the tips of her fingers gently.

"And will you ask me to sneak out at night and rendezvous with you too?"

I leaned in and said, "Better yet, I'll climb up to your

balcony and abduct you—whisk you away to Neverland, like in *Peter and Wendy*!"

"Only if I let you," Dulceña said. "I'm no Wendy, you know. I have my own adventures in mind."

Her declaration startled me. I had never thought about Dulceña's plans for herself outside of my love for her and my desire to marry her someday. "What kind of adventures?"

"Oh, there's so much to consider! The possibilities are limited only by what we dare to dream." She looked out to the horizon. "Just think of it, Joaquín. Out there, past the valley and beyond the gulf, is a whole other world with different countries and different cultures and different perspectives. Did you know that in Africa there are immense herds of wild beasts that roam the plains as far as the eye can see? Someday, when all this nonsense with the Plan de San Diego is over, when our world is right-side up again, I am going to travel. I'm going to pack my bags and go see this great big world and write all about it, like those reporters in the magazines my father reads."

"Yeah, well, there are countries where women aren't allowed to travel alone," I said, feeling my face flush even as I spoke the words.

Dulceña turned away from me then. "You don't understand," she whispered.

"No. I do. I do understand," I said. "You want to be free to explore the world on your terms. But what would you have me do? Forget about you while you travel all over the world in search of adventures?"

"No, of course not. I just want you to remember that I have free will too." The dimples on her cheeks deepened as she smiled up at me. "Let's just promise we'll always respect each other's dreams."

"Of course!" I said.

A loud knock on my bedroom door jolted me out of the bittersweet memory. It had been months since I'd been able to see Dulceña at school. I rushed across the room and grabbed my hat.

My mother called out from the hall, her voice concerned, "Joaquín? Are you all right?"

"Yes. Yes." I dug my left boot out from under the bed and slipped it on.

"Your food is getting cold," she said as I opened the door and squeezed past her, kissing her temple before I hurried off.

Our two young maids, Sofia and Laura, approached me as they carried fresh linens up the stairs. Wondering if either one of them had anything to do with the letter tucked safely inside my pocket, I made eye contact with each of them. Their eyes glistened and their faces flushed brightly. Embarrassed, I hugged the wall, making way for them. They glanced at each other and then rushed up to the second floor, giggling.

On the first floor, Doña Luz went into the dining room with a fresh pot of coffee. I didn't think she had anything to do with Dulceña's secret letter. She couldn't have gotten away so fast that I wouldn't have seen her in the hall. No. I would have to wait for another day to figure out how the letters were getting to me. I wasn't too worried about it. I was just glad someone was on our side.

As it turned out, the letter would have to stay in my pocket longer than expected that day. Before we were even done with our desayuno, the first and most important meal of a working man's day, Manuel came into the dining room and announced that someone was waiting to speak to Papá.

My father put his fork down on his plate and asked, "Well, who is it, Man? What do they want?"

"It's Captain Munro, Patrón. He says he needs to talk to Gerardo."

"Flora's boy?" Mamá handed the pot of atole to Doña Luz, who hurried out of the room with it like it was on fire. "What in heaven's name for?"

"Let me take care of this," Papá said, wiping his mouth and putting the napkin beside his plate before getting up.

I pushed back my chair and walked quietly behind my father until we were standing side by side on the porch. Captain Munro had dismounted and was standing next to two other Rangers. I didn't recognize them, so I figured they must be new to his company. Because of the rebellion, Munro's company had grown exponentially. Most of the new men were sent to him through the ranks. Others, however, were handpicked from among his friends. Consequently, a lot of his men didn't have any military training. Their only qualifications were their animosity for Mexican bandits and their willingness to do whatever Munro said without question.

"What's going on, Munro?" Papá stepped down and shook the captain's hand. "I hear you want to talk to one of my workers?"

Munro nodded. "I need to have a word with Gerardo Gutierrez. We have reason to believe he was involved in an incident at the sugar mill late last night."

"An incident?" Papá asked. "What kind of incident?"

"A group of Mexican revolutionaries crossed the river into Texas last night. They met up with a group of tejano rebels in Hidalgo County and then headed this way intent on burning down our mill. What they thought they were accomplishing, God only knows, but we have witnesses that say Gerardo was involved." Munro took a toothpick out of his shirt pocket and rolled it between his fingertips, like he wasn't sure whether to pick his teeth.

"Gerardo wouldn't want to burn down the mill," my father replied. "Those Mexican revolutionaries are trying to gain notoriety, to call attention to their working conditions as laborers down there in Mexico and up here. But Gerardo has nothing to gain from that. He has a good life here at Las Moras, where he gets a fair day's pay for his work." Papá put his hand on the porch rail and leaned against it gently while Munro waited for him to finish his thought. "Gerardo doesn't strike me as the type to run around with revolutionaries. Sure, he's young, his ideals might be a little muddled, but a rebel? No. I don't think so."

"Well, he was at Colonia Calaveras at dawn, drunk and disorderly, talking about hanging out at the mill last night with a gang of rebels and even having the protection of La Estrella," Munro said. "I'd say he and I have a lot to talk about."

Papá sighed. He sounded tired, almost defeated, as he turned to Manuel and said, "Go get Gerardo. We'll get to the bottom of this right now."

"I'm not sure you understand, Ace." Munro licked his thin lips and smiled grimly, making his leathery skin stretch taut across his gaunt cheekbones. It made me think of a pit viper or a copperhead, all coiled up and ready to strike. "I'm not here to work this out with you and Gerardo. He's coming with us."

"So it's settled then. There's no way around it?" Papá pressed his lips together as he waited for Munro to confirm his intentions. "This is a bit much, don't you think? Do you even have an arrest warrant?"

Munro didn't answer my father. He just fixed those strange golden eyes of his on Manuel and said, "Just make sure he brings his horse. Unless he wants to walk all the way back to the station."

It didn't take but a few minutes to get Gerardo. He'd heard about Munro's visit and was halfway up to the main house when Manuel caught sight of him. Together, Gerardo and Doña Flora, our laundress, walked up to our porch. His two younger brothers were trailing behind them while Manuel followed them all, leading Gerardo's saddled horse.

Munro tipped his hat at Doña Flora, saying, "I'm sorry to have to do this in front of your other niños, señora, but the law's the law." Then Munro turned away and waved to the two other Rangers, who seized Gerardo and handcuffed him.

Doña Flora screamed and cried when Munro's men reached for Gerardo's forearms and began to cuff his wrists together. Gerardo said, "Son, for your illicit activities at the mill last night, publicly proclaiming yourself a rebel and disturbing the peace in Morado County, I am placing you under arrest."

For his part, Gerardo didn't resist. He just stuck out his chest, spit on the ground right in front of Munro, and said, "Yeah, I was at Colonia Calaveras early this morning. But I was there to see my girl, Apolonia. I wasn't disturbing no peace."

"Who else was with you up at the mill last night?" Munro asked.

Gerardo frowned. His mouth twisted sideways into a wry smile. Then he shook his head and said, "I don't know what you're talking about."

"I'm talking about you and your compañeros trying to blow up the mill. Who else was there? Who was with you?" Munro demanded, pushing Gerardo in the chest until he stepped back from Munro.

"That wasn't me," Gerardo insisted. "I told you. I was at Calaveras with my girl. How could I be at the mill if I was with her all night?" He stared Munro down with hooded eyes, avoiding Doña Flora's increasingly worried expression. The charges were much worse than him spending a night out with Apolonia, but his mother couldn't have been happy to hear about it. Good girls, girls from decent families, were always chaperoned, and everyone knew Apolonia Morales had no mother or female relative to enforce that social rule.

One of the deputies behind Gerardo shoved him forward. "What about all this nonsense about La Estrella?" he growled.

"Well, La Estrella—" Gerardo started to speak, but then he stopped and looked up at my father like he wasn't sure he should answer the question. Papá stared him down the way he used to stare me or Tomás down when we were young and we stepped out of line. It was very intimidating, and I could only hope Gerardo knew how much trouble he was in, not just with the law but also with my father, who didn't put up with nonsense from anyone. My mother, however, pulled on her shawl and hugged herself more tightly with it, turning her head sideways. It was clear Mamá didn't know what to say that might help Gerardo, whose eyes were gleaming. "La Estrella is the protector of the people," Gerardo said softly as the Rangers leaned in to listen. "It doesn't matter if they're Mexican or tejano. She helps everyone."

Munro cleared his throat, spit on the ground beside him, and spoke to Gerardo again, "And you're not afraid to be associated with Mexican bandits or tejano rebels and charged with treason?"

"There is no crime in speaking her name. Everybody talks about La Estrella." Gerardo lifted his chin, unafraid to speak about the legendary figure whose nickname had become synonymous with rebellion.

"La Estrella is a myth—a bedtime story," I said, stepping forward to stand between Munro and Gerardo. "Nobody really expects her to materialize. She gives the people something to talk about, that's all. Gerardo didn't mean anything by it. He was probably just trying to impress his girl or something."

"La Estrella is real!" Gerardo shouted, his tone passionate. "She's flesh and blood—as alive as you and me! Someday, Joaquín, you will come to understand why everybody loves her. She's a hero. She would die for our gente."

"M'ijo, por favor. Don't say things like that," Doña Flora begged. She reached for her son, but Munro put his hand up to stop her.

"Son, violent delights have violent deaths. There is nothing more dangerous than idolizing a rebellious woman. I'm sure it feels good to have such a female smile softly at you when you join her cause and conceive and commit crimes in her name, but there are repercussions, muchacho." Munro took a step back. His golden gaze swept around the small crowd, his tone and expression designed to intimidate all of us. "La Estrella is a fugitive. She has a price on her head. Anyone who aligns themselves with her will answer to me. The looting and vandalism that sympathizers and insurgents get up to in other counties doesn't go on here. I will not allow you to disrupt the order that my men and I have worked so hard to establish!"

Gerardo lifted his head and took in the same crowd as Munro. His mother was crying into a pañuelo she had pulled out of her apron, while his little brothers clung to her skirt behind her. My parents were standing together beside me by then. Mamá had come down from the porch and threaded her arm around my father's while Munro ranted about La Estrella. The campesinos who'd drifted up from the barn, wondering in fear at what the Rangers were doing, hung their heads and shuffled their feet in silence. Our maids, Sofia and Laura, peeked out from the house windows, terror gleaming in their bright eyes. "What?" Gerardo asked, turning back to Munro. "Are you going to arrest everyone who admires La Estrella? Then you're going to need a lot more men."

"I've heard enough." Grabbing Gerardo's shoulder, Munro turned him around and shoved him at his men. The Rangers put Gerardo on his horse and rode away, leading the animal by its reins as the cuffed young man gripped his saddle horn uncomfortably.

The lawmen weren't even out of sight before Doña Flora was gripping Papá's arm, begging him to help Gerardo. "Please, please," she kept saying. "You have to do something. They're going to kill him like they did his father! Please, Patrón. You have to help him!"

Doña Flora had come to Las Moras six months ago, begging for shelter after her husband was killed in Cameron County by Rangers who acted more like vigilantes than lawmen. With her husband gone, she'd taken on the task of raising her sons alone, working harder than most any other woman at Las Moras. During the day, she laundered our clothes and linens at the main house and the servants' quarters. And on the way home, she went out to the field house to collect laundry from our campesinos when they came in from working the sugarcane fields in the evenings.

"There's nothing I can do right now, señora." Papá shook his head. "Munro has a job to do. He has to uphold the law. He has Gerardo's own careless words to use against him, and God knows that's enough evidence to convict anyone these days. No lawyer in Monteseco would dare take the case. Not now."

I felt sorry for Gerardo's mother as she hung her head. "They're going to kill him. I just know they're going to kill him." Her shoulders began to shake then, softly at first, then more and more vigorously. It broke my heart, and I wanted to turn away and go back in the house because I knew Papá was right. There was nothing we could do right now.

"Go home, señora. Go home and take care of your other children. The best thing we can do right now is wait. The law's the law, and we have to let these things take their natural course. I'll go into town and post bail for him on Monday. Trust me, Gerardo will have his day in court. Munro has always taken care of us," Papá said. Then, because the rest of the men were standing around gawking, he addressed them too. "Let's get back to work. We have a cattle drive to prepare for."

Even though I wished things hadn't turned out that way, that Papá hadn't been powerless to help Gerardo right there and then, nobody expected him to interfere with the law. It would only get him arrested too. Letting Munro take Gerardo that morning was best for us and also for Las Moras. Papá would do the right thing come Monday morning. Even if he had to hire a lawyer out of Edinburg, he'd take care of Gerardo.

"Let's go!" Manuel said, waving the men to the stockyard. "You heard the boss. Back to work, everyone."

As the men and women went their separate ways, I couldn't help but be angry at Gerardo for putting his family through this. I didn't disapprove of his sneaking out to see Apolonia. I was guilty of sneaking out to see Dulceña myself. No. It was his rebel mouth that infuriated me. It was reckless to run around town shooting his mouth off about La Estrella. Everyone who worked for us knew about her, whispered her name in awe, but never in public, and never to Munro's face. If I'd been Gerardo's older brother, I would have given him a fat lip for putting Doña Flora and her boys through this misery. But Gerardo was nineteen, a year older than me, and he wasn't my brother.

In a way, I was lucky my brother was a priest. At least neither he nor I were ever going to break Mamá's heart.

Letter from Dulceña,
Friday, August 20, 1915

J—

¡Cómo te extraño!

I miss giggling and clinging to your arm as I did when we would walk in your mother's garden with her faint footsteps following close behind because our parents were still friends. I miss the sound of your voice quietly reading poetry to me. I miss twirling the silky softness of your blond locks around the tip of my index finger as I listened.

So much has been taken from us. We are but wooden marionettes, you and I, dangling from precarious strings, tangled up in the cruel conspiracies and political plots of devious men—dancing to the tune of their whims, permanent smiles painted on our faces while we waltz around in circles!

The moon is fading fast, mi amor, and I can't help but wonder—will I see you at the masquerade tonight? Mateo and Fito already have invitations. Now, so do you and I.

Te amo,

—D

CHAPTER 2

ALONE IN MY ROOM THAT AFTERNOON, I opened the envelope from Dulceña. Inside I found a brief letter and an invitation to Lupita's quinceañera taking place later that night at the dance hall in the town square. I must have read and reread the letter from Dulceña a dozen times. My heart beat wildly against my chest at the passionate tone of her written words.

After reading it yet again, I laid it beside me on the bed and skimmed through the invitation she had enclosed with it. Addressed to *Romeo del Toro*, the invitation gave specifics for attending the themed party with a masque ball in place of a regular baile. I was to pick up my mask when I presented my invitation at the door. That seemed simple enough.

Mateo and Fito had talked about going to the party for days, but I hadn't been interested then. Now I would have to send word with either Sofia or Laura for my friends to wait and not leave without me. It would put my mother at ease to know I wouldn't be going into town alone.

After sending Mateo and Fito a message, I bathed and put on my best clothes, and even threw on the slim black tie I wore to church on Sundays. As I combed my hair in front of the mirror, I wondered what could be so important that it would make Dulceña take such a risk as to ask for us meet in public. Even if there were masks involved, we wouldn't have the freedom to talk alone. We'd be lucky if we got in a dance or two without her parents figuring out it was me behind the mask. Although they hadn't been able to stop us from speaking to each other at school, they wouldn't condone our socializing at a baile. Not without a formal apology from my father for the way he had treated them two years earlier.

By the time I went downstairs, my parents were sitting quietly in the parlor. My mother assessed my outfit and asked, "What's going on, Joaquín? Why are you all dressed up?"

"I'm going out with Mateo and Fito," I said, clearing my throat and fussing with the cuff of my new dress shirt.

"A dónde?" Papá asked, putting aside the magazine he was reading. "Is there some special event going on in town I don't know about?"

"Mateo and Fito want me to go into Monteseco with them; a girl they know is turning fifteen. It's going to be a hell of a quinceañera, from what I understand." I leaned over and fussed with my boots. *I should have polished them,* I thought as I scraped a spot of dirt off my left heel with my fingernail. "Mateo's girlfriend is going to be there," I continued, straightening up again. "He hasn't seen Conchita in days, so he really wants us to go to this thing. I'm not really in the mood for a dance; I'm just trying to find something to do to take my mind off everything."

Mamá turned to our housekeeper, who was clearing out the evening's coffee cups. "You know anything about this, Luz?"

"Ay, sí. Lupita's quinceañera." Doña Luz nodded, placing the dishes on a tray to take them back to the kitchen with her. "It's going to be very different, not like a real quinceañera— young people are going to have to put on máscaras con plumas on top of their heads." She waved her hands around her head, as if they were feathers.

Mamá giggled a little. "A masque ball?"

Doña Luz clapped and pointed at Mamá. "¡Sí, that's it! That's what the invitation said." She frowned and shook her finger, going on a tangent that was a familiar topic around the kitchen table. "I'll never understand why people waste all their money on quinceañeras they can't afford. They end up asking everyone they know to chip in, just so their daughters can waltz around in a fancy dress. If I had daughters—"

"If you and I had had daughters, Doña Luz, I suspect we'd call in every favorcito we had coming to us to make their party special and unique," Mamá said, patting Doña Luz's arm.

"Well, I better get going," I said, turning toward the front door. "Mateo and Fito are waiting for me."

"Wait!" Mamá waved at me frantically. I turned back

around. "Maybe you should stay home tonight. You saw what happened to Gerardo—"

"Mamá, por favor. Don't act like that," I interrupted her. I hated it when she treated me like a little boy who needed her permission to leave the house. "I'm a grown man. Besides, I'm not Gerardo. I'm not joining the rebellion. It's just a birthday party."

"Joaquín, m'ijo." Mamá stood up and came to hug me around the waist. "I know you're a young man and you need to get out sometimes, but couldn't you just stay in for tonight? There will be time for this kind of thing later. There's always something going on on the weekends in these parts."

Mamá let go of me with a sigh and busied herself pinching something off the sleeve of my shirt. To my surprise, my father got up to join us. Letting out a little sigh and placing his hands on her shoulders, he said, "It'll be all right, Jovita. Don't worry. I'm sure the boys won't go any farther than Monteseco. The town square is safe and close enough to the sheriff's office should anyone get out of line."

"Oh, no. We'll be fine," I said, not feeling too much guilt about meeting Dulceña in secret. Tomás would say that omitting facts was the same as lying, but I couldn't help it. It was a sin I was willing to commit.

Don't forget to tell that to Tomás at confession, my conscience said, and I promised I would let my brother chastise me in the confessional at the Capilla del Sagrado Corazón early Sunday morning before mass.

"Just be careful, Son." Papá pulled Mamá off me and into

his arms. She chided him quietly for letting me go off tonight as Papá said, "Stay with Mateo and Fito. There is safety in numbers. And try to not to stay out too late. I want you to go into town with me tomorrow and see about bailing Gerardo out. That outta be easy enough. Judge Thompson owes me a favor."

"Don't worry, Papá," I said. "I'll ride into town with you in the morning, no matter how late the boys want to stay out tonight."

For as long as I could remember, Mateo, Fito, and I had been inseparable. When we were young, our fathers kept us busy cleaning stables, feeding the animals, and weeding the gardens at Las Moras after school. We were happy to do our chores, as long as we got to do them together, because working with friends was so much easier than working alone or with strangers.

Unfortunately, that changed the day Mateo and Fito dropped out of school right after their sixteenth birthday. Mateo wanted to earn money so he could marry Conchita as soon as he turned eighteen.

Fito didn't have a girlfriend, but he seized the opportunity to drop out of school with his brother. He always shadowed his brother's actions. If Mateo did it, Fito had to do it too. I can't say I blame either one of them. They knew their lot in life was to toil in the fields, and they didn't want to waste any more time in school when they could be earning a living and helping their family prosper. It also didn't hurt to have their own money to spend when they went into town on the weekends.

When he first got to Las Moras, Gerardo Gutierrez had joined our friendly working group, but then his attitude changed. Being older than us and not from around here, he had different ideas about my father's friendship with the Rangers. When I questioned his loyalty to my father and Las Moras the way he questioned Papá's loyalty to tejanos, he pulled away from the group. Back then, I could only speculate that he'd been embarrassed to be caught talking badly about the man who had taken his family in when they'd needed it most.

That conversation never sat right with me, but I didn't tell my father about it. I didn't have to; I knew why Papá kept Munro around. "It's good to know where the snake likes to lay in the brush. It's the only way to survive," he said every time my mother complained about one of Munro's "friendly visits" to Las Moras.

It took a while to get to the quince. I was quiet for most of the ride, letting Fito and Mateo do most of the talking. It wasn't unusual. I was always the discreet one of the bunch. At Lupita's quinceañera, several of her cousins stood at the dance hall door handing out plumed masks. "I hope this helps you find your Juliets!" a hostess said as she handed me mine.

"I can't wait to see my Conchita," Mateo said, putting on

a red mask. "Hey, Joaquín. You think I should ask Conchita to give Dulceña a holler? Maybe your girl could get out here for a quick twirl around the dance floor. What do you say? Should I ask her?"

"That won't be necessary." I pulled the strings of my purple mask to fasten it to my head. It was still too loose, so I looped the string behind my ears and tightened the knot.

"Why not?" Mateo wiggled his mask over his face until he could see me better.

Fito, who was carrying his mask around like he didn't know what to do with it, turned to me then. "What's the matter? You two get in a fight or something?"

"No, that's not it." I walked past the foyer and stood at the entrance of the dance hall. Before us was the most extravagant birthday party I had ever attended. Lupita's parents weren't rich, not by any means. It was obvious her parents had called in many favors from friends and family. The live music was not being provided by the usual conjunto group, but a long-tailed band. The músicos were Mexican, but they weren't local, certainly no group I'd ever seen before.

The decorations were beyond extravagant. The whole room was swathed in wide colorful ribbons. The swatches of cloth extended from the ceiling at the center of the room, billowing outward in every direction. At the edge of the ceiling, the giant ribbons were fastened with enormous bows and dropped downward, elegantly draping the walls until they dusted the floor. Every table had a different-colored skirt, and on every runner lay a huge elaborately decorated chest with bedazzled fans; long beaded necklaces; and assorted jewels the guests could crown and pin on each other, layering them on one after another until they looked like royals.

As we moved into the warmly lit room, staying in the shadows by skirting the cold stucco wall, masked girls dressed in rich, luxurious, long dresses walked past us, giggling with their friends. Some of the more sedate ones sat at elegantly draped tables with their sisters and mamás, waiting to be asked to dance by the masked boys milling around the room.

Every one of the guests wore contoured masks adorned with lentejuelas, delicate sparkling sequins in a rainbow of colors. The girls' masks had long, colorful plumes that trembled and quivered with every word they whispered as they goggled at the room.

"Then what's going on? Why don't you want her to come?" Mateo asked when we found a clear spot along the wall to linger. "Are you dumb or something? It's the perfect opportunity to meet up with her. You could make ojitos at each other all night long and nobody would ever know because we're all wearing masks."

I pointed straight ahead to a girl with a matching purple mask. "She's here."

Fito, on my right, craned his neck to see where I was pointing. "What? Really? When did you arrange this? You sneaky possum!"

"Never mind that," I said, unable to concentrate on Fito.

No matter how much my loyalty pushed me to be honest and real with my friends, there was no way I was going to tell them about my secret correspondence with Dulceña. To disclose our most guarded, most intimate secret would dishonor my love and respect for her.

"Well, all right. I guess you know what you're doing," Mateo said, patting my shoulder and pushing me forward a little. "Go on then. Go ask her to dance."

I shook my head and tightened my mask, taking in a long deep breath. As I took a step in her direction, she stopped, turned around. I couldn't see her eyes, but her lips lifted a little at the corners. My heart beating wildly against my chest, I held my breath and froze in place.

Her cousin, Irma, put her hand on Dulceña's shoulder and whispered something in her ear. Dulceña's lips parted and her teeth sparkled as she smiled that generous, full smile I had grown to love. My pulse quickened. Without taking her eyes off me, she pushed the girl away gently, lifted her skirt to keep the hem off the dance floor, and started to inch around other guests in the crowded room.

I moved forward too, slowly, until we were face-to-face in the center of the dance floor amid an array of couples swaying to a gentle waltz. There were so many people that we didn't have to work at getting close.

"Are you my Julieta?" I asked. Grinning, I offered her my hand.

She smiled and giggled nervously before taking it. "I don't know," she said. "Are you my Romeo?"

"You are stunning," I said, and she winked and curtsied before me.

Dulceña took my hand. "What took you so long?" she asked. "It's almost eleven."

"Oh, you know my mother. She had some *concerns,*" I whispered as we positioned ourselves among the couples.

"We're being watched," she whispered, leaning into me as we took to the floor and swayed with the music. "Mamá is intrigued, but Madame Josette knows exactly who you are."

I scanned the room as we turned in the waltz. Doña Serafina sat at a table to our left. "I think Madame Josette is trying to distract her," I whispered, sweeping Dulceña farther away from the two women. "Where's your father?"

"Against the far wall, to your right." Dulceña dipped her head in that general direction.

Don Rodrigo was talking to Mr. Simmons, our neighbor over by Las Moras and co-owner of the sugar mill. "He looks busy."

"Yes, but not for long. He'll be joining Mamá soon, and they will want to know who I'm dancing with," Dulceña whispered. Taking my lead, she twirled beautifully under my uplifted hand. The ease of our movement together surprised me. We hadn't had occasion to dance with each other in more than two years, not since our parents stopped socializing. It felt good to hold her in my arms again.

"So what do you want to do?" I asked, spotting the nearest exit.

"Listen, we have to talk," Dulceña said. She took the lead

and turned us so that my back was to her party's table. "There's something I need to tell you. But not now. Not here."

"What do you want to do?" We moved to the rhythm of the music, stepping forward and back with ease.

Dulceña leaned in so that our cheeks were almost touching, but not quite. "Meet me at midnight in our secret spot. There will be a big display of cuetes in the plaza at midnight. I can sneak away then." We switched positions and moved within view of her parents. Don Rodrigo stood up as if he was about to leave. Doña Serafina put her hands on Don Rodrigo's arm and held him back, speaking in his ear.

"What?" Why would she want to meet in the woods? There were bandits and Rangers out there. "No. It's not safe."

"Midnight. Be there—it's important," she whispered. Then she let go of my hands and backed away from me between the other couples, mouthing, "I love you."

No. We shouldn't. We can't. The words got stuck in my throat. I didn't get a chance to say it because Don Rodrigo was coming my way. Dulceña squeezed through the throng of dancers, disrupting their well-counted steps until she got to her father. She grabbed his hand and said something, likely very sweet and witty. Don Rodrigo smiled, and they started to dance.

"Let's go, Romeo, time to move." Fito put his hand on my shoulder and pressed me to move. "You can't stand here all night. Not unless you have a dance partner."

"Yeah." I pushed my way through the crowded dance floor and came up for air on the far side of the dance hall. Dulceña twirled under her father's arms, unaware of the dilemma brewing in my heart. I didn't want to disappoint her, but I should have refused to meet her out there at night. Doña Serafina was still sitting with Madame Josette at their table. I couldn't hear Dulceña's mother's words, but her mouth lifted into a wistful smile, then she turned her face away.

As soon as Don Rodrigo took Dulceña back to the table, Geronimo, a young man who'd graduated the year before us, came up and offered Dulceña his hand, asking her to dance with him. She shook her head and sat down instead, ensconcing herself modestly between her mother and Madame Josette.

I was visibly tense, my body straight and taut, and I had the urge to run. Fito patted me on the back. "At least you got to dance with her once," he said. "Come on, let's go get something to drink. It's hot in here."

"No. I have to get out of here."

"What?" Fito asked, following me as I made my way to the front door. "But we just got here. Joaquín, wait."

I didn't wait for Fito. It wasn't quite yet time to go to our secret meeting spot, Arroyo Morado, but I just couldn't stay there and watch Dulceña dance with someone other than her father. Because that's what was about to happen. She would be asked to dance many more times throughout the night, and to please her parents, she would give each boy a couple of turns on the dance floor. Etiquette dictated that she dance no more than twice with each suitor—asking a young woman to dance more than twice would indicate a young man was officially courting her. Her acceptance of the third dance would mean she was interested in him as a suitor. I just couldn't stand around, watching that scenario play itself out. Not that I thought she would ever dance more than twice with any of the young men in Monteseco, but it would still be too hard to watch. It was better to just walk away.

I rushed out of the dance hall and into the dark summer night, throwing off my mask as I jammed my hat on my head. I ran off to the corral where we'd left our horses, then got on my horse and rode out of town at a gallop. The hot summer breeze caught my hat and whisked it off my head. I didn't lose it, tied down as it was, but I left it off, lying flat against my back as I slowed down and turned my horse, taking the road that ran to Las Moras south of Monteseco.

I stopped at the covered bridge just outside town. From the bridge, there were a number of directions one could take in order to find some excitement. There were several small towns both to the east and west of the creek and a few more down southeast, along the border of the Rio Grande, but I wasn't going much farther along Arroyo Morado. Less than half a mile past the bridge westward along the creek, there was a small slope in the land. I stopped at the oak tree with a giant limb shaped like an alligator. Its wide-open mouth signaled the clearing I'd been searching for.

Here I dismounted. Tying my horse to the oak, I pushed through the thick brush and heavily clustered mesquites until I came to an alcove, a tiny recess where my brother and I used to swim when we were younger. Those times were long gone, but recently the swimming hole had become the secret meeting place for me and my Dulceña.

Ever since she'd left school, it was where we saw each other. We didn't meet there often, only when it became absolutely necessary, and never this late at night. Most of the time we met early in the morning or in the middle of the afternoon after Madame Josette had been dismissed for the day. On those rare occasions, she'd send me a letter very early in the morning and I'd skip school to meet her at the creek.

That night, the air in the clearing was hot, oppressive, and the gibbous silver moon hung low in the sky over the bank of Arroyo Morado. I had at least another hour before Dulceña would arrive—in my hot-headed escape from the dance, I hadn't considered I'd have nothing to do while I waited. I just knew I wanted to be there by the time she arrived. The waning moonlight bounced off the tops of the dense growth of pecan trees deeply rooted along the edge of the creek and wavered wistfully in the dark water before me.

The silence of the night reminded me of another ominous evening. I was eight years old at the time, and by all accounts, I shouldn't have been there. But for some childish and ridiculous reason, I had picked Arroyo Morado as the perfect place to live when I'd decided to run away from Las Moras. I couldn't remember why I ran away that night, only that I did.

The wind had howled all around me as the storm that had threatened to come all afternoon caught up with me. I remembered standing on the edge of the water, a skinny boy, afraid, but just mad enough not to turn around and head back to Las Moras when the furious storm became violent.

As the skies had opened up and the rain crashed into me, I inched down the incline, hoping to find shelter from the raging winds. Then, as if in slow motion, my feet slid out from under me, my legs gave out, and I couldn't support myself. The water was cold, colder than I remembered it from the swimming lessons my brother, Tomás, had given me all summer in that same spot.

"Help!" I had cried, my voice swallowed up by the roar of the water and wind. "Help! Socorro!" I swam for my life, but made little headway against the current. Then, because I could think of nobody else in the world stronger and more courageous than my big brother, I had called out to him. Again and again, I called out, "Tomás! Tomás! Help me, Brother! Help me!" Weighed down by the rain, I bobbed in the current, which soon swallowed me. I went under, taking mouthful after mouthful of water as I panicked.

I don't know how he was able to find me, but Tomás was suddenly there. I didn't see him arrive, just like I didn't see him jump in after me. I only felt his strong arms as he wrapped them around my chest and pulled me upward with him, and then he was dragging me out of the creek. As he sat me down on the water's edge, I started spewing out the muck clogging my lungs, immensely thankful to have a brother who loved me that much.

"Why would you do this? Why, Joaquín? Why?" he kept asking me as I clung to his soaked shirt, trembling.

"I'm sorry!" I said, burying my face into his shoulder and closing my eyes, wishing the white flames of lightning and blasts of thunder would come to a halt. "I'm sorry!"

The memory faded as I stared at the murky waters before me, thinking that Tomás wouldn't approve of what I was doing out here tonight any more than he had approved of my actions that terrible, dark night so many years before.

Thanks to him, I had survived that incident. But what if something happened out here now? What if bandits came along? What if we ended up seeing something or hearing something that would embroil us in treasonous acts? If we couldn't tell anyone, would we be accused of conspiring with rebels, as Gerardo had been? Tomás had no way of protecting me or Dulceña if that were to happen. As far as he knew, I was safely back at home at Las Moras, reading a book or writing poetry in my journal as I did most nights.

I sat musing on that terrible night for as long as it took the moon to travel its own width across the sky. Just as I started to wonder how much longer Dulceña would be, I heard something move quietly in the brush. I turned around and saw her. She was standing just inside the clearing. She started walking toward me, and I stood up. I couldn't make out her face because she was wearing a shawl over her head and shoulders, but I didn't have to. I knew it was her. My heart only beats wildly for one girl in Monteseco.

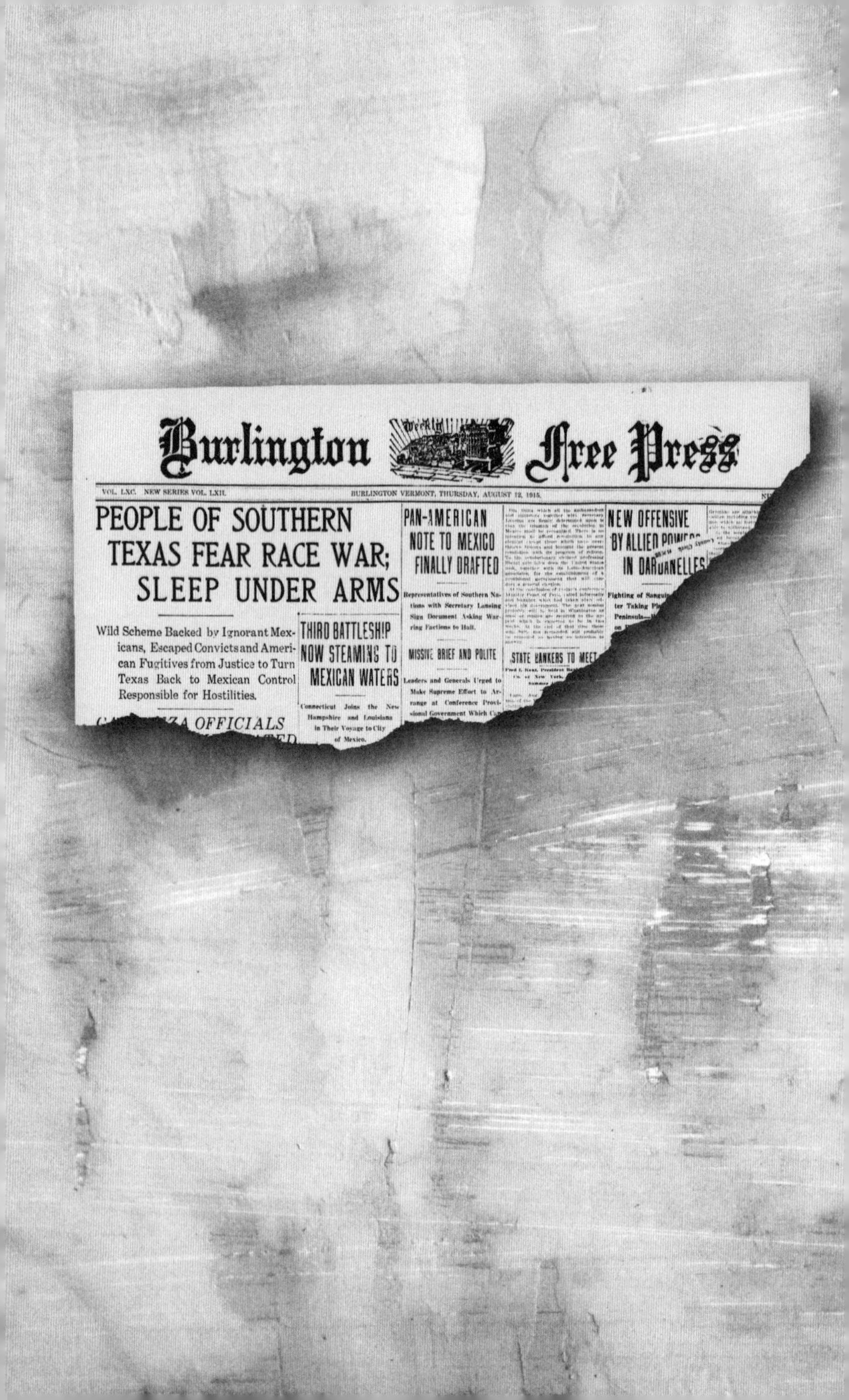

Burlington Weekly Free Press

VOL. LXC. NEW SERIES VOL. LXII. BURLINGTON VERMONT, THURSDAY, AUGUST 12, 1915.

PEOPLE OF SOUTHERN TEXAS FEAR RACE WAR; SLEEP UNDER ARMS

Wild Scheme Backed by Ignorant Mexicans, Escaped Convicts and American Fugitives from Justice to Turn Texas Back to Mexican Control Responsible for Hostilities.

OFFICIALS

THIRD BATTLESHIP NOW STEAMING TO MEXICAN WATERS

Connecticut Joins the New Hampshire and Louisiana in Their Voyage to City of Mexico.

PAN-AMERICAN NOTE TO MEXICO FINALLY DRAFTED

Representatives of Southern Nations with Secretary Lansing Sign Document Asking Warring Factions to Halt.

MISSIVE BRIEF AND POLITE

Leaders and Generals Urged to Make Supreme Effort to Arrange at Conference Provisional Government Which

STATE BANKERS TO MEET

NEW OFFENSIVE BY ALLIED POWERS IN DARDANELLES

Fighting of Sanguin
ter Taking Pl
Peninsula

Chapter 3

"We shouldn't be here," I said. It was the first thing that came to my mind when I saw her standing there in the dark.

"I had to see you," Dulceña said, stepping all the way into the clearing.

"This is dangerous," I whispered. Her eyes gleamed in the dark, reflecting the pale, wavering moonlight. "It's not proper." That hadn't stopped us before, but meeting in the daylight was one thing. Nighttime meetings were another thing altogether. There was something more than dangerous about a nighttime meeting. The whole thing felt sordid, and I wanted to get it over with and escort her home as soon as possible.

Dulceña reached out to me. I took her hand, caressing her fingertips as she said, "I'm not afraid of being alone with you. You would never do anything to damage my reputation."

"Of course not," I said, clutching her hand tightly between mine. "It's just that I can't help but wonder what is so important that we had to meet here, so late at night. We should go to town, find a quiet place to talk. It's not safe here. Not now."

"No," Dulceña whispered. "My father would kill me if he found out we were together. But I had to warn you about the Rangers. Did you read the paper today?"

Dulceña's hands were cold. I rubbed them gently between mine. "No. My father—well, you know. But I don't understand what the paper has to do with us."

"Not us," Dulceña said. "This concerns you and your family. There was a story about the incident at the mill in the paper today. You do know about the mill, don't you?"

I nodded. "Munro and a couple of his men were at the ranch today," I said. "They took Gerardo Gutierrez, but he claimed to have nothing to do with what happened at the mill. I don't understand why anyone would want to blow the mill up, anyway. Gerardo was just meeting his girl near there."

"Oh, but he did have something to do with it," Dulceña whispered. "This is big, Joaquín. Bigger than anything that's happened in Monteseco in a long time. You see, several men escaped the authorities. The story said as much, but what wasn't in the paper, what my father wouldn't dare print, was that some of the escaped men were local ranch hands—men from Morado County who are so frustrated, so angry over this matanza, this indiscriminate slaughter of our people, they're ready to burn down any business owned or operated by Anglo immigrants. To them, the mill is yet one more way the white man profits from our oppression."

"What are you talking about?" I leaned in to catch her eye. She was talking so quietly that the sounds of the night and the running water nearby made it hard to hear her.

"My father was at the station this morning, waiting to interview Munro, when the Rangers brought in their prisoners. The Rangers wouldn't give my father any information about the identity of the men in custody, but he overheard the two prisoners talking to each other when they thought they were alone."

She took a deep breath. "Joaquín, they said they hoped their friends made it back to Las Moras all right."

I dropped her hands and stepped back, my breath sucked out of me.

Dulceña waited for me to recover before she continued, "If it's true that some of your workers are conspiring with rebels, it could mean real trouble for Las Moras."

I turned to stare at the creek waters, letting the news wash over me. None of it made sense. We sold our sugarcane at the mill. The owner, Mr. Simmons, was a friend of ours. My father kept company with all types of people, from business owners to lawmen. It was in his best interest to keep peaceful relations with everyone in town. And as far as I knew, we didn't have any rebel sympathizers working at Las Moras. "It's going to be okay," I told her. "Munro is my father's friend. He'll take care of us."

Dulceña came closer and put her hand on my shoulder. "Joaquín, listen to me. I know your father trusts the Rangers.

But this rebellion has changed Munro. His politics have shifted. As it stands, he wouldn't think twice about arresting your father and shutting down Las Moras if his men try burning the mill down again. This is serious."

"But that's not right," I said, turning sideways to her. "My father can't be held responsible for what our men do outside Las Moras."

"But he will be. That's how Munro operates," Dulceña insisted, tossing the shawl off her head. "You have to tell him what's going on. You have to make sure your father understands. He must find out who the troublemakers are and turn them in before it's too late and they end up finishing what they started."

I thought about Papá, about how honorable he was, about everything he believed in, and I knew in my heart that wasn't going to happen. "He won't do it," I said, more to myself than to Dulceña. "He won't take sides." It was one thing for him to allow Munro to arrest Gerardo—he had no control over that. It was something else entirely to ask him to turn his men over to the Rangers.

"Then Munro will go after him," Dulceña said.

The tiny pain that had started at my temples was suddenly throbbing behind my eye sockets. I thought my head would explode from the pressure of it. "No," I said. "They're friends. Munro and my father have been friends forever."

"Munro has no friends, only allies and pawns. The minute he thinks your father is harboring insurgents he will go after him with a vengeance," Dulceña said. "He's vowed to protect the people of Morado County from rebels, and that includes anybody harboring them."

Whether the people of Morado County wanted his protection or not was Munro's unspoken promise. Dulceña was right. The thought of seeing Papá handcuffed and taken away for "harboring insurgents" gave me a chill. I could see it, my father's demise unfolding before me, because unlike Papá, I didn't trust Munro.

There were many reasons I didn't like Captain Munro. None of them had anything to do with his position or his power. All of them had everything to do with that strange way he had of looking right through anyone he didn't see as an equal.

How many times had I felt his strange golden eyes lift off his playing cards to settle on me, pinning me to my seat like a needle through an insect? And how many times had I watched Mateo and Fito tug at their collars and squirm because Munro was doing exactly the same thing to them? Even my brother, Tomás, who was always sunny and bright, seemed to darken when Munro sat on our patio drinking brandy and playing poker with our father.

Dulceña pulled me out of my dark thoughts by lifting her hand to my face, turning my head. "Make no mistake, Joaquín, Munro is ruthless. The best thing your father can do right now is find out who was at the mill last night and turn them over to the Rangers."

"Don't worry," I said. "I'll find out exactly what's going

on. If it's true and rebels are hiding out at Las Moras, I'll find them myself."

"What? You can't do this alone!" Dulceña furrowed her eyebrows. "Please, please promise me you won't do this. Not alone."

Thin sheets of clouds passed overhead, obstructing the moonlight, and suddenly we were enveloped in mist. "It's the only way it's going to get done. My brother's a priest, so he can't do it, and my father . . . well, he just *won't* do it. No. It's up to me to make sure Gerardo's accomplices don't jeopardize our livelihood."

"It's not fair." Dulceña pulled at the shawl around her shoulders like she was suddenly cold. "This is all wrong."

"That's funny," I said, reaching up to take her hand in mine. "I always thought you and your family would be siding with the rebels at a time like this."

"What do you mean?" Dulceña asked, cocking her head sideways.

I cleared my throat, my mouth suddenly dry. "I mean your father seems to . . . understand . . . to sympathize with tejanos who've become rebels after losing their lands to greedy Anglo immigrants. It's what he leans to . . . the stories he chooses to print."

"We're not on any one side in particular. We're on the side of truth and justice," Dulceña said, squeezing my hand in hers. "And it would be an injustice if Munro and his posse took down Las Moras and your family lost everything because of a few misguided souls. Mexican bandits and tejano rebels don't understand the damage they're doing when they destroy businesses and raid ranches and farms, just as much as the Rangers can't see that dragging men into the brush and hanging them without a proper trial is not upholding the law."

"This world is going to hell," I whispered, suddenly feeling the burden of her words weighing down on me. "It's all falling apart."

As the clouds crawled away, the moonlight caressed Dulceña's cheekbones. I could count every thick eyelash fanning out of her lowered eyelids. She stepped in, coming closer than I'd expected. I had been alone with her out here before, four or five times in the last few months, but not like this, never like this, pressed against each other, with every inch of our bodies touching.

"You're trembling," Dulceña whispered. "Are you cold?"

"No." My voice was low, my mouth parched.

"You want to go?" she asked. Her dark eyes were gleaming, full of that fierce moonlight and something else, something deeper, more significant.

"No," I said, mesmerized by the luster of her black hair, the glimmer in her brown eyes, the fullness of her lips.

Dulceña wrapped her left arm around my ribcage and placed her cheek on my shoulder. "Then what do you want to do?" Her face was inches from mine, and her breath was warm and soft—a whisper against my neck.

"I want to kiss you," I said, at once shocked and shamed by my boldness. I hadn't meant to make such an admission, to be so atrevido. I admit I am daring, even impulsive by nature, but I never revealed all of my emotions, not to my parents, not to Mateo and Fito, not even to my brother, who despite being eight years older than me was my closest ally.

Dulceña didn't say anything. She took my hand and placed it gently at her waistline. Spurred on by her audacity, I leaned in and kissed her softly. We stood like that for uncounted minutes. Locked in that embrace, we let that sweet, intoxicating kiss take us to another realm, a safe place far away from the border and the Mexican revolutionaries and the tejano rebellion.

"Ay, isn't that sweet?"

Dulceña and I jerked away from each other at the sound of the gruff, mocking voice.

The shadow of a man crouched in the brush at the top of the incline at the clearing's edge. The long barrel of his rifle was pointed straight at me. I lifted my hands instinctively.

"Hey, Pollo! Guess what I found?" The man yelled in English, which told me they were tejano rebels or local outlaws. The realization did not put me any more at ease than if they'd been Mexican revolutionaries who had crossed the river to wreak havoc on our borderlands. Someone came up behind our assailant, cutting his way through the dense brush with his heavy boots.

"What you got, Rogelio?" the one called Pollo asked.

"Two little birdies, just a huggin' and a kissin'—so, so sweet." Rogelio laughed as he sang the words.

“Well, get ’em outta there,” Pollo said. “Take ’em up to the jefe.”

“You heard ’im.” Rogelio stood up and waved his rifle, showing us where to move. “Let’s go!”

Rogelio and Pollo walked us at gunpoint with our hands over our heads, half out of our minds with fright, all the way up the patchy trail to the old tree where Dulceña had tied her mount next to mine. Half a dozen scruffy bandits were milling around the area, while a couple of them rummaged through our saddlebags.

“¡Siéntense!” Pollo said as one of the ruffians untied our horses and led them away.

“Please, don’t hurt us!” Dulceña said. “Take whatever you need. It’s yours. The lantern. Here, take this blanket, please.” She pointed to a blanket she had tossed over one of the tree limbs. “It’s very comfortable!”

A heavy-set bandit with thick, hairy eyebrows ripped it from the tree limb, sniffed it, and then said, “Oh, that’s nice. Real nice! The jefe is going to like you, chiquita. He’s going to like you a lot!”

His remark brought about depraved snorts from the rest of the men. Dulceña, suddenly understanding their implications, physically recoiled from their laughter, seeking refuge beside me.

“Don’t be scared,” I said, putting my arm around Dulceña’s shoulder and pulling her in close. “I won’t let them touch you.”

“Well, listen to him!” A young, skinny bandit wearing a

red shirt sneered as he circled around us. "Qué macho, and he doesn't even have a mustache. How old are you, boy? Fourteen? Fifteen?"

I rolled back my shoulders and stuck out my chest. "I'm not a boy. I'm eighteen." I'd be damned if I was going to let these thugs lay even one filthy paw on my sweetheart. I'd die before I'd let them touch my Dulceña.

"And you?" Pollo asked. "How old are you, señorita?"

"That's none of your business!" I said, putting my arm out in front of Dulceña. I don't suppose there was any harm in letting them know she was also eighteen, but it stoked my fire that they would ask such an impertinent question of her.

"Look at what I found." An old man with a white beard came up the trail clutching my spare clothes. He dropped my mochila, my new leather saddlebag, on the ground beside the oak tree.

The young man with the red shirt ripped my clothes out of the old man's hands and said, "Let me see those."

"You can take all of *his* things, Chavito," the old man told him. "But I'm keeping the girl."

"Shut up! Both of you," Pollo said. "The jefe is coming."

"What's going on?" a rich, heavily accented voice called out from the darkness as their jefe's tall, imposing frame came into view.

"Not much, Carlos," the bearded old man said, folding Dulceña's blanket in his thick, leathery hands with the delicacy of a cleft-clawed armadillo. "Just a couple of kids, out for a good time, about to go for a swim, no doubt."

Carlos regarded us for a few seconds before zeroing in on my mochila sitting on the ground to the left of us. Without saying a word, he picked it up.

"Take it," I said as he held the satchel up to the lantern.

"Well, thank you. Don't mind if I do." A crooked grin formed just under Carlos's thick mustache, but his dark eyes bespoke his lack of amusement at my remark. He tossed my mochila at Chavito and nodded. The young man started rummaging through it.

"There's a good hunting rifle and a new saddle on my horse," I said. "You can have them too if you like. All I ask is that you let us go. We're no threat to you."

"He's telling the truth," Dulceña said, pulling her blue shawl over her arms and wrapping it modestly over her shoulders. She was conscious that the glow emanating from the lantern hanging from the tree limb was drawing unwelcomed attention to her figure.

"Well, whaddya know. He's a poet." Chavito was standing behind us, directly under the glow of the lantern, thumbing through my journal. "Oh, he's good." He pulled the lantern down and brought it along with the journal for his boss to inspect.

Carlos took my journal and examined it under the light provided by his goon. He furrowed his thick eyebrows, concentrating as his eyes roamed over a poem, and then he flipped to the first page, reading my personal information with interest.

"These your poems?" he asked, lifting his dark, menacing eyes to meet mine, my journal still open between his hands. "You're Joaquín del Toro?"

"Sí," I admitted, lifting my chin, letting him see I had nothing to hide. That journal was full of my deepest personal thoughts and dreams, but I wasn't about to let these outlaws make me feel ashamed of them.

"What should we do, Jefe?" asked one of the bandits.

Carlos looked at the first page of my journal again, snapped it closed, and toyed with it, as if weighing his options before he gave the command: "Let them go. Give them back their things."

"Thank you," I said as Chavito handed me my clothes. I wasn't going to ask why.

"Take your things and pack your horses. And tell no one of this." Carlos tossed the journal at me. I didn't take my eyes off him as I caught it against my chest.

"We won't say a word, promise," Dulceña said, stepping back and away from the bandits.

"Go!" the gang leader yelled. "You don't belong out here."

El Sureño

Vol. XXI | Monteseco, Texas | Friday, August 20, 1915

ONE DEAD, TWO ARRESTED AT MORADO CREEK SUGAR MILL

—Pandemonium Continues—

Tejano Rebels Dead Set on Keeping Morado County Texas Rangers Busy in Monteseco and Surrounding Areas. Captain Elliot Munro

DANGER IS INDISCRIMINATE: AFFECTS ALL SOUTH TEXAS

MORADO CO. — The people of South Texas don't know who to trust when both the lawmen and outlaw are willing to kill at will good and the bad pose a threat Mexican descent. The Texa reprieve. When th

CHAPTER 4

WE WERE NEARLY BACK TO THE main road when two mounted figures came out of the woods in front of us. When I first saw them, I thought the rebels had changed their minds and come after us again. It wasn't until they called out to us, identifying themselves as Morado County sheriff's deputies, that I realized we were not being hunted down.

"What are you two doing out here?" one of the so-called deputies called out. I couldn't see their badges in the dark, and because I couldn't tell if they really were deputies, I pulled my rifle off my shoulder and laid it sideways before me next to the saddle horn.

"We're heading home, sir," I said as they approached and circled us. I caught a glimpse of a deputy's badge and my pulse quickened.

Dulceña had covered her head and the lower part of her face with her rebozo. As we made eye contact, I gripped the reins tightly in my hands until my palms felt bruised. The sheriff's office worked closely with the Texas Rangers. Papá was definitely going to find out about our midnight escapade.

"Heading home?" I recognized Deputy Slater as he leaned forward in his saddle, trying to get a better look at us in the dark. We wouldn't have been at a disadvantage if the rebels hadn't kept our lantern. "You Ace's younger boy?"

"Yes, sir, I am," I said, nervously. I'd heard tales of what Rangers did out in the chaparral. Out here in the darkness, where lawmen can't tell Mexicans and tejanos apart, the Rangers were ruthless, shooting first and asking questions later. It was exactly why I had been worried about our late-night meeting in the first place.

"This your sweetheart, Joaquín?" Slater asked, sidling right up to Dulceña's mount, trying to catch a glimpse of her covered face.

Before I could answer, Dulceña shook her head. "That's none of your business," she said.

"This is Dulceña," I said. "She's my parents' goddaughter."

"Well, don't you two know there's a rebellion going on?" Slater asked. "Outlaws hide out in these parts. It's not safe to wander the woods at night."

"Yes, sir, we know." I looked sideways at Dulceña, who was sitting quietly in her saddle. "We should really get going. Her parents are probably worried sick about her by now."

"I'm sure they are," the second deputy said, and as he came toward me, I recognized him. His name was Davis, and he was new to Morado County.

When Slater came over to sit between me and Dulceña, she averted her eyes, turning her face away from the deputy. Slater reached over to Dulceña's horse and stroked its mane for a moment. "Maybe we should escort you two into town—make sure you make it there without any trouble."

"No!" I said—too quickly, because both deputies turned their attention to me at the same time. "No. It's fine. We'll be all right." I tried to sound competent, up to the task of getting Dulceña home safely without assistance.

I didn't want to come off as paranoid, but I just didn't trust them. Lawmen were just as dangerous as rebels in South Texas these days. Reports from Hidalgo County and Agua Dulce had been running in the rumor mill, of lawmen—Rangers and deputies alike—taking girls away under the pretense of escorting them home and then violating and brutalizing them, oftentimes leaving them for dead in the campo. Since I didn't know Slater and Davis personally, I wasn't about to let them "escort us home."

Davis's mount snorted, and he yanked at the reins, smiling. "Wait a minute. Are you two running off together?"

"No, of course not!" Dulceña's pitch rose in agitation. "I was out for a ride this evening and decided to visit Las Moras. It got to be too late to ride back alone."

Slater cleared his throat fiercely. Coughing something up, he spat on the ground in front of Dulceña's mount. "Stop teasing her, Davis," he said. "Come on. Let's get this caravan going."

Dulceña shrunk a little inside her rebozo as Slater took

the reins from her and began to ride off with them in tow.

"There's no need to take her reins away," I said as I started to follow. "She can manage her own horse."

Davis suddenly sidled up to my left and reached over to me, "Where do you think you're going?" he asked, grabbing me by the back of the neck. He pulled me toward him, and I twisted against him until we both fell off our horses, hitting the ground with a heavy thud.

Somewhere in the darkness, I heard Dulceña scream, but Davis had me facedown on the dirt, flat against the ground. I wrestled against him. His right arm wrapped around my throat, cutting off my airway, and his knee pressed against my back, keeping me still while he tried to choke the life out of me.

"Dulceña?" My voice sounded small, weak to my ears.

When she didn't answer, I closed my eyes and anchored my right shoulder in the dirt, pushing my knees into the ground at the same time to gain momentum. When I felt Davis's arm give a little, I pushed off, lifting us both off the ground. I twisted around until I had him on his back so that I could scoot over him, easing myself out of his chokehold in the process.

On my feet a moment later, I reached for my horse's reins, hoping my lead would get me to Dulceña in time. Then Davis, on his knees beside me, pulled his gun.

"Stay!" he ordered. My skin prickled, and every muscle in my body tightened.

I froze.

Davis started to stand.

Given a moment of distraction when he wobbled on one knee, I threw myself at him. Davis flew backward. I yanked his pistol from his hands as he went down, throwing the gun into the brush and dropping on him in one motion.

I didn't think. I just reacted. Papá had taught me how to wrestle and fight to defend myself since I was twelve years old. Pugilism had been his favorite pastime as a youth, so he trained me well. Though I'd never expected to use them in defense of my life, the moves came naturally now. I hit Davis in the side of the jaw with a few quick left jabs before delivering a solid punch with my right, exactly the way I had practiced with Papá.

Once Davis was laid out on the ground, I ran into the brush in the direction my horse had taken when he'd gotten spooked by all the squabbling. I found him standing between two trees. He shook his head and snorted when I clicked my tongue and approached him. I stroked his mane once, to soothe him, before mounting. Then I grabbed my rifle and rode into the thicket, in the direction Slater had taken Dulceña.

Just a few yards on the other side of the brush, Dulceña was fighting off Slater's attack as he tried to pin her against the trunk of an old oak tree. Without hesitation, I fired a warning shot into the night air and aimed at Slater's back. Slater spun around, pulling Dulceña in front of him. She was pale with fright, and I could tell by her swollen cheek he'd beaten her up quite a bit. I dismounted, because if I was going to shoot, I wanted to make sure I was standing on firm ground where I had more control of the situation. Holding his pistol to her temple, Slater yelled, "Throw your weapon down, boy."

The sight of Dulceña with a bloody lip and bulging left eye was enough to send me over the edge. I kept my rifle aimed at him. I wanted nothing more than to shoot him, but I didn't have a clean shot. I thought about it for a moment, considered shooting at him anyway, but then he yelled again, "Now! Before I change my mind and kill you both."

I didn't get a chance to lower my weapon. Davis came out of the shadows behind me and hit me in the head. My head exploded with pain and I fell to the ground.

"What should we do with him?" Davis asked, pressing his gun against my head.

Slater took a deep breath, as if considering what to do next. Then he pushed Dulceña back to the tree. "You stay there, or you both die tonight. Understand?"

Dulceña nodded, and Slater walked over to me, tapping his thigh with his gun.

"Joaquín del Toro," Slater said. "You should've stayed down, boy. You're in over your head here. What are people going to *think* when we take you in for raping and killing this pretty young thing?"

The thought of them getting away with rape and murder put knots in my stomach. "You're not smart enough to pull that off." To prove my point, I spat on his boots.

Slater tossed his gun to Davis and pulled me up by the

collar of my shirt. When I was on my feet, he pushed me back and swung at me. I let him have the first punch. His fist barely skimmed the rim of my jaw as I moved my head sideways, shifting with the punch to minimize the impact.

Then I ripped into him, jabbing his jaw three times before taking him by the shoulders. I kept him close so that it was his back Davis would hit if he tried to shoot me, throwing body punch after body punch.

"Slater!" Davis screamed. "Do I shoot him?"

"No!" Slater shouted as he struggled against me. "No! No! Whatever you do, don't shoot! I can . . . take him . . ."

"Oh, hell!"

Davis threw down the guns and tried pulling me off Slater. Almost immediately, we all went down to the ground, struggling in a mass of arms and legs. Together, both deputies were getting in more and more punches on me, which fueled my rage. I punched blindly, not caring where my fists landed, as long as flesh pounded flesh.

Suddenly, a shot rang out, and we all froze. Still clutching Slater's shirt in my fist, I turned to see Dulceña holding a deputy's pistol in each hand, pointing at us. Her figure was tiny against the darkness, but her feet were firmly planted on the ground, shoulder-width apart. She was ready to shoot again.

"Get off him," she said, waving the gun in her left hand in the general direction she wanted the deputies to move.

As Slater and Davis rolled off to the side, I clutched at my forehead. Sometime during the scuffle, I had hit my head hard against a rock, and the sting of it suddenly caught up with me. Dulceña spoke again. "You two stay where you are. Don't even breathe. Are you all right, Joaquín?"

"Yeah." I got up and walked over to check on Dulceña's wounds. "The question is, how are you doing?"

She handed me one of the pistols. "I'll live" she said, leaning into my arm with a sigh of relief. "Should we tie them up?"

The sound of approaching horse hooves caught everyone's attention. As we all turned, my older brother, Tomás, came crashing into the clearing followed closely by Mateo and Fito. They kicked up a cloud of dust as they came to a quick stop that made Tomás's sorrel whinny, rear up, and beat at the air with his white forelegs.

All three men jumped off their horses. While Tomás came over toward us, Mateo and Fito made quick work of grabbing Slater and Davis and pushing them to the ground, making them lay there with their hands behind their heads. Tomás winced when he prodded my head wound, but he let out a loud, exasperated breath when he inspected Dulceña's face.

"It's not too bad. The swelling will go down in a few days. I just hope your lip doesn't scar." He took the gun from Dulceña and handed it to me. I pointed it at the deputies on the ground.

Inching over to me while keeping his gun aimed at the deputies, Mateo asked, "You feeling okay, Joaquín? Not seeing two of everything, are you?"

"No. I'm fine," I said, touching my forehead again and flinching at the pain that was becoming sharper by the minute. "What are you all doing here?"

"What do you think we're doing? You left without telling anyone where you were going." Tomás's voice changed. He was suddenly grit and stone, hard, the way he used to be when I was growing up. Even though I wasn't a boy anymore, his tone still affected me. I suspected it would always be that way. "Mateo and Fito were worried about you. They couldn't go back to Las Moras without you. How would they explain your whereabouts? You shouldn't be so inconsiderate of your friends, Joaquín. Perhaps if you had stayed with them, none of this would have happened."

"I know," I said. "I'm sorry."

"Never mind that," Tomás said. "What happened here, exactly?"

My brother's eyebrows furrowed more and more as I recounted the harrowing events of that night, leaving out the meeting with the bandits for fear of incurring more of his wrath. I swear my brother cringed when I pointed out Dulceña's disheveled hair and torn dress to validate my story.

"You two are going to have a tough time explaining this to Sheriff Nolan after I have a talk with him," Tomás said to Slater and Davis, who were now sitting up on their knees next to each other, hanging their heads. "I suggest you get on your horses and start heading into town."

"We can't let them go," I protested, upset but not shocked by his decision. Tomás was always trying to help people out.

"We have to take them in. Tell the sheriff what they did."

"We don't have any authority here," Tomás said. "These might be Nolan's men, but we all know who's really in charge. It's Munro we'd have to talk to, and I doubt Munro would believe you over them. You know how he is. He'd do anything to keep law and order, even if that means covering up for his men when they run rampant."

"He's right," Mateo said, his dark face twisted with disgust. "Unfortunately, it's your word against theirs, and lawmen are never wrong. Not around here, they ain't."

"We have to get you home," Tomás said. "You're both bleeding, and we need to get some ice on Dulceña's face to bring down the swelling. And if I know Mamá, she'll want to help her clean up before we call for her parents."

"But—"

"But nothing," Tomás interrupted me. "Take their guns. Make sure they have no other weapons on their mounts, and let's get you both back home. It's going to be a long night at Las Moras."

Excerpt from the Hand-Book of Etiquette for Ladies by an American Lady, 1847-1915

the gentleman to the lady, not the lady to the gentleman.

III.

An introduction at a ball for the purpose of dancing does not compel you to recognise the person in the street or in any public place; and except under very peculiar circumstances such intimacies had better cease with the ball.

When in
tion the nar
ure to do th
embarrassm
duced, and
better to sa
did not hear
unpleasant

As a gen
introductior
from relatic

TRUE POLITENESS.

A

HAND-BOOK OF ETIQUETTE

FOR

LADIES.

BY AN AMERICAN LADY.

Chapter 5

When we got back to Las Moras, my father called Munro and we all met in the sala, the more intimate family room in the back of the house, away from the impersonal foyer and the grandeur of the main parlor. Dulceña's parents sat together on the big couch with their daughter snuggled between them. My mother had taken care of Dulceña's wounds. Other than a swollen lip and a few scratches on her face, my beloved looked like she always did, composed and smart, completely in control of her emotions.

It was strange having both our families gathered together in the sala again. Not since that fateful Easter Sunday when my father had lost his temper had the Villas visited our house, much less sat across from each other in this, the most familial room in our home. But I couldn't take any joy in the situation. Dulceña's wounds made me regret the circumstances that were bringing us together.

Mamá, beside me on the love seat, rested her hands on my right arm, and fussed with my hair. My father and Tomás were standing by the stone fireplace next to Captain Munro, as he asked questions and put together the details of the attack. We all knew it was a long shot, but my parents had insisted on calling in Munro and trying to make him do something about the attack.

While Captain Munro, Tomás, and Papá sorted things out, Mamá checked my head wound one more time, gingerly testing the bandage. Then she kissed me and hugged me tight, saying, "Gracias a Dios you're all right. I couldn't bear it if anything happened to you. ¡Eres mi alma—mi corazón!"

Captain Munro asked me a few more questions about the incident. Why were we there? What was the purpose of the meeting? Who else was at the creek? I was as honest and truthful as I could be when I answered him without making any remarks that might tarnish Dulceña's reputation or give Munro any information about the concerns we had over our ranch hands before I had an opportunity to alert my father. As far as Munro was concerned, we were just talking, visiting with each other away from the chaos and commotion of the quinceañera.

"You have to understand," Mamá said, coming to our defense. "They've been friends since they were out of the crib. We practically raised them together. They played together year after year, in school and in this house. It can't be easy for them, this . . . separation."

Munro took stock of us as we sat together in discomfort. "And that's it?" he asked. "That's the whole story."

"Yes, sir, that's it," I said. "We just wanted to sit down and talk, away from the drunken partygoers in the plaza." Of course, I didn't mention the earlier incident, when we were accosted by rebels. I couldn't tell anyone about that, not after the information Dulceña had bestowed upon me earlier that night. I couldn't be sure what the Ranger would think if I told him the rebels let us go soon after they found out who I was. There were all kinds of implications there, and I didn't want Munro to come to the conclusion that we were in league with tejano rebels.

Dulceña didn't mention the rebels either. It's not that Dulceña's deceptive, but she probably wanted Munro and his posse to concentrate on the deputies. She'd want Slater and Davis arrested and imprisoned for what they tried to do to her.

"Well, Ace, we have to face it. My hands are tied," Munro said, walking over to stand by the window. "I don't have many options here."

"What do you mean, you don't have many options?" I asked. "What are you talking about?"

Papá turned around to face the Ranger. "Damn it, Elliot!" he said. "I'm not trying to make trouble for you, but those boys have to be punished. You can't let them get away with this."

"Yes, but we can't let this get out either," Munro interrupted. "Don't you understand? If this got out, it would ruin the girl's reputation."

"That's outrageous!" Mamá said, leaving my side and standing up to face the captain. "How could it ruin her reputation? She's done nothing wrong. She's the victim here!"

Munro turned around to stare down Mamá. "You and I know she had no business being out there at that time of night."

At the Ranger's words, Doña Serafina let out a small, startled cry. Don Rodrigo stood up, his chest puffed out, his eyes narrowed and bright. "I would be very careful with my words if I were you, Captain. Very careful."

"I'm not saying it's her fault," Munro said. "But the fact is she put herself in this position and now we have to face the repercussions of her lack of propriety. If she had never left the ball, if she had stayed with you, with Madame Josette even, she would not have been attacked. But she went out into the woods, in the middle of the night to meet a young man. Alone. Well, there's nothing—absolutely nothing—anyone can say that can account for that lack of judgment on her part."

"But Slater and Davis shouldn't get away with this!" I said, standing up too. "Her reputation shouldn't keep you from punishing her attackers. Those two are rapists! Her reputation should be the very reason for going after them!"

"And let people speculate, spread rumors, whisper when she passes by?" Munro asked, clenching his right hand as he spoke. "Is that you want, son? You want that girl to live with this for the rest of her life? Because that's what'll happen. People around these parts, they never forget anything. They never let things die. That's the problem with these—these—"

The Ranger's words had ignited a fire inside me and I could feel myself getting hotter and hotter, boiling over with rage as I said, "—with these *Mexicans?*"

"Joaquín!" Mamá cried out, shocked. I clenched my teeth to keep myself from yelling out everything else I was thinking. I knew Papá would never admit it, but Munro was a bigot. It poured out of him from every pore—his abhorrence for mejicanos. I'd heard it all my life from the campesinos at Las Moras. Mamá sensed it. Tomás suspected it. Everyone except Papá saw Munro for what he really was.

Munro glowered at me with gold-flecked brown eyes, poisoned arrows honing in on their target. "I was going to say—that's the problem with these *small towns*. One pain is lessened by another's anguish."

"I'm sure you were," I said, refusing to be thwarted by his golden stare.

"Now, let's not let our tempers get the best of us." Tomás paced the room for a moment. "Captain Munro is right. This incident could cause irreparable damage to Dulceña's reputation and status within the community. He has to find a way to punish the men without involving Dulceña."

My mother pulled on my forearm to get me to stop staring at Munro. I turned away, and she stood between me and the Ranger, near the doorway.

"So what are you suggesting?" Mamá asked, looking across at the captain.

"The way I see it, there's only one thing we can do," Munro said. "We make Sheriff Nolan deal with these men.

I'll see to it that he punishes them accordingly. I'll tell him to make sure this doesn't become public knowledge. If your family doesn't press the issue, Rodrigo, the least his men can do is keep their mouths shut."

"What about me?" I asked. "What if I press charges for their assault on me?"

Munro turned his full attention to me. "These aren't common criminals we're dealing with here. They are officers of the law. You're better off letting me take care of this. Like I said, I'll have a talk with Nolan. Let him know what's expected here."

"I don't know, Captain," Tomás said, shaking his head. "I think you're tempting the devil. If these men don't get what's coming to them, if they're not dealt with publicly, it could further aggravate the racial tensions we're already experiencing. Things could get ugly. What do you think, Papá?"

"I think you should hang 'em!" I said, my voice quivering with rage. "That's what the sheriff would do if it was one of us." I silently dared Munro to contradict me.

"I think you better let me do the thinking," the Ranger said. "Now if those boys are brought up on charges, they're going to start telling stories, trying to defend themselves to gain sympathy. They might even try to make you out to be the bad guy, Joaquín. There's no telling what kind of tales they might fabricate to keep their necks from the noose. No. I think you better let me handle this. I'll talk to Nolan, and we'll get those boys straightened out."

Suddenly, Dulceña was on her feet. She walked over and

stood right under Munro's nose. "Why are we still standing here pretending you're going to do anything about this?" Her eyes brimmed with thick tears. "Everyone here knows you're going to cover this up. You've said as much. As long as men like you rule this world, women like me, innocent women, will have no justice. Do you think I care about my reputation? I don't care what people think or whisper about me. All I care about is making things better for our people, and if that tarnishes my reputation, then so be it. I will not be victimized by your goons!"

Munro's eyes almost bulged out of their sockets. "Young lady! You mind your manners and remember your place!" He pointed his index finger in her face. "Don't you ever talk to me like that again."

I moved around Mamá and got right up behind Dulceña. "Now, hold on! Dulceña has a right to her own opinion."

Papá agreed with me for once. "Joaquín is right. Now, all we're saying—all we're asking—is that you do your job, Elliot. Arrest those men. Deal with them to the fullest extent of the law. Before they do this again!" Papá rapped his knuckles on the coffee table for emphasis.

"There you go again!" Munro turned on my father. "Why are you questioning my authority? I don't need you to tell me how to deal with this. I make the law around here. And I will enforce it in whatever way I see fit! This is *my* county and Monteseco is *my* town. Nolan does what I say. Judge Thompson does what I say. There is no higher power than me in Morado County. Now, if I say I will take care of it, then by God, I will take care of it. Those boys will be brought in. I will investigate. I will dole out the orders, and my orders will be followed. By you and everyone else around here! Understand?"

My father's face fell, become ashen. "What happened to you, Elliot? You used to be a good man."

I was about to remind everyone that Munro answered to the law of the land, not the other way around, when Munro pointed at me and Dulceña. "This happened! Things like this make my job a lot harder than it has to be. I can't be expected to hold up my end of things when you let your brood run amok. Now, if I were you, Rodrigo, I would take my daughter home and make sure she doesn't get out again. Make sure she understands this is what happens to young women when they sneak around at night como prostitutas."

Dulceña threw her arms in the air, pounding on Munro's chest with her clenched fists. "You filthy, disgusting—"

I started toward the Ranger too, but my father pushed me back to the door. At the same time, Doña Serafina shot out of her seat and rushed over to pull Dulceña away from the captain. "Dulceña! ¡Hija, por favor! Cómportate! Please don't stoop to his level. No matter what anybody says, you are a lady, una señorita de familia decente! This isn't solving anything." Then, looking over at her husband, she said, "Vámonos, Rodrigo. It's time to go home."

"It's time for you to go too!" I said, addressing the Ranger while Papá held his hand firmly down on my shoulder, stopping me from moving toward Munro.

"Well!" Papá said, unaffected by the Ranger's narrowing eyes. "You heard my son. Your business here is done."

As Dulceña and her family rushed down the hall and out the front door, my father and the Ranger measured each other up, assessing their next moves. Then, Munro pulled his hat down halfway over his forehead and said, "Yes, it is. I have an interrogation in the morning that requires my attention. I've given Gerardo Gutierrez too much leeway. It's time I got to the bottom of things with your ranch hand, Ace. Joaquín. Señora. I will see myself out."

My father didn't say another word to the Ranger. He was stoic and firm, standing his ground as Munro slithered down the hall and slipped out of our house, closing the door behind himself quietly.

Letter from Joaquín,
Saturday, August 21, 1915

D—

¡Tengo miedo de perderte! The conflict with the rattlesnakes in the brush has sown in me a fear so dark and powerful it overwhelms me. A corded vine, thick and tight, has sprouted, punctured through my chest, crept along my torso, and wrapped itself around my throat like a noose. Thoughts of losing you cause my lungs to strain, my heart to race. I may not make it through another night without seeing you again, making sure that you—that we—are all right. ¡Por favor, no te olvides de mí!

Te amo,
—J

Chapter 6

Saturday morning, my father woke me up early and told me we needed to go into town to see what we could do to help Gerardo out. He wasn't going to wait until Monday before trying to get him out of jail. He didn't trust Munro, not after his parting words the night before, and frankly, neither did I. It's true what they say—when you let rattlesnakes crawl on your belly, you're going to get bitten, and Papá had played possum too long by allowing Munro to "take care of us" under the guise of friendship.

When I remembered we were going into town, I ran upstairs and picked up the note I'd written to Dulceña in the wee hours of the morning, when I had been feeling so wretched I couldn't get to sleep. I'd planned on finding a way of getting the note to her come Monday morning, but there was no sense in waiting, especially if I could get it to her earlier. It wasn't urgent. Just important. She needed to know how miserable I was. How much I regretted everything that happened the night before. How much I still loved her.

Because Papá had a big delivery of lumber to pick up, he decided we needed to take the wagon instead of driving the Packard into town. I rode in the wagon with my father, while Manuel, Mateo, and Fito trailed behind us on horseback.

By the time we got into Monteseco, I was itching to get out of the wagon and find a small boy I could hand a peso to and say, "Here, go give this envelope to the pretty girl in the print shop." Her father never suspected anything was amiss because Dulceña was technically in charge of opening and sorting through the mail at *El Sureño*. If Mateo's girlfriend, Conchita, was around, I would give her the note. She would rush over for a quick chat during her break from waitressing at Donna's Kitchen and slip it into Dulceña's hands when Don Rodrigo wasn't looking.

When we got there, Papá and I went into the jailhouse while Manuel and the twins went to check on our order at the lumber mill. Papá stepped up to the clerk's window and asked for the amount of the bail on Gerardo Gutierrez.

Nacho, the old clerk who had worked at the jailhouse as long as I could remember, scrambled with some papers on his desk, mumbling something that I didn't quite catch. Papá frowned at him, and the clerk repeated himself. "I'm sorry, Don Acevedo," he said, forcing a crooked little smile onto his face. One of those nervous smiles people get when they're uncomfortable. "But you can't bail him out."

"What do you mean?" my father asked. "Where is he?"

Nacho's eyes flickered back and forth between the door and my father before he continued. "There's no bail on Gerardo. Not allowed."

"No bail? There has to be a bail!" Papá said, his eyebrows drawn so close together over his piercing eyes they almost touched each other on his forehead.

"No. Not if the judge thinks he might run," Nacho said, his voice low and meek, like he was afraid of delivering the bad news to my father.

"Run where?" my father asked. "What for?"

Nacho shuffled his feet, repositioned himself behind his little window, and scratched his head. "Oh, I don't know. To Mexico, maybe," he said. "To join the revolution. Might be he takes off and hides out with his friends out in the chaparral. There's a whole lot of places a rebel like him might run off to. Who knows, he might even run off to join the Sediciosos!"

My father frowned. "But he hasn't even had a trial yet!"

"Gerardo, a Sedicioso?" I asked. "That's not true, is it, Papá?"

It was hard to imagine Gerardo as a Sedicioso. The Sediciosos were a fearsome rebel gang run by Aniceto Pizaña, a prominent tejano rancher who, after a brutal attack by Rangers on his ranch, Los Tulitos, earlier in the month, had taken up arms, recruiting men and making good on the promises outlined in the Plan de San Diego. They were said to be responsible for a number of incidents involving the destruction of railroads, bridges, and other infrastructure in South Texas. They'd sworn to take out anything related to the white settlers to make sure they got their message across: tejanos were not going to be oppressed, much less enslaved, not in their own land—the land that had been stolen from them and their ancestors. Even my mother conceded their argument, reminding us every now and then this was our land long before the conquest. "Forget the Spanish land grants," she'd say. "We don't need a piece of paper to stake our claim on this country. My hair, my skin, the color of my eyes is proof enough. My ancestors—our ancestors—were here first!"

"No. Gerardo wouldn't run with that lot," Papá said, shaking his head and waving his hand in the air dismissively. "He's too green for that kind of outfit. Besides, Los Sediciosos keep to their territory. Their business is down in Hidalgo, Cameron, and Starr Counties. They've never entered these parts."

Nacho shrugged and said, "Well, those are the charges."

"Let me talk to him," Papá said. "I need to let him know we're taking care of this. I promised his mother I'd get in to see him."

Nacho took in a long breath and let it out in what sounded like a defeated sigh. Then he fussed with his papers again and said, "Nope. No visitors allowed either."

"That's not legal. Any two-bit lawyer in town will tell

you that." My father's voice was suddenly quiet and deep, menacing. He stood with his hands on the sill of the iron-grated window that separated us from Nacho and thought for a moment. Then, without saying another word to Nacho, my father turned around and walked to the door. "Come on, Joaquín. Let's go."

Outside the jailhouse, my father put his hands on his waist, hooking his thumbs in his belt loops. A bunch of Munro's men coming out of Donna's Kitchen caught his attention.

"Where the hell's Munro?" my father mumbled, more to himself than to me.

"They always have a late breakfast at Donna's," I said, guessing he was considering confronting the Ranger. "Same place he always is at breakfast—sitting at the corner table by the window."

My father let out a long-held breath. Then he gritted his teeth and pushed his hat down over his forehead. "Go to the mill. Get Manuel. Tell him what's going on."

I didn't have to go all the way to the mill. By the time I ran down to the end of the street, Manuel and the twins were already turning the corner. "Papá's at Donna's, talking to Munro. They wouldn't let us bail out Gerardo. They wouldn't even let us see him. Papá said to—"

I hadn't even finished telling him the rest of the message before Manuel turned to the twins and said, "Get the wagon and horses. Bring 'em over to the café. I'll go check on your father," he said to me.

Mateo, Fito, and I rushed off and retrieved the wagon and horses. I pulled the wagon around and tied it up across the street from the café, at the general store, and Mateo and Fito tied their horses beside the wagon. When everything was secure, we started across the street.

That's when I caught sight of Slater and Davis a few buildings down from us. Slater was too busy entertaining Davis and the rest of Munro's posse standing in front of Nina's Dress Shop to notice us. My suspicions were confirmed: Munro and Sheriff Nolan had done nothing to get us justice. Slater and Davis weren't acting like doomed men. Slater's face bore no signs of worry or distress, and nothing about his demeanor said he'd received any kind of reprimand or suspension. In fact, he was as happy as a lark. Both he and Davis were standing around like they didn't have a care in the world. Except for the black eye I'd given him, it was as if nothing had happened. Worse yet, both he and Davis were standing around like they didn't have a care in the world.

"I knew it," I said, disgust roiling up inside my belly. "I knew nothing was going to happen to them."

"That's not all," Mateo said, putting his hand on my shoulder. "Slater's been shooting off his mouth all morning. I saw Conchita on my way to the mill, and she said he's been telling all his friends you tried to beat him up because you caught him and Dulceña having a good time at Arroyo Morado."

"What! That filthy son of a—" Fuming, I took off running across the street with the twins right behind me.

"Stop! Joaquín! Wait!" they screamed, but I wasn't about to stop. Slater had another beating coming to him, and I didn't need anybody's permission to give it to him.

I stepped onto the boardwalk just in time to catch Slater in the act, smacking his lips, saying, "Yes, sir, she's a good kisser, that sweet little Dulceña!"

Enraged, I rushed at him with all the ferocity of a bull. I plowed into him so hard we fell into the street, kicking up a cloud of dust as we hit the ground. I rolled over and got on top of him, pounding his face again and again. Davis and the rest of the lawmen stood over us. They hooted and hollered, yelling, "Come on, Slater!"

"Get up!"

"Hit that *bean-eater*!"

"Hit him!"

But I was not about to let that happen. As I punched away at Slater's bloody face, no one tried to stop me. They wouldn't have been able to anyway. The locomotive inside me was running full steam ahead. It wasn't until I heard Papá's distinct, long-winded whistle that I halted. Holding Slater down on the ground under me, I saw Munro and Papá running down the boardwalk in our direction.

"Boy, what do you think you're doing?" Munro asked, pulling me off Slater.

Papá turned me toward him. He tested the scrapes on my face gently with his fingertips and sighed deeply. Manuel reached down, picked up my hat, dusted it off by slapping it against his leg, and handed it back to me. Frustrated, I pushed my hair back and shoved my hat down on my head. On the ground, Slater moaned and coughed, rolling over on his side to spit out blood. Then he put his fingers in his mouth and pulled out a jagged tooth.

"Jesus! What a mess!" Munro said, shaking his head in disgust.

"He had it coming!" I exclaimed.

Slater was a pathetic sight, writhing on the ground, acting as helpless as a slimy worm on a fishing hook.

"I didn't do nothing, Capt'n," Slater proclaimed, spitting up some more blood for effect. "He just come out of nowhere."

"I had to do something!" I said. "He's been spreading rumors! Lies! About Dulceña! I couldn't let him get away with that. He can't talk like that. Not about her. Not about my Dulceña."

Slater stood up, grabbing at his side as he continued. "I didn't do nothing. I was just talking to my friends when he come up on the porch and took a swing at me for no reason at all. You can ask these guys if you don't believe me."

Munro didn't have to ask, because Davis jumped in and corroborated Slater's story. "Don't know what he's crying about. Slater and us, we was just minding our own business and then here comes Joaquín bustin' things up, gettin' all mad for nothin'."

"That's not what happened," Mateo said, stepping forward

to speak to the Ranger directly. "Slater's been saying some vile things, making Señorita Dulceña sound like a loose woman, when we all know she's anything but."

"I'm not lying," Slater said, pressing his palm against his left nostril, trying to stop the bleeding. "You're just jealous 'cause your negrita's no better. Or didn't you know your little chocolate doll likes the white boys too?"

"Shut your mouth, you ignorant pig!" Mateo said, spitting at Slater's feet. "Conchita would never get near a filthy tlacuache like you!"

Slater stepped back. "Shut your own mouth, *messy-skin*!"

"You call him that one more time and I'll tear your tongue out!" I pointed a finger in Slater's face.

"Now hold on!" Munro stepped between me and Slater again, holding out his hands like an official in a boxing ring. "Nobody's going to do anything. This stops now!" Then, turning to my father, he said, "I don't want to tell you what to do, Ace. But your boys are out of control. Might be they've been influenced by rebels, same as Gerardo Gutierrez. I'd straighten them out before they gets themselves in too deep."

"That's bull! Gerardo is not a rebel," I said. "This wouldn't have happened if you'd done your job!" I said, mustering up the courage to tell Munro what I really thought about his refereeing.

"Joaquín!" The terse tone of Papá's voice told me he'd had enough. A good son doesn't talk back to his father in front of another man, and I was trying my best to be a good son.

So I clenched my teeth to keep myself from saying anything else until we were alone, until we could sit down and hash this thing out. If it was me, I'd tell Munro exactly what he could do with his opinion.

"What's going on here, Ace?" Munro took his hat off and wiped the sweat from his brow with a handkerchief before tucking it inside his shirt pocket. "What kind of potrillos are you raising in your corral? I suggest you take your son home before he gets himself arrested."

"Or killed!" Slater popped off one more time from behind Munro.

"You keep your trap shut! You're in enough trouble already!" Munro pushed Slater away from him in disgust and turned back to Papá. "Let's get these boys away from each other, Ace. You deal with yours and I'll deal with mine."

Papá's voice was low and gruff, his words quiet as lit dynamite. "Fine. Make sure you take care of it this time."

"Oh, I'll take care of it, all right," Munro growled at my father. "Don't you worry about that. These boys. The business with Gerardo. It's all going to get sorted out! I just hope you're as prepared for what's coming as you think you are."

"Is that supposed to intimidate me?" my father asked, lifting his chin. "I've got nothing to hide."

Munro's lips pulled back against his cheeks slowly, like they were being drawn against their will, revealing an unsightly row of long, yellowing teeth. He looked like a calaca, a desiccated skull, smiling eerily. "We'll see what Gerardo has to say about that," he said, then he tipped his hat and walked off. "Come on, boys. Let's go talk to Nolan."

Manuel said the lumber wouldn't be ready for pick-up until Monday morning, so Papá and I got in the wagon and sped down the dirt road toward Las Moras. Manuel and the twins kept a respectful distance behind us, giving me and Papá room to speak about the incident in front of Nina's shop. But my father wasn't in a mood to speak. The fast pace he was keeping said it all. He was furious.

We drove like that for at least twenty minutes, both of us fuming in silence. "I'm sorry, Papá," I said after my blood had stopped boiling enough to let me think straight again. "I didn't mean to cause any more trouble. I know you've got enough to worry about with this mess with Gerardo, but you have to understand! I couldn't let Slater just get away with dragging Dulceña's reputation through the mud like that."

Papá shook his head and slowed down a bit before he finally spoke to me. "I just wish you weren't such a hothead, Joaquín."

"What was I supposed to do?" I asked. "Curl up and hide in my shell like a cochinilla? I'm not a cowardly bug, Papá. I can't do that! That's not how you brought us up. You've always said a man stands up for what's right. And protecting Dulceña's good name was the right thing to do, even if you're still mad at Don Rodrigo. I guess you know by now, she's my sweetheart, and I have to protect her. It's my fault she's in this mess. I shouldn't have agreed to meet her. Not there. Not at night. So now it's up to me to make sure nothing else comes of this."

"I understand what you're saying, Joaquín," Papá said. "I didn't expect you to roll over and play dead. You did what you had to do. You stood up for Dulceña, defended her honor. That's what a gentleman would do. Anytime. However, there comes a time when a man has to decide how he wants to be regarded by society. You need to learn to think before you act, Son. You can't solve every problem with a fistfight."

"I guess we disagree on that," I said.

My father kept his narrowed eyes on the road, his lips tight, before he finally said, "Yes we do."

Secret Message from Dulceña, Sunday, August 22, 1915

J—

You will never lose me! Estamos enlazados—our hearts are tethered.

Forever Yours,

—D

Chapter 7

Because of all the nonsense with Slater, I wasn't able to send Dulceña my letter while I was in town, but I managed to give it to Mateo, who handed it over to Conchita during service on Sunday morning. I couldn't very well be the one giving Conchita a note in church, but Mateo managed it with ease. It was a good thing, because I got an immediate response.

That very afternoon, I found a tiny note tucked within the folds of my napkin at dinnertime. I wasn't expecting it to be there, not so soon after having sent her mine, so it fell to the floor when I pulled my napkin open. I wasn't quick enough to snap the small, pink envelope onto my lap without calling attention to it. Time stood still as it fluttered down silently before landing on my boot, but I managed to kick it off and slide it under the table with my foot before anyone noticed.

Doña Luz stood between me and Mamá, who was sitting to my left, and neither of them saw me reach down and pick it up with my napkin. I left it sitting on my thigh for a while, being careful to wipe my hands gently, without taking the lacy material off my lap, until I was able to tuck the note discreetly into my pants' pocket.

Immediately after dinner, I ran up to my room and read the meager message. It was a sweet note, and it felt good—our connectedness. But I had so many questions, so many concerns. Was she suffering any criticism from the vile rumors Slater had been spreading in town? How was she feeling? Had her lip started to heal? Did she miss me? The note just wasn't enough. I needed to see her.

I went downstairs to check on my parents. Tomás, who hadn't left after dinner, had joined them in the library. I walked in and sat down with the rest of my family, waiting an eternity for them to finish their business, watching their every move with a sharp bird's eye, como halcón. It seemed like Papá took more time than usual with the ranch bookkeeping that evening. I sighed often and scribbled poems into my journal, while Mamá read newspaper stories and Tomás worked on a sermon.

Just when I thought Mamá was almost done, an article in the *Maverick*, a small paper out of Eagle Pass, caught her attention, and she read it aloud. "Listen to this, Tomás, 'Most assuredly, it is La Estrella who will go down in history as the true spirit of the rebellion. Her willingness to go outside the law, against her neighbors, risking her life to help feed and clothe our tejano brothers in arms, is the reason we are still fighting the evil lawmen of South Texas who would do anything to subjugate our people as they struggle to protect their families and keep their ancestral lands from being stolen from under their feet. Our courageous women are our secret weapons, and it is because of them that we will win this fight.' "

"That's daring!" Tomás put his Bible on the coffee table to his left. "You don't usually read that kind of story in English. Only papers written in Spanish carry those kinds of editorials. Did A. V. Negrados write that?"

"Sí. I'm going to clip it," Mamá said, putting the paper aside and reaching for her scissors. From what I had seen lately, although A. V. Negrados was a new voice in South Texas, she was quickly becoming one of Mamá's favorite reporters. She was always clipping her stories and putting them into her scrapbook. "This article proves just how courageous tejanos are becoming. That's something the Rangers will never understand."

"Or accept," Tomás said. "You should be careful with that notebook of yours, Mamá. It's not necessarily the kind of thing you want Munro to find if he gets a wild hair and decides to raid Las Moras."

"Tomás is right," Papá said. "We're in no position to keep things like that in the house anymore, mi amor, especially now that Munro and I aren't seeing eye to eye. The way he's handling this business with Gerardo . . . Well, it just shows me what he's really made of. We can't trust him. I would prefer if you got rid of that scrapbook of yours. God only knows what he would make of that."

Mamá gave Papá a look that said she wasn't about to have that discussion with him. Her scrapbook was one of her most prized possessions. She clipped every news article regarding La Estrella like the woman was some sort of religious icon for her. I never thought much about it, except that Papá was right. Under the circumstances, and the irrational behavior Munro had been exhibiting, the scrapbook might become evidence of insurgence in his eyes.

"The Texas Rangers think they can dictate how we act and think. But they won't defeat us." Mamá put the newspaper aside distastefully, like the mere mention of Munro raiding Las Moras had soiled it for her. "Those who rush stumble and fall. Even their brutality will never break our spirits. We are tejanos mejicanos. We are familia. We will always stick together. Our spirits, our hearts, that is something they can never take away from us."

"Well said." Tomás smiled and went back to work on the sermon he'd been drafting on the couch.

Even after my brother left, I stayed up writing in the library, waiting for everyone to go to bed. It was almost eleven when I was finally able to leave the house without being questioned. I wondered if Dulceña would even be awake by the time I made it into Monteseco.

It took me almost an hour on horseback to get to Dulceña's house. I left my palomino tied to a mesquite just outside of town, behind the lumber mill, and walked over to her neighborhood on Fourth Street. After jumping over their side fence, I stood in her backyard throwing dry, hardened chinaberries at her window. When she finally emerged, I climbed the jacaranda tree up to her balcony as quietly as possible, careful not to wake up anyone else in her house.

"What are you doing here, you crazy guy?" Dulceña pulled at my hair, like I was a mischievous child. Then she put her hand on the nape of my neck and pulled me in close for a tender kiss.

I kissed her softly—although her lip wasn't swollen anymore, I could tell it wasn't completely healed.

"I needed to make sure you were okay," I said. "That you were on the mend. Your note didn't say much, and I wanted—no, I *needed* to see it for myself."

Dulceña smiled, that soft little smile that belonged only to me, the one that said, *I love it that you love me.* "Well, I am," she whispered, putting both arms around my neck and kissing me again. "You are too much, Joaquín! Coming here, at this time of night!"

"Thank you, I love you too," I said, keeping one hand on the cold iron bar of the balcony between us and another one on her waist.

Dulceña's face suddenly changed, a dark little frown crossed over her brow, and she toyed with the collar of my shirt before she finally said, "Listen. I know you love me, but you really should be more careful."

"Well, I am standing ten feet off the ground holding on to this railing with only one hand," I said, grinning. "Wanna let me in?"

"You know you can't come in," Dulceña whispered,

playfully hitting my chest with her fist. "My parents would kill me if they knew I was out here with you right now. Sweetheart, you have to stop doing crazy things."

"What are you talking about?" I asked.

"I'm talking about what happened in town this morning," Dulceña said. "Outside Nina's shop."

A white-hot ball of anger swirled in the pit of my stomach at the thought of Slater still walking around town with a badge on his chest, as if he knew anything about integrity. I was angry at Slater, angry at Munro, angry at the rebels . . . but more than anything, angry at the Rangers and settlers for forcing tejano rebels to fight for rights that were already theirs. It was their fault we were in this mess. They had created the whole situation. Why couldn't they leave my family and our friends alone? We had no part in this. But none of that was Dulceña's fault, so I stuffed the whole mess back down and swallowed my rage. "Oh, that," I whispered.

"What were you thinking?" Dulceña asked, her brows knitted close together over her big brown eyes again.

"I was thinking that I'll rip that badge off his chest and carve his eyes out with it if he ever so much as glances in your direction again," I grumbled.

To my surprise, Dulceña lowered her eyes and was suddenly very quiet. Concerned, I swung my leg over the railing and jumped over onto the balcony to take her into my arms. She nestled into me, wrapping her arms around my waist and putting her head under my chin.

I kissed her forehead. "I've upset you," I said, remorse suddenly gnawing at me. "I'm sorry if my words hurt you. I didn't mean to make you cry."

"I'm not hurt," she whispered, sniffling delicately. "I'm angry! I'm angry that they hurt me. I'm angry that they hurt you. But more than anything, I'm angry that nothing is being done to them. They're both walking around town while I have to stay inside until my face heals so no one will ask questions about what happened. The thought of having people talk about me is too much for my mother to handle. But she's right, I am a señorita, and older women with young daughters especially are bound to talk. They would use me as an *example*, someone to point to so they could tell them what not to do, which makes it all even more unfair. Slater is the criminal, but because of *convention*, because of *etiquette*, because of societal norms I had no part in creating or supporting, I'm the one serving time!"

"It's okay, let it out. You have every reason to be angry." I wiped a tear off her cheek with my thumb.

"I keep reliving that night over and over again in my head," she said. "There was a moment there, when Slater wrapped his arms around my throat, before you arrived—I was powerless. I am ashamed to admit it, but at that moment, when he first hit me, I wanted to kill him. I've never wanted to kill anyone before in my life, but just then, I did."

"You have nothing to be ashamed of," I said. "You didn't do anything wrong. And you're not a victim. You were the one who took the guns and stopped them from finishing me off, remember?"

"I'm ashamed of having to keep this a secret!" Dulceña leaned back from my embrace, grasping my shirt in her fist. Her eyes glistened with unshed tears. By the tightness around her jaw, she was trying hard to be brave. She shouldn't have to be hiding, much less feeling ashamed. She should never have been put in this position. "Aiding in the conspiracy to keep things quiet for the sake of my honor makes me sick to my stomach. I hate being part of all this."

"You don't have to be a part of it, mi amor," I said. "I'll take care of it. I'll take Slater out if he wags his tongue again. I don't care what happens to me. I won't let him ruin your reputation."

"No. Please don't do anything rash. You've already put yourself in too much danger." She squeezed my hands for emphasis. "I don't want Munro's posse coming after you any more than I want them coming after my own family, and they would. You can bet on that."

"But we'd be letting them all get away with this!" I said. "Because it's not just the deputies who are getting away with this, mi amor. Munro and Sheriff Nolan also share in that guilt. They're as much to blame for their men acting como salvajes. Someone has to make them pay!"

"My father says letting them go free is the best thing anyone can do for them right now," Dulceña said. "He says bad people never stop doing bad things. Water always runs to water. They'll get what's coming to them eventually."

I nodded. "Papá says sometimes you have to let a vicious dog think he's loose for a bit, give him a little leash. He'll just run around in circles until he gets all tangled up in his own rope and hang himself."

Sighing contently, Dulceña wrapped her arms around my waist and snuggled up to my chest. I was about to kiss her again when we heard her bedroom door open.

"Dulceña?" Doña Serafina called from inside her room.

"You have to go!" Dulceña said. I didn't hop over the railing right away. Instead, I stole one last kiss from her before throwing my legs over.

"Hurry!" She pushed me away, almost making me fall off the balcony. "Be careful!"

"Dulceña, Hija? Are you out there?" Doña Serafina asked, her voice getting closer to the balcony as I started climbing down the jacaranda tree.

"Coming, Mami," Dulceña said as I reached the ground. I hid behind the tree, pressed snugly against the wall of her house.

"What are you doing out there?" her mother asked Dulceña once she was inside the room.

"I couldn't sleep," Dulceña admitted. "It's that moon. It's so close tonight—like having a giant lantern shining into my room."

Doña Serafina went to the balcony door, where she poked her head out and surveyed the garden. I had managed to skulk along the wall to the right of the balcony, discreetly hidden behind a massive bougainvillea.

"Then you should try closing the door and drawing the drapes." Dulceña's mother glanced up at the moon before turning around to talk to her. "You'll catch a cold, standing out here breathing in this mal aire. Come on. Let's get you back to bed."

I stayed in the garden for a few more minutes, to see if Dulceña would come back out and we could finish our conversation. Then I saw a gas lamp light up downstairs, so I bolted out of the yard, jumped over the fence where I'd come in, and ran down the alley toward the edge of town.

THE RONAN PIO

'The Oldest Newspaper on the Flathead Indian Reserv

Entered as second-class matter May 12, 1910, at the post-office at Ronan, Montana, under the Act of March 3, 1879.

VOL. VI. NO. 16. RONAN, MISSOULA COUNTY, MONTANA, AUGU

MEXICANS KILLED BY TEXAS RANGERS

SEVERAL OUTLAWS REPORTED SLAIN IN FIGHT NEAR NORIAS, TEXAS.

AMERICANS ARE REINFORCED

Special Train Carries United States Soldiers to Aid Ranchmen—300 Mexicans Cross Rio Grande, According to Sheriff.

Harlingen, Tex., Aug. 10.—Five American ranchmen were wounded two of them seriously and sever Mexican outlaws were reported k in a fight between Texas ran American ranchers and Mexican bandits at Nori miles north of Lyfor county, according to received here from N ber of casualties to th is said, could not be as ing to darkn

The ted Nor

To Reject British Contention.

Washington, Aug. 10.—Urged by American exporters, the state department was quickly completing its tentative draft of an answer to the British refusal to cease interference with American shipments. In brief, it was understood, the British will be told the American Civil war blockade precedents they cited are not in point. At that time, it will be asserted, the United States government held up no European shipment which it did not know was intended, when shipped, for the Confederacy.

BUMPER YIELDS REPORTED BY ALL THRESHING CREWS

Threshing way the cou

GERMANS MENACE WARSAW RAILWAY

TROOPS ARE NOW W OF LAST EXIT ING

BIG G

Total A Pittsburgh fifth lic

Chapter 8

I didn't know much about politics or revolution, but I knew trouble when I saw it. And the next morning, when Manuel came running up the steps of our house asking for my father, I knew something must have been snapping at his heels like a ravenous coyote.

Mamá, who had been sweeping the porch, set her broom aside in the door frame. "Manuel, qué pasa?"

"It's rebels, Doña Jovita," Manuel said, fear warbling his voice. "They're through the gate and heading up here."

I walked to the edge of the porch. "Rebels?" At the south end of the property, two men were always posted at our gates. "How many of them? Why did the guards let them through?" There was no sign of them yet, but we didn't have a clear view of the south side from the porch of the ranch house.

Mamá ignored my questions. A frown marred her forehead. "Are you sure it's rebels? Did you see them yourself, Manuel?"

"Sí. I saw them from the water tower. It's them all right.

There's no time to waste, señora," Manuel said, pointing toward the south gates as if the rebels were already upon him. "I need to let Don Acevedo know."

"Need to let me know what?" Papá asked, his tall, stout frame blocking the door.

"Rebels, Patrón. Coming up to the house right now." Manuel twisted his slouch hat in his hands as if it might come apart.

Papá peered to the west, beyond the mesquite and huisache tree line to the empty horizon. "Now? In broad daylight? Are the Rangers after them?"

"No," Manuel said, shaking his head. "I didn't see anyone after them. We have to hurry, Patrón."

"The women and children!" Mamá crossed behind Papá to grab her shawl off her rocking chair and put it over her shoulders. "Go to the fields, the laundry room, the farmhouse. Find them all—wherever they are. Get them together, Manuel. Take them to . . . take them—"

"—to the barn?" Manuel finished her thought—my mother was too flustered to finish it herself.

"¡Sí! ¡Sí!" she said, turning to Papá for confirmation. "To the barn, ¿verdad, Acevedo?"

"The barn?" I asked, puzzled. My father nodded, and Manuel took off running behind the house, toward the servants' quarters. "We'd be safer in the house and on the roofs. We can take better aim from higher up, don't you think?"

My father turned to me and said, "Don't ask questions, Joaquín. Just do as your mother says."

"But it makes no sense to hide in the barn!"

My mother headed off down the wide dirt road that led to the big barn.

I ran into the hall and pulled a couple of rifles and pistols off the gun rack. When I came back, I handed my father a rifle and his pistol belt and buckled mine around my waist, hoping Papá couldn't read the worry on my face.

"Come on, Joaquín. We have to go, Son."

As we left the porch and took to the road on foot, a cloud of dust rose up through the woods from the south, getting bigger and bigger as it approached. It was a group of rebels riding hard toward the main house. My stomach twisted with apprehension as Papá and I followed my mother's hurried steps all the way down to where Manuel, Fito, and Mateo were herding some of the women and children who lived at Las Moras into the barn.

When I stepped inside, I found only a few of the women and children had been brought into the fold. But when I asked Mamá where the rest of the womenfolk were, she shushed me. "Not now, Joaquín. Please, just trust me," she said.

Doña Flora ran up the road, waving her arms, yelling for Manuel to wait for her.

I hated when my parents did this, treated me like a kid. I was a grown man. She had no business shushing me. Although I didn't like it, I thought better of resisting or questioning her any further. It would be inappropriate to argue with her in front of the help. It was a conversation for another time.

"Por favor, let me in. I have to talk to them," Doña Flora begged Manuel. He moved slightly aside and let her squeeze past him with her two younger sons. Once we were all in, Manuel closed the doors and we stood quietly huddled together beside the haystacks, saddles, sawhorses, wheelbarrows, and small tool crates in the back. Like chicks in a locked henhouse, we blinked, our sight adjusting to the dimness inside the barn.

The sounds of approaching horse hooves startled our horses, who snorted and pawed restlessly at their stall floors. Papá and Manuel clucked their tongues and spoke soothingly to them as they stood waiting at the front of the barn. One of the younger children whimpered and started to cry. Doña Flora put her hands on her sons' shoulders. She leaned down and whispered something I couldn't hear. Some of the other women did the same, while Beatriz and Teresa, our two field house cooks, picked up their young ones and cooed to them, rocking them in their arms.

I made sure my rifle was loaded and readied myself for whatever happened if the rebels broke through the doors after they were done pilfering the farmhouse and the rest of the grounds. Mamá came to stand beside me. She put one hand on my left arm and the other over my right hand as it hovered over the trigger. "Wait," she whispered. My father was standing quietly beside Manuel. Neither one of them was holding a weapon. I didn't understand how they could all be so calm at a time like this. My heart was thumping in my chest and my hands were sweating as I gripped my rifle.

Outside, horses came to a stop. Men talked quietly as they dismounted. The spurs on their boots clicked and clanged as they milled around in front of the barn. The shadows of their feet moved back and forth under the door frame, their steps pronounced but unhurried. A barn owl hooted and whistled. A thick drop of sweat ran from my temple down the side of my face and I shrugged, wiping it off with my shirt collar.

And then the door opened, letting in the morning sun one slow, hazy ray at a time.

Then Carlos and his men came barging through the door, mean and dangerous in their filthy clothes, with their hands resting over the pistols on their belts. I moved my hand, and then Mamá stepped in front of me, blocking me. I aimed the rifle at the floor.

Suddenly, there was a rush of movement and joyful squeals and laughter as the women and children ran to greet the bandits. "¡Papi!" Teresa's son shouted as he and Teresa rushed in and hugged Chavito.

Chavito grabbed her and called her amor mío. He kissed her on the lips while their son clung to his left leg, his face pressed against his father's thigh.

Beatriz had called Pollo "Guelito" as she hugged him and handed him her youngest daughter. "Say hi to your abuelito, m'ija," she said.

My head was spinning as I turned this way and that and saw nothing but welcomed hugs, lingering kisses, and tearful, warm smiles. But nothing prepared me for the surprise of my life, the moment when Mamá walked over to Carlos, put her arms out, and said, "¡Hermano!"

Carlos wrapped my mother in a bear hug and picked her up off the ground as she kissed his scruffy cheeks and cried out for him to put her down. Confused by the realization that Carlos was my mother's brother, I raised my eyebrows at my father, who was smiling broadly at their reunion.

Even after he put my mother down, Carlos couldn't stop grinning, his upper lip lost under his thick mustache. At that moment when he grinned at us, he was different than I remembered him from our encounter at the creek. He was smaller, shorter. More human.

Papá put his hand on my shoulder and squeezed. The hair on the back of my neck stood on end as I continued to mull over the fact that Carlos was my uncle. But why didn't I know him? Where had he been all my life?

"What's the matter?" Mamá caressed my cheek. "Are you in shock? Can you talk? This is your tio Carlos, Joaquín. He is my father's son from his first marriage. Our families weren't close—our mothers did not get along. That's why you've never met him. But wars tend to unite people, especially if they are familia, verdad, Hermano?"

Carlos patted my mother's hand. "Joaquín and I have met, Jovita. At that creek outside of town, the other night."

"You mean that night with Dulceña?" Mamá's eyes widened and her hand lingered on my arm.

Carlos grinned down at my mother. "But don't worry. He

wasn't the least bit afraid of us. He is most definitely your son, Estrellita."

"Joaquín?" Papá's eyes narrowed. "Why didn't you tell us?"

My mind reeled for a moment. I had been holding my breath, so I filled my lungs with air before I spoke to my mother. "I'm sorry. I'm just a little— Wait," I said, as I tried to make sense of the situation. "Did he just . . . did he just call you *Estrellita*?"

Mamá put both hands on the sides of my face, anchoring me with her eyes. Her thumbs grazed my temples for a second. Then she lifted her chin and said, "I'm sorry I haven't told you what I was doing, that I have been helping the rebels, providing for them, taking care of their families, harboring them at Las Moras. But it was for your own safety—you understand, don't you? We were waiting for the right time."

"We?" I cleared my throat and looked to my father for an explanation.

Papá nodded to my mother. "Your mother is right. This is definitely the right time to let you know what's been going on. This conflict has brought us all closer together, and now is as good a time as any to let the lawmen of Morado County know exactly where we stand, what side we're on in this fight. A lot has changed in the last couple of years. Things are not so black-and-white anymore."

I swallowed hard before asking, "You mean . . . we're in league with bandits? Was Munro right? Were our men really attempting to blow up the mill?" My whole body tensed up.

I'd promised Dulceña I'd root out and turn in any rebels hiding out at Las Moras, but I couldn't denounce my own mother and father. No way I would ever turn them over to Munro or any other lawmen for that matter. I loved them too much.

"No, of course not!" Mamá reassured me. "These men are a little rough, but there are no ruthless criminals at Las Moras." My mother moved aside and slipped her right hand into the crook of my elbow, hooking our arms together as if we were about to step onto a dance floor at a baile or quinceañera. "Your uncle Carlos and I have reconnected as more than brother and sister. We are united as tejanos mejicanos, the true children of this land we all love so much. We are what Munro would label *rebels* only in that we are willing to do whatever it takes to protect our families. Up to now your father has had to keep up appearances, pretend to be neutral, for the sake of this property, our home, the land of our hearts, but he understands and supports my commitment to our people."

"I'm sorry we don't have time for a more proper, less hurried introduction," Carlos said, interrupting my mother with an urgent tone that startled me. "But I'm afraid Las Moras might be compromised."

"How?" my father asked, his eyes shining in the dimness of the barn.

"Munro and his posse took Gerardo Gutierrez on the road to Hidalgo County at dawn today," Carlos said. "We all know Gerardo and his friends weren't really planning to blow anything up. They were there trying to stop the real culprits from bombing the mill. But it was all a setup. Gerardo was a patsy in Munro's plan. He used him to flush us out. That's why I sent two men out to follow them, in case they took a detour, like Rangers tend to do these days."

"Is he all right?" Doña Flora broke away from the crowd and came forward, wringing her hands. "They haven't hurt him, have they?"

"I'm sorry, señora," Carlos whispered, lowering his voice respectfully. "But my suspicions were right. Munro and his posse never planned on transferring Gerardo down to the jail in Hidalgo. They pulled off the road as soon as they got far enough from town to be out of sight. They were going to hang him. He probably sensed that, or maybe they told him. In any event, somehow he got loose and attacked Sheriff Nolan."

"What do you mean, he attacked the sheriff?" I asked, afraid of the answer even as I asked the question. "How? With what?"

"He disarmed Nolan and shot him with his own pistol," Chavito said, putting his arm around Teresa and pulling her in closer.

Doña Flora put her hand to her chest. "So what are they going to do to him? Did they bring him back to Monteseco?"

Carlos shook his head. "No," he said. He took a deep breath, and slowly let it out. "I'm sorry to have to tell you this, señora, but they didn't bring him back. They strung him up. Left him up there on an old oak tree, hanging on the side of the road for everyone to see."

"No! No!" Doña Flora's cry was more like a long-winded wail. She stumbled back and steadied herself against a nearby water barrel. Mamá left my side to comfort Gerardo's mother, who clung to her and wept, shaking uncontrollably. Teresa and Beatriz went over to help comfort Doña Flora. They wrapped their arms around her and stroked her hair and hugged her tight while they whispered soft, sorrowful condolences.

"Let me go! Let me go!" Doña Flora kept wailing. "I can't do this! I can't leave my baby out there like that!"

"We won't leave him out there," Mamá said, hugging Doña Flora to her chest like she was her very own sister. "We'll cut him down and bring him home. We'll take care of him—just like all the others. I promise. Don't worry about that."

"How can I not?" Doña Flora cried, sobbing into her shawl. "I am in hell, and Death is my heir."

My mother's promises to Doña Flora slowed the blood in my veins. I grew numb with shock and something else, something cold and foreign. The emerging details of my mother's secret life as La Estrella sent tiny shivers down my spine and raised goose bumps on the skin of my forearms.

Pollo broke the solemn silence that had started to settle over the crowd like a mourning shroud. "The Rangers are holed up in the sheriff's house with Doc Hammonds," he said. "Last we heard, they didn't expect Nolan to live through the night. It's got the whole lot of them all riled up."

"We should open the hole," Papá said.

"Open the hole?" Fito asked.

Teresita's daughter clung to her mother's skirt. "What hole, Mami?" she asked.

I looked at my friends, Mateo and Fito, for the first time since we entered the barn and realized the younger children were just as baffled by everything that had transpired as we were.

"Yes," Mamá said, moving out of the way of the men. "It's time."

Manuel and Papá pulled a crate of tools away from the wall. Mamá removed a wooden slat from the floor directly under where the crate had been sitting, a spot I'd never seen uncovered. Papá helped her, and together they pulled on a rope that brought the slat up.

Dirt and debris fell off to the sides and hinges squeaked as the secret slat came up. Manuel helped lock it into place with an iron rod. Then he reached down and helped Papá take a large crate out of the hidden compartment under the floor.

Carlos knelt down, dusted off the top of the crate, and opened it, revealing a huge cache of weapons. A second crate revealed rounds and rounds of ammunition. Enough ammunition to wage a war.

Excerpt from Joaquín's journal,
Monday, August 23, 1915

RINCHES

Lawmen have
been given free will
—orders to shoot
mejicanos on sight
in South Texas.

My blond hair
and freckled face
afford me a few seconds
to save myself.
A moment of hesitation
from a Ranger
buys me enough
time to speak out,
to clarify who I am,
establish that I belong
on this side of the border.

"Those Rinches," I hear
campesinos gripe,
throwing their fists
in the air.

"They are bloodthirsty
salvajes, Godforsaken
fiends—hijos de Satanás!"

From the stables
to the corrals,
to the banks of the Río Bravo,
Rangers are infamous
for their cruelty.

My brother, Tomás,
has seen them
resting their forearms
on their rifles
as they scan the horizon
with sharp, color-blind eyes.
Desert lizards,
trying to discern between
the shades of brown
—distinguish that
which lives and breathes
and separate the brown skin
from the brown earth,
the brown brush,
the brown bark.

Rinches—without
their badges, their sins
would shame the Devil
and make the angels cry.

Chapter 9

Although many of the rebels took their new weapons and returned to the brush, not all of them left. Because we had no way of knowing what Gerardo had disclosed before he was hung, my parents decided that Carlos and some of his men should stay and help guard Las Moras. "We'll need the manpower," Mamá said. "I wouldn't put it past Munro to raid our ranch. Not after today."

"Are you sure about this?" I asked my mother as Manuel and Papá distributed the weapons in the crate to both rebels and campesinos.

Mamá pushed back a lock of my hair, placing it behind my ear gently. "I've never been more sure of anything in my life," she said. "We have to prepare ourselves for the worst, Joaquín—purgatory, torture, hell itself. We can't be caught off guard. Munro's taken off his mask. He's shown us that we are nothing more than another target. It's time he saw what *we're* made of."

"Yes, but aren't we overreacting a bit?" I asked. "I mean,

these men are rebels—*real rebels*—from out in the brush—and you're not just taking their families in or giving them food and supplies anymore. We're actually arming ourselves and joining forces with them! Don't you think we're asking for trouble here? We're risking more than Las Moras, Mamá. We're risking our lives!"

"Son, we can't sit back and wait for the storm to arrive before we tar the roof and fix a broken window," my father said, overhearing. "Only a fool refuses to take precautions. Your mother is right. Munro has set his sights on Las Moras. Otherwise, Gerardo would still be alive. We have to make sure we're ready for an attack."

The same apprehension I was battling was also reflected in the eyes of the rest of our ranch hands when we met them at the field house. Those whose regular duties included the security of Las Moras had resolutely taken their weapons and formed groups to patrol in. However, some of the campesinos were used to toiling the land and working hard without resisting the system. They were farmers, not fighters. These men and women weighed the guns in their hands as if they didn't quite trust themselves to use them when the time came to fight. But as they handled the weapons, loading bullets, holding them up, peering through the site holes, the women were no less determined than the men to figure it out.

"Don't be afraid," Mamá said "These men are not bandits or rebels. They are not evil minded. Please understand they are our friends and as our friends they are here to defend us."

"They are more than our friends," Papá said. "These men have strong ties to Las Moras. These men are more than friends. Their families work and live here. And now, they're here to help protect us. But they can't do it alone. We have to help ourselves. Every one of you knows how to load a rifle and pull a trigger. We've all hunted rabbits, ¿verdad? We've all shot at targets here and in the campo. This isn't anything you can't handle, and with any luck, you won't have to use your weapons."

Carlos slung his rifle across his arms. "Don Acevedo is right, but you never know when disaster might strike. I came home one night and found my wife crying because she didn't have the papers to prove we owned the land our house was built on in Hondo. They had been lost in a fire, years before, and her family had never replaced them. Without those documents, my wife and I had no way of proving the land was ours. No one would help us. Lawyers refused to take our case. County officials wanted United States paperwork, when the only paperwork we had before the fire was from Mexico, a hundred years ago when our ancestors were granted the land. And then the Rangers made sure my wife and I moved out." He paused, a memory he obviously didn't want to relive coming to the surface. "They hung my sixteen-year-old son in our own backyard."

Carlos wiped his face, shuddering a little. "My wife never wanted to set eyes on that house again after that. She went home to her parents in Matamoros, and I've been roaming around ever since, helping displaced families when I can, defending others who might be suffering the same fate, fighting off Rangers and deputies every chance I get."

Pollo stepped up beside Carlos, patting him on the shoulder. Everyone listened in horrified silence. "It was Rinches took my son-in-law," Pollo said. "Beatriz's husband. They dragged him on a rope behind a horse all over Hidalgo County—made an example out of him for *questioning* the law, after arresting him for loitering when he dared to meet in public with other tejanos." Laws like that—banning tejanos from gathering in public places—hadn't made it to Morado County yet, but rumors from other counties came over from time to time, reminding us that such things were not so far away. "It broke Beatriz's heart—but it toughened mine. I have no shame when it comes to fighting off lawmen. The way I see it, if they can kill an innocent young man in the prime of his life, drag him so long and hard his own wife couldn't identify his body, they can do the same to me."

Pollo's voice rose, determined. "But I'm not going to just lie down and expose my belly like a mutt. I won't let one more Ranger take another one of my family members without a fight. I'll take up arms. I'll shoot lawmen. I'll do whatever it takes to make those políticos up north get the message and send someone to get these demonios tejanos off our backs!"

"Sí, I understand what you're saying." Josue, an old ranch hand with a crooked back and missing teeth, weighed a pistol in the palm of his hand. "But I've never aimed at a man before, much less a lawman. What if I kill one of those Rinches? I don't want to hang. I'm too young to die."

At his words, the whole lot of them laughed. I thought about what we were asking them to do for a moment. Seriously thought about it. And even though I had just promised Dulceña the night before that I wouldn't do anything rash, I knew what my parents were asking was not rash. If anything, it was the only option Munro had left us.

Like it or not, the Ranger was no longer on our side. After questioning his authority and demanding that he do his job, we had become his enemies. And while he had everything to gain, we had everything to lose, especially now that I knew who my mother really was. We couldn't let Munro discover my mother's secret identity. La Estrella meant too much to her people. It was our responsibility to make sure she stayed safe.

That's why Carlos and his men had shown up at Las Moras. They were making sure she had the protection she needed so she could continue to comfort and provide for her people.

"You're right, Josue," I said, addressing the whole group. "Nobody here wants to hang for shooting a lawman, but the fact is the Rangers are hanging men for a lot less than that. Today, you might have to defend your right to be left alone. I might have to shoot at a lawman to defend my land, my home, my right to live. I know that sounds crazy, but it's come to that."

"Joaquín is right," Mamá said. "Man or woman, old or young. I urge you to help us protect yourselves and your families. I urge you to help us fight for your rights."

After hearing my mother's words, the rest of the campesinos filled their pockets with ammunition and assumed their assigned posts—the men back to the fields and cow pasture, the women and children back to their work in the house or in the gardens and fields, but every adult well armed and prepared to respond at a moment's notice when the need arose. The talk in the field house had filled them with courage, and they walked around patrolling the perimeter of our property with their shoulders rolled back and their heads held high.

Many hours later, I stood high up on the lookout tower to the left of the front gate with Carlos and Manuel, while Papá and Pollo stood on the right tower. We were all heavily armed. And even though I knew it was necessary, I couldn't help it. The whole thing gave me an odd, uneasy feeling. My hands stayed sweaty and my index finger twitched every time it grazed the trigger guard of my weapon.

After a while, Mamá rode up to us with a group of armed men and women behind her. "Ready for the next shift?" she called out to my father, who started to climb down from the tower. Pollo followed him.

I'd never seen my mother in this light. She was like a soldadera, a true warrior woman, fighting in the Mexican Revolution. I had seen pictures of soldaderas in the paper the last few months, with their belts of ammunition hanging across their chests and rifles resting in their arms, solemn and grave and ready to go into battle to fight for justice.

My mother was less conspicuous. Her rifle rested on her back from its shoulder strap, and she wasn't wearing an ammo belt. My father stood beside her mount, talking quietly to her, even laughing a bit, as they kept an eye on the road that ran in front of Las Moras.

At that very moment, just as I was beginning to think nothing was going to happen on our watch, we saw a cloud of dust moving slowly up the road toward us, like an ensnared dirt devil. At first, the devil made little progress, like a lazy little breeze. Then, as the minutes ticked off, the devil grew bigger and bigger, gorging itself on dirt and debris, gaining momentum as it galloped toward us, until there was more than dust in its midst and there appeared before us a group of pale riders—Munro's posse. Their serpent eyes fixed on us as they rode up to our gate and pulled on their reins, making their breathless horses twist sideways, shake their heads, and whinny in protest.

"How can I help you, Elliot?" Papá leaned casually onthe flank of Mamá's horse. Too casually.

Munro nodded past the gate at the wide expanse of Las Moras. "We're here to check the premises."

"Now hold on there," Papá said, extending his hand in midair. The Ranger's posse pulled on their reins and stood by, waiting for Munro's response. "Why do you have to check the premises?"

Munro took his hat off, shook the trail from it, and began fanning his face. Mamá reached for her rifle, and I pulled mine up against my chest.

"You're harboring insurgents," Munro said. "Gerardo Gutierrez told us as much."

"Gerardo?" Papá's brows furrowed and his green eyes narrowed. "Now, was that before or *after* you pulled off the road to execute him without trial or evidence?"

Munro wasn't taken aback by my father's question. His expression didn't change as he looked to the right and then to the left, up and down the length of our fence, where Carlos's men were posted every twenty yards as far as the eye could see. "I don't have to give you any explanations. Suffice it to say Gerardo confessed to treason. Now, I'm seeing a lot of new faces out here with you. You want to explain that?"

"Sure," Papá said, nodding with a little frown. "As soon as you show me a warrant."

"You know very well I don't need a damn warrant. Not if you consent. That is, of course, unless you have something to hide, like who these men are, where they came from, and what they're doing here?" Munro's reptilian eyes glistened with pride and something more—something menacing.

"These men are hired help," Papá said. "These are perilous times, Munro. You know that better than anyone. I need to make sure my place is well guarded, especially now that I have to go on the cattle drive. It shouldn't surprise you that I should want to protect my land and my family in my absence."

The captain took his time adjusting his hatband before he addressed my father again. "Well, I guess you won't be needing our services this year," Munro said.

I hadn't thought about that, how every year Munro posted men at Las Moras when Papá and his riders drove the herd up to Fort Worth. It always bothered Mamá, but she put up with it. Although she didn't like Munro, she had respected my father's decision to cultivate a mutually beneficial friendship with the captain. The Rangers offered protection and a certain amount of immunity against the racial prejudices and crooked politics in Morado County. For his part, my father's friendship lent integrity and respect, even esteem, to Munro and his company.

"No," Papá said. "After what you and your men did to Gerardo, I would have to say your services are no longer welcome here."

Munro's lean cheek paled as he stalled. Finally, he said, "Gerardo was an insurgent, a rebel hiding out on your property, and on those grounds I have every right to search the premises, to make sure there are no other fugitives hiding out here."

"Then you're going to need to see the judge, because I'm not opening these gates without a search warrant," my father said, holding firm to his resolve.

A moment later, a horseman moved his mount from out of the group and rode up, stopping directly in front of my father on the other side of the gate.

"Excuse me, Don Acevedo," the young man said. "I don't know if you remember me, but my name is Miguel Caceres. Judge Thompson appointed me as acting sheriff to Morado County for now, at least until the next election. As you can see, Slater and Davis are no longer with us. They were dismissed because I'm trying to make sure we do things right from now on. You're absolutely right about the search warrant, señor. But we would appreciate it very much if you gave us permission to inspect Las Moras. We promise not to take too much of your time."

"What are you doing?" Munro asked, pulling on his reins to keep his mount from moving around under him. "Who told you you could speak?"

"Well, he's right," Sheriff Caceres said, turning to Munro. "He doesn't have to let us in without a search warrant. The law's very clear on that."

"Son, in case you haven't figured it out, I am the law!" Munro's eyes bulged with rage. "Now, either you shut up, or I'll have you swinging from a branch next to that traitor Gerardo before suppertime. If you don't know how to take orders, there are plenty of men in this outfit willing to take your place. Now get back there and let me do my job."

"You're wrong, Munro!" I called out from atop the tower. "Sheriff Caceres knows what he's talking about. You should listen to him."

"Are you ready to let me take care of my business?" Munro asked Caceres, fixing him with a demonic stare.

The sheriff was silent for a moment, but the longer he sat there, the more Munro's posse focused on him. Their eyes lingered on his face while their hands rested on the butts of their holstered pistols. Then, seeing that he was outnumbered, Caceres clicked his tongue and rode back to find his place among the rest of Munro's men.

"So that's it, then?" Munro asked, turning his attention

to my father again. "You're not going to let us in?"

Papá took a deep breath and nodded. "This is my territory, Munro. You may rule out there, but I rule in here. I am not some young defenseless boy you can drag off the road and hang on a whim. I will not be disarmed, arrested, or lynched like so many other tejanos who've fallen victim to the bogus accusations and panic that the Plan de San Diego has brought to our borderlands."

"I hope you understand," Munro said, pointing at the gate and down at the men who were guarding it. "You're setting yourself up for some dark days. I can't protect you, not if you won't cooperate."

"That's fine by me," Papá said. "But make no mistake, Munro, this is my land, and I will defend it."

12 THE SUN, SUNDAY, MARCH 14, 1915.

MODERN AMAZONS OF MEXICO KEEP ARMIES ALIVE

Whole families of the war women of Mexico travel under box cars.

Soldaderas Rustle the Grub for Fighters and Thereby Effect Gigantic Saving for Leaders

By JANE DIXON.

"IF the women want to vote let them get out and shoulder guns!"

So say the voters of our fair and free land who are averse to sharing the privilege and plunder of the polls with petticoats.

"No one should have a voice in the government of a country who can't get out and fight ...

... to put off washing the dishes and rush to the front, where she picks up the gun of some soldier whose trigger finger has been stilled forever, and stands shoulder to shoulder with the men, ...

"When the army is transported by train what then?" I asked.

"You shall see for yourself," one of the agents of the Villa government promised. "Some of the troops will be coming into Juarez to-morrow. They have come up from the interior by train. We'll go over and see them."

War Women Equal to the Hardships of Soldiering Fight in Front Ranks With Husbands

Chapter 10

That evening, Mamá, Tomás, and I were about to walk out the back door. "Wait!" Papá loomed in the hallway. "What's this I hear about you going out to give Gerardo last rites?"

"We have to go," Mamá said, unhooking her gray cloak from the coat rack and throwing it around her shoulders. "It must be done now, tonight, before the zopilotes do too much damage. Besides, most of the lawmen, including Munro, will be busy attending Nolan's funeral tomorrow morning. They won't know what we've done until well into the afternoon. Gerardo's body will be buried deep under Mexican soil by then."

Papá shook his head, coming to stand between us and the back door. "I can't let you do this."

Mamá fastened the wide black buttons of her cloak, her fingers flying down the front of the dark material. "We have to." She held a hairpin between her teeth and talked through it as she pulled her hair together. "I promised Flora we would take care of him. Please don't get mad, Acevedo. We have to do this."

"Mamá is right," Tomás said. "We have to act now. Before dawn. By tomorrow there won't be much of him left. Don't worry, Papá. God will be with us."

"This has nothing to do with God!" my father boomed. "Don't bring Him into this. Not now, Tomás. It's not fair."

"Fair?" Tomás narrowed his eyes. "Whoever said any of this was fair? Is it fair that Munro has turned against you? Is it fair that yet another innocent boy is hanging in the brush, or that women and children are huddled together in makeshift huts, hungry, wounded, and scared, because the Rangers have taken to terrorizing them on a daily basis? No, Papá. None of this is fair. But it's the right thing to do. The decent thing to do."

Turning to my mother, Papá changed his tone of voice, speaking softly. "Jovita, por favor. Try to be reasonable. What you are doing, what you are asking me to consent to, is too dangerous. You heard what Munro said before he left. He's going to have men watching over that body at every turn. Nothing would please him more than to capture La Estrella. Don't you see? You are the grand prize. He's laid out his trap, and you're planning to walk right into it."

"Munro doesn't know anything," Mamá said, tucking the hairpins deftly into the chongo she had pulled together, holding it in place on top of her head. "Not when it comes to La Estrella. He's too busy trying to keep up appearances.

His biggest concern, his *only* concern, is his reputation as *the law of the land*."

"Exactly." My father took my mother into his arms and spoke to her softly, face-to-face. "He doesn't have to suspect anything to figure it out. He just has to catch you doing this to put two and two together. And what would be more reputable than becoming renowned for bringing down La Estrella? You'd be the biggest feather in his cap. Is that really what you want? You want to give him that much power?"

"Don't treat me like I'm a child," Mamá said, putting her hands on Papá's chest and pushing him away. "Don't you think I know that? But I'm not about to let fear stop me from doing what's right for Flora and her family. I have two sons. I wouldn't want them to be left out there to be mutilated by beasts. Why should Gerardo suffer that fate if we can do something about it?"

Papá released my mother as she struggled to get out of his embrace, glancing at me and Tomás. "They're my sons too, you know. I wouldn't . . . I could never let that happen."

"Good," my mother said. "I'm glad you understand. Just as I understand that you can't take part in this. You're needed here as much as I am needed out there. When all this started, when my own sister left and went back to live with my mother in Monterrey because she was scared of the Rangers, you said you understood. You promised you'd let me do whatever was necessary to help my people. You promised you'd never be part of the problem."

"I'm not trying to be part of the problem, Jovita." Papá

spoke in a quiet but firm tone that said he wasn't ready to acquiesce to my mother just yet. "What I don't understand is why it has to be *you* who does this. Why can't you let Carlos and his men go out and get Gerardo's body? Isn't that why they came to Las Moras, to make sure nothing happens to you?"

Mamá took my father's hands and kissed them. "I know you love me, and you're worried. But there's nothing to be afraid of. Carlos and his men are my decoys. While they're keeping Munro's men busy, Tomás and I will be getting the body. We'll be in and out quickly. We've done it before. *Many times.* Trust me. We can do it again."

"It'll be all right, Papá," I said, trying my best to sound confident. "I'll be there to help them."

My father let out a short, exasperated breath that made his nostrils flare out. He opened his mouth as if he was about to say something else. Then, as if he thought better of it, he put his arms around me and Tomás, kissed our temples, and said, "Take care of your mother. Take care of yourselves."

Then he let us go and moved aside to let us through.

I felt guilty as we left the house, knowing that we were leaving him there alone to worry about us. *How many times has he had to do this?* I wondered. Worried about Mamá? Stepped aside so that she might go out and "do the right thing"? How many times had he swallowed his pride and stayed behind to protect Las Moras because he couldn't be in two places at once? The question remained in my head long into the journey as we traveled on horseback through the woods, avoiding the roads.

"Mamá," I whispered as we squatted in the darkness, our horses tied behind a thick cluster of huisaches, listening for Carlos's signal that we could rush in and take Gerardo's body. "Has Papá ever come with you? Has he ever ventured out to help the rebels too?"

"No," Mamá whispered. "Your father and I, we have different ways. He's not as keen on the idea of fighting the law, not in subversive ways. But then again, he's never had to. Your father's a good man, Joaquín. He has integrity and a good heart, but rebellion and revolution are not in his blood."

I could see what she meant. My mother was born in the United States, but her mother, Abuela Rosa, was born in Mexico. After my maternal grandfather, Aurelio, passed away, Abuela Rosa went back to Mexico to take care of her sister who had fallen ill. Abuela Rosa still lives in her family's rancho in Monterrey. Papá's family, on the other hand, has owned Las Moras since the times of the Spanish land grants. They are true tejanos, original settlers of Texas, and as such, they've always believed in cultivating friendships with local law enforcement and politicians. My father's father, Abuelo Tomásito, who passed away when I was five, was even mayor of Monteseco for a while in the late 1880s.

I was about to ask Mamá if she could see anything, when we heard a group of horsemen rush toward us. Startled, I jerked and hit my head on a tree branch. Mamá put her hand on my head and pulled me in close, shushing me quietly. I clamped my hand over the knot forming on the top of my head. The horse hooves beat rhythmically against the earth as they galloped by.

I couldn't make anything out from our dark hiding place, but the hooting and hollering told me it was Carlos and his men, riding past us like the devil himself was lashing after them. No sooner had they gone by than another group of men galloped by us. They weren't as fast, and instead of rushing on to catch their prey, they slowed down a few yards away, lingering in the brush.

"Where did they go?" one of them asked.

"North, I think. Come on, we don't want to lose them," another answered. The Rangers were scouring the brush so close we could hear their horses' heaving breaths in front of us. My heartbeat roared in my ears, and I had to remind myself to breathe.

"This way! Let's go!" And with that, the horsemen rode off, intent on catching Carlos and his men. After they were gone, we stayed put for a while, listening for Pollo's signal, which came within minutes, a low, owlish triple hoot that he repeated just like he'd shown me before we rode into the chaparral.

Mamá prodded me with her elbow. "It's time." Tomás and I rushed over to get our horses, then we all mounted and rode out.

It didn't take long to locate Gerardo's body. If the cries of scavenger birds flapping their wings in the dark had not done so, the sickly stench of death would have led us right to him. Mamá passed me a plaid handkerchief. I followed her lead and covered my nose and mouth with it.

"You sure that's him?" I asked, when we rode up to the site.

"Yes," Mamá said, dismounting before the corpse. I stood in front of Gerardo and touched the tip of his worn-out boots.

"Help me lift him," I said, grabbing his legs. Together, Tomás and I hefted Gerardo's limp body while Mamá used a sharp pocketknife to cut the noose on his neck, releasing him.

"Hurry," Mamá said. Tomás and I made short work of placing him across the saddle of the extra horse we'd brought along for this purpose. I helped Mamá tie him down, and then we rode off toward Calaveras, traipsing through the darkest, densest part of the brush. Staying off any roads would help us avoid any deputies or Rangers who might have given up on the chase and come back to check on the body. Before we left the site of Gerardo's death, I had obscured our tracks with a branch so come daylight the Rangers couldn't just track us after a few hours.

After traveling southeast for about half an hour, we broke through the thicket. Mamá stopped. We stood atop a cliff overlooking a small, darkened village in the woods, a tiny neighborhood made up of a cluster of jacalitos, rough-made huts that housed the poorest among us.

I could barely make out the grass huts, with their thatched

roofs and stick walls and fences, in the darkness of the night, scattered down a crooked dirt road. We had arrived at Calaveras, the place where our displaced people went to live after they were run off their properties, where they disappeared to when they had nowhere else to go. Calaveras wasn't necessarily the best place to live. The jacales were remnants of old Mexico, relics of a time and a place that no longer existed, much like the people who went to live there.

When we entered the village, Doña Flora, her two younger sons, and Gerardo's girlfriend, Apolonia, were waiting for us at Doña Flora's comadre Petra's house. Apolonia cried out and began to sob, but a wail escaped Doña Flora's lips when we brought down Gerardo's body. Even more heartbreaking, when we laid him on the floor just inside Doña Petra's kitchen, Doña Flora threw herself onto her son and wept, wheezy sobs that clawed their way out of her chest like wounded lechuzas.

Wanting to feel something—anything—besides the numbness that had taken over my heart, I pressed my fingertips into my dry eye sockets. But no tears came, no sobs racked my body, no emotion overcame me.

I was empty inside.

"There's no shame in crying, Son," Mamá whispered. Gerardo's two younger brothers were crying even as they tried to console Doña Flora.

Tomás and Doña Petra had laid down an old weatherbeaten tarp on the butcher table in the kitchen. I helped them pick up Gerardo's body and place it gently over the tattered cloth. I bent my head as Tomás placed his hand on Gerardo's forehead and administered last rites. When Tomás stepped away, Apolonia reached down and caressed Gerardo's face. She pushed his hair off his forehead, placed it gently behind his ears, and then leaned down and kissed him before she left, crying softly into her cupped hand.

"You don't have to stay for this," Mamá said as Doña Petra put a pot of hot water on the table beside Gerardo's body. The next step was to wash his body, to prepare it for burial. "You and Tomás can go stand outside and wait for us to finish. We won't take long."

"You should go home now, Doña Jovita." Doña Flora caressed Gerardo's face and then undid the buttons of his shirt with the gentleness and reverence only a grieving mother would have. "We're just going to clean him up a bit before we bundle him up and take him home to Matamoros for the burial."

"No," Mamá said, a deep crease forming over her brows. "This will go quicker if I stay to help. I'll feel better once he's tucked away in the wagon and Pollo and Chavito are transporting him down to Mexico for you."

I didn't go outside. I stayed in and held the water bucket, watching Mamá and the other three women lovingly scrub down Gerardo's body, limb to limb, and head to toe, until he was as clean as they could get him. Then Mamá concocted some sort of medicinal balm to mask the scent of death and keep the bugs away. Tomás and I stepped back and gave the women space to move around the table and rub Gerardo down with the thick balm before dressing him and wrapping him up in a clean sheet.

When the body was ready, Tomás went outside. He whistled, a long, extended sound that echoed in the darkness. Within minutes, Pollo and Chavito rolled up in a rickety old wagon that groaned as it stopped behind Doña Petra's jacal. Tomás, Pollo, Chavito, and I moved Gerardo's body quickly into the bed of the wagon. Then Pollo and Chavito took it down the dirt road, where Mamá said it would be covered over with sacks of old clothes and boxes of unwanted knickknacks, disguising it as the belongings of a father and son on their way back home to Mexico.

Doña Flora and her sons would wait until morning to get on another wagon and cross the border a few hours behind it. It was a well thought-out plan. One that, unfortunately, the people of Calaveras were used to orchestrating.

As soon as Gerardo's body was gone, Mamá, Tomás, and I left Doña Petra's shack and headed down the dirt road to another jacalito a few hundred yards away. A young boy was waiting for us on the porch, and he ran up and opened the stick gate for us. We walked up to the tiny hut and were welcomed by an elderly woman who took Tomás's right hand and kissed it. Then she hugged Mamá and thanked us for coming.

Inside the woman's home, the oil lamp sitting on the table in the small room offered little light, but my eyes were drawn to the bed where a young woman lay on her side with her back to us.

"How is she, Doña Sarita?" Tomás asked. Mamá walked across the room and sat on a rickety chair by the bedside.

Tomás and the old woman hovered over Mamá. "She's not eating," Doña Sarita said. "And she won't stop saying she wants to die. I don't know what to do, Padrecito. She's my only granddaughter. I don't want to lose her."

"Adelita," Mamá said, putting her hand on the girl's hand to get her attention. "Are you awake, m'ija?"

Adelita turned over and sat up, slowly. Her long, loose hair was covering most of her face as she shook her head and whispered, "Sí."

"How do you feel?" my mother asked, and Adelita shrugged. "The fever's gone. Your hands feel warm, but not hot like before. How's your head? Does it still hurt?"

When Adelita shook her head slightly, Mamá tried to gingerly push her hair aside. That's when I understood what she was talking about. The left side of Adelita's face was battered to the point of disfigurement. Mamá turned around to give me a murderous glance, because without even intending to, I had let out a small sound that showed my horror.

"What happened?" I stepped closer to the bed to hand my mother her medicine bag. Mamá had no medical training, but she had learned to stitch cuts and cleanse wounds well enough, out of necessity. The nearest physician, Doc Hammonds, lived too far away to travel all the way to Las Moras every time someone had an accident. Mamá tended to the people that worked and lived at Las Moras. She knew how to care for anything from insect bites to dysentery.

"Rinches," a voice rasped. Behind me, an old man sat on a cot on the other side of the room. "They had their way with her, just like they did with the Robles girl last week."

Doña Sarita sat down on a chair on the other side of the bed and took her granddaughter's hand. "It's not enough that they hang our young men," she said. "Now they're coming after our girls too."

"Rangers did this?" I asked Tomás. "Did they report it?"

"You know better than that." My mother opened her medicine bag and took out gauze and a small bottle of red iodine to clean the wound. "There is no trust, no faith, no honesty in men, especially not when they join the Rangers."

As my mother tended to the poor girl's swollen face, a new wave of anger for Dulceña, at what had nearly happened to her, arose in me. How could any man do this to a girl? I couldn't reconcile it. "I don't understand why they come after our women," I said, more to myself than anyone else. "Isn't it enough that they take our fathers, our brothers, our friends, and hang them in the brush?"

"They know our men are our strength," Doña Sarita said. "But women—well, women are our corazón. They go after our girls to tear us apart, to keep our hearts from growing strong."

The old man at the table cleared his throat. "At least they didn't kill her like they did that Gonzales girl last month."

"Killed!" The declaration should not have shocked me, given recent events. Yet it did. "How many girls have been attacked?"

"Five," Doña Sarita said. "Two of them are missing, but they were good girls and too young to run off with some boy. We all know the Rinches killed them. There's no way of finding out where they dumped their bodies, though. They could be anywhere out there in the monte. God rest their souls wherever they may be."

"Amen," Tomás said, crossing himself.

"Amen," Mamá and Doña Sarita whispered, but I couldn't join them in their faithful show of respect. My heart was too angry. When I thought about what could have happened to Dulceña, how much worse the attack on her could've been, my heart thundered and my stomach twisted itself into knots. If they had raped her— killed her—dumped her body, well, I wouldn't be alive. I'd be dead too, but I would've taken some Rangers with me. I'd be hanging from a tree for sure.

As we rode back home that night, my heart seethed with rage as I thought about Slater and Davis and what they were doing to the people of Calaveras. I couldn't even be grateful that Dulceña had escaped the worst of the same fate. All I could think about was how much I wanted to get back at Munro and his posse.

—FROM JOAQUÍN,
SATURDAY, AUGUST 28, 1915

D—

Eres mi alma—mi corazón!

Thoughts of you swirl in my mind every time I close my eyes. There is so much I wish I could share with you—so much I cannot divulge in these dark times! A lot has changed since we last saw each other. The world has flipped on its axis, and I find myself turned upside down on my ideals, my values, my personal beliefs.

I am sorry I have not made more of an effort to see you, to speak with you, to hold you tight and reassure you of my love. But there are things I must do, things I must take care of, before I see you again. I have to make sure the darkness that lingers in our midst, casting its sinister shadow over Las Moras, looming over our people, is dispelled. I have to act, now, before we all perish.

Tuyo, hoy y siempre,
—J

Chapter 11

After watching the Ranger station and following Slater and his deputy friends for days, I was still seething with anger and resentment. Ignoring my mother's pleas, I came up with a plan. Three nights later, I was squatting low to the ground and unfastening the gate of the Silver Hoof Corral behind the sugar mill, on the outskirts of town, when I heard footsteps. The horses snorted and moved around nervously, while every muscle in my body tensed. There was no one patrolling the corral. My observations led me to believe that wasn't part of the nightly routine, and I knew for a fact the corral boy was asleep—I could see him from where I was squatting—so I could only assume it was a Ranger coming back for his horse.

As heavy boots stepped carefully over snapping twigs and crackling pebbles, I reached for my pistol. I drew it out of its holster slowly, intent on using it if I had to. I couldn't think of a story to explain my presence there, so I figured I was going to have to flee. I froze as the footsteps grew closer.

"Joaquín del Toro," a hushed voice whispered in the darkness.

I recognized the man who came forward from the shadows and crouched down beside me. "Carlos!" I whispered, relieved. He was holding a gun in his right hand. He wasn't pointing it at me, but I wondered why he had drawn it. "What are you doing here?"

"Me?" Carlos asked. "Well, I'm a rebel, so I'm up to no good, of course. But what about you? What's this all about?"

"I'm taking care of the Rangers' horses," I said.

"Looks shady to me." Carlos tested the knotted rope on the gate as he spoke. "You trying to steal these horses, son?"

"Why does that shock you? You stop people in the chaparral and take their things from them all the time," I said.

Carlos was silent, but only for a moment, before he explained, "Stealing from vagrants and ruffians isn't the same as stealing from lawmen."

"I don't see how it's any different. They're the same breed—outlaws and lawmen," I said. Then I pointed to the rope. "Besides, I'm not stealing them. I'm just going to cut them loose. Release them."

Carlos cocked his head and thought about it for a second before he asked, "Why would you do that?"

"To torment the lawmen." I continued to work through the knot. It was the least they deserved, after all they'd done lately. "I'm going to take their beasts south of town, to the border. With any luck, I can coax them to run across the river into Mexico."

"And what's that gonna accomplish?" Carlos asked.

I finished untying the rope and pulled it through, separating the gate from the fence. "Well," I continued, "the way I see it, if Munro and his posse are busy rounding up their horses, they won't have time to round up Mexicans, much less go chasing after our girls."

"And you're doing this all by yourself?" Carlos put his gun back into its holster, then stood up, watching for signs of our discovery. "You know you can't do this alone."

"I'm not alone." I opened the gate, then crept around the corral for my horse. Carlos followed. "You're here. And if I know you, you have half a dozen men with you."

Carlos laughed softly, deep in his throat. Then he came over and patted my horse's nose. "So what?"

"Oh, don't pretend you all were out here stargazing," I said. "You knew what I was up to. The question is . . . are you here to help me?"

"This is madness, Joaquín," Carlos said, shaking his head as I mounted.

"All right then, step out of the way," I said.

At the sight of me on my mount, drawing out my pistol, Carlos swore, "Oh, hell!"

I fired my gun into the air three times and screamed at the top of my lungs. Carlos jumped aside as the lawmen's horses leaped into action, bolting out of the corral at top speed. I chased behind them, using my hat to spook them out of town.

The wind whistled in my ears as we galloped after the

remuda, trying to keep them together. A few of them went by the wayside, but most of them formed a herd that ran southeastward from town.

At first my horse was galloping after them, but after a few minutes, we were beside them, and suddenly, we had surpassed them, together a whirlwind of muscle and mane that ran through the chaparral, a many-hoofed, roaring beast. The ride was more than exhilarating. It was downright intoxicating.

As I'd hoped, a team of horsemen sprinted out of the woods. The mounted men sped up, flanking the remuda on either side, not trying to stop us, but racing alongside as if their goal was the same as mine, to get them to Mexico as soon as possible.

From the ranks, a leader emerged by my side. I recognized him in the dark. "I knew you couldn't stay away," I yelled at Carlos as we raced ahead.

"Does your mother know you're crazy?" he yelled back.

"'Course not!" I said. "That's what makes it so much fun!"

"Boy, you and I need to have a talk about what constitutes fun!" Carlos snapped his reins and made his mount move ahead of me. I let him take the lead, figuring he knew the territory better than I did.

We continued heading south, slowing down, keeping a strong but steady pace until we got close enough to the river, an earthy, wet mud smell intensifying in the warm summer air. When we reached the edge of the Río Bravo, we came to a complete stop.

Pollo and Chavito rode up to meet us. We split up, trotting half up and half down the riverbank, scouting a good place to cross.

"Down here." Carlos signaled for us to bring the remuda along. The men snapped their reins and slapped their legs against the ribs of their mounts and we drove the lawmen's horses into the river. The dark waters of the Río Bravo were calm and warm, inviting. It wasn't too deep either. I barely got my boots wet before we were on the other side.

"Let's go!" Carlos hollered, and we all galloped after him, driving the herd of horses into the campo.

"Where are we taking them?" I asked when Carlos slowed to a leisurely trot.

"Up into the hills," he said, keeping a steady pace as he talked. "Those Rinches and their deputy friends will never find them if we can get them to Chelito."

"Chelito? Who's that?"

As we traveled, Carlos told me that Chelito's real name was Consuelo Zaragoza Morales de Limón. She was a Soldadera, a former tejana who'd fled to Mexico after her father and brothers were murdered and she and her mother had been forced off their ranch in Monteseco fifteen years before. She was now in command of a band of fifty-two Mexican revolutionaries, an all-female troop holed up in the hills of northern Mexico. However, to my uncle Carlos, she was simply Chelito.

Deeper into the hills, we came upon a campsite hidden within the folds of a huge ravine. A large group of wild warrior women came out of the cavernous dwelling to welcome us.

"Carlito! Cariño mío, where have you been?" Chelito called. Her long, thick white braid moved softly side to side as she walked to us. "I haven't seen you in almost a year!"

"Working hard to keep you in luxury, as you can see." Carlos nodded back to the herd of horses Chelito's women were already inspecting and petting behind us.

Chelito's eyes twinkled and crinkled at the edges. "Are those for me?" she asked.

"Who else?" Carlos reached over and pulled on one of her trenzas, like she was a little girl. Chelito grinned and slapped his hand away playfully.

"And who's this?" she asked. Time and hard living had not taken the fire out of her eyes. Although her face was heavily creased, her gaze sparkled with life.

"This is your benefactor," Carlos began. "The herd is a gift from him. He was going to cut them loose, but I told him I knew someone who would really appreciate them."

Chelito narrowed her eyes at me for a moment, and then she smiled, a tight-lipped smile that revealed nothing. "You a horse thief?"

"No, ma'am," I said. "I just thought the lawmen in Monteseco needed to be taught a lesson." I'd intended to make the Rangers scrabble in the brush looking for their horses, but the idea of making the horses disappear altogether did appeal to me.

"Amen!" Chelito said, then she unhooked a canteen from

her belt, took a small drink, and handed it to me. “Have a drink. You’ve earned it.”

I took a long, thirsty swig only to choke on what I can only describe as a gluttonous, bitter alcoholic muck.

“You all right there, son?” Chelito asked, pounding forcefully on my back as I coughed and snorted the fiery liquid straight out of my burning nostrils. My windpipe was aflame, and my lungs clogged with red-hot cinders.

“Let me guess,” Carlos shook his head. “You never had pulque before.”

“No,” I said, puckering at the sour, yeasty residue lingering in my mouth.

“Ay, m’ijo, you’ve been missing out,” Chelito said. “Here, have some more. It’s sweeter the second time around.”

I took another swig and swallowed the volcanic stuff down quickly, handing the canteen back to Chelito before she insisted I have any more of it.

“Come on in, pásenle a lo recogido.” Chelito took the canteen and led us up a dirt path. We made our way up the small hill, where women lingered at the mouth of the cave.

It was dark inside their dwelling, but my eyes adjusted quickly to the dim light. Every nook revealed the remnants of the women’s somewhat domesticated lives. There were floral skirts, drab shawls, and light-colored undergarments drying out on recumbent clotheslines that extended from one end of the small cave to the other. The simple bedding on the dirt floor was neat and tidy, like it would be if they had real beds.

A small fire burned low and quiet, and I could smell coffee brewing in the tin pot sitting on an iron grate over it. There was even a set of crates piled up two by two, one set on top of the other, with a lacy tablecloth spread over it, and a thick, unlit candle at the center.

"Don't let her get too close." Carlos sat down on a crate next to me and Chelito, who was studying my hair as she ran her fingers through it. "She's a sirena! She'll draw you in, ply you with sweet words and small swigs from her jug, and then she'll break your heart." He winked at Chelito.

"Break your heart? When have I ever?" Chelito reached across me and smacked his arm.

"Always," Carlos teased. "In all these years, you've never kissed me. You just keep me waiting like a schoolboy."

"Oh, behave yourself! Now who's this child? Do I know his parents? I don't recognize the hair. But those eyes," she said. "Well, those eyes are legendary, aren't they?"

"Well, you're right about that. This is Joaquín, the youngest son of Acevedo and Jovita del Toro, from Rancho Las Moras," Carlos informed her as I squirmed beside her.

Chelito touched my hair again and said, "So you're Jovita's son?"

"You know my mother?" I asked, intrigued by her familiarity.

"A long time ago, when she was a young girl," Chelito said. "We played in the same fields, picked flowers together, gazed up at the stars, and made promises that—"

"Joaquín is not a stargazer, Chelito," Carlos said. "He's

more like his Papá in that respect. He's just started to see things our way."

Chelito cocked her head sideways to stare at me again. "Oh, but it was always there. I see the light of La Estrella in his eyes. Even his smile is his mother's, isn't it? And judging from his actions, he's got his mother's spirit también."

"La Estrella. You know about that?" I asked. As I thought about my mother, I wondered just how long she had been known by that name. Was she helping these women too? Was she a revolutionary like them?

"Well, I wish we had time to discuss Joaquín's rebellion, but we have to get going," Carlos said, shifting as if to rise.

"But you just got here," Chelito said. "Stay. Rest. Let the horses get their wind back. I'll pour you some good, strong coffee, to help keep you awake for the ride home."

So we stayed for a while, rested over a couple of hours by the campfire. The women plied us with aromatic coffee. Carlos teased them all, outright flirting with them, asking them for a kiss or a hug, but none of them paid him any mind.

While the men lay down and chatted with each other by the fire, I sat on a dusty zarape on the ground and leaned back against a battered trunk. I killed time, writing a poem in my journal, waiting to get back to my life and the only thing on my mind: Dulceña.

Excerpt from Joaquín's journal,
Thursday, September 2, 1915

IN DREAMS

In my dreams, I run with beasts—
we run rampant, como remuda,
into the thickness of the chaparral.
Darting off, their necks stretch
forward and lengthen until the stars
on their faces touch the sky.
The diamonds on their chests contract,
expand, harden them. Their withers grow
hair that fluffs and flickers, and we fly
into the fog, in and out of the mist,
like locomotives on fire.

In my dreams, I run with beasts—
caballos moros, blancos, y negros.
Their hooves eat the dirt beneath us,
spitting out the bones of the earth
as we gallop back to a place in time
where mount was monarch
and man could only watch
and marvel at him from afar.

We swallow the wind in giant gulps
as we pass man by, leaving
him farther and farther behind.

In my dreams, I run with beasts—
capricious ballos, beautiful and strong.
Their ears sit back, almost flush
against their skulls, as we spring out
of the brush. We run along the dim horizon,
wade through arroyos, climb over
deep ravines. We rush through valleys,
dash through deserts, traverse montes,
and somewhere in the Sierra Madres
we come upon Zapata and his insurgents.
We sprint over campfires—a pot of beans
spills, sputters, and bursts into flames.
Zapata shakes his head and smiles,
bedazzled by the swiftness of the shadows
we cast upon canyon walls.

In my dreams, I run with beasts—
sweaty mounts with foaming coats
and heavy snorts, worn, weary mammals
with rebellious, seditious hearts fleeing
on instinct, running toward the light.

We outrun coyotes, stomp on vipers,
and spook lechuzas, and all the while
my thoughts return to you, like buitres
circling overhead, always going back
to the United States, back to hostility,
back to oppression, back to resentment.

Chapter 12

Because my horse got spooked and I fell into the river when we were crossing back, I got to Las Moras completely soaked. Fito was taking care of the stables that night, so I didn't have to explain to him where I was going when I left. But when I got back, he did tell me to be careful because Tomás had arrived earlier in the evening and hadn't left yet.

Worried I might get in trouble for leaving the house in the middle of the night without telling anyone where I was going, I snuck in through the back door. With any luck, Tomás was spending the night and already asleep, so I wouldn't have to talk to anyone. I slunk through the kitchen, down the hall, until I came to the banister of the main stairway. That's when I saw the light coming from my room. To my surprise, Tomás was sitting on my bed waiting for me.

"Join me, Joaquín," he said, shifting the book he'd been reading and placing it on his lap. I breathed a thankful sigh of relief when I saw it wasn't his Bible. It was hard having a priest for a brother. I was especially worried about having to talk to him tonight, because I knew for a fact I was going to have to lie to him, and I was sure lying to a priest had to be one of the biggest sins a man could commit. "Odd time for a swim, don't you think, Hermanito?"

"It was too hot in here," I said. "I couldn't sleep."

"Hmm," Tomás frowned. *Here it comes,* I thought, cringing. *The Lecture.* "You shouldn't stay out so late." Tomás lifted the delicate ribbon from the crease of the book and flipped it over and away from the page. "It's hotter out there than it is in here."

Tomás put his book aside, got up, and came over to me. He stood before me in his black shirt and black pants, his persona less like a priest and more like a brother as he put his hands on my shoulders.

"Please don't lie to me," he said, gripping the back of my head and tugging at my hair as if I were a pup. "I know about the horses. Now, please, tell me. Why would you do something like that?" Not wanting to lie to my brother, I hung my head instead and didn't say anything else, hoping he'd let me go to bed without any more fuss. "Am I talking to myself here, Joaquín?" Tomás asked, giving my hair another tug.

"No." I eyed the place on his shirt where his priest's collar would have been if he'd been wearing it and wondered if lying to your brother when he's dressed down was less of a sin than if he was all decked out in his priestly garb.

"Now, we both know this isn't the first time you've snuck out of the house to see Dulceña since that night," he said. "But this thing with the horses, it's . . . well, it's insane."

I jerked. Not many people knew about my secret meetings with Dulceña. Mateo and Conchita would never let it leak out. Other than the unknown person delivering her messages inside the house, I could think of no one else who would turn me in to Tomás.

"Who told you?" I asked.

Tomás tightened his lips for a second, then he let out a deep breath and said, "Mamá. She sent for me."

"Mamá knows? ¡Ay Dios mío!" My head was suddenly pounding, and I could feel myself stiffen. I pressed my hand against the muscles in my neck and started rubbing the tension away.

"Of course," Tomás said. "You think Mamá doesn't know what's going on in her own house? Come on, Joaquín. She's too smart for that. She's just letting you think she doesn't know. But she's been keeping an eye on you the whole time, keeping me abreast of the situation. Listen. I wasn't going to say anything either, but you've never been this late getting back. We're getting worried, Joaquín. Well, what have you got to say for yourself?"

"Nothing," I said, scuffing at the floor with my wet boot. Making eye contact with him would have most certainly been my undoing. "Does Papá know?"

"Yes." Tomás put both hands on the sides of my head, gently forcing my head up. "You know they don't keep secrets. Except from us, of course. But not from each other."

I turned away from him. I longed for Tomás to walk out that bedroom door, wished he would go back to the rectory and let me deal with my own life on my own terms. "I'm sorry it came to this, Tomás," I said. "But a man's got to do whatever he can to protect the woman he loves. You're a priest. You wouldn't understand."

"You're wrong, Hermanito." Tomás came to stand behind me, but didn't touch me again. "I understand that you want to protect Dulceña, but stealing horses isn't going to fix anything."

"Not in the long run, but for now they can't go anywhere. It'll be a few days before the Rangers can move around and go after our people again," I reminded him. "And by then, I'll figure something else out. Something to keep them from attacking. It's the only way I know to fight back, to cripple them. You saw that girl at Calaveras. You saw Dulceña that night. Our people are suffering, our women especially. It's our duty to protect them."

Tomás nodded and paced the room, thinking.

"This is my doing." Mamá stood just inside the door of my room. Her hair was half pinned on the top of her head, and she was holding her robe closed over her chest with her hands. "I was afraid I might have given you the wrong impression by taking you to Calaveras. You have to understand, m'ijo. Not all rebels are innocent underdogs. There are dangerous men out there too, Joaquín, cold-blooded killers and rapists, predators worse than Slater and his kind. You could get hurt if you don't know who to trust, who to work with."

"Is that why you sent Carlos after me?" I asked. "Because

you think I don't know how to defend myself? I know what I'm doing. I'm not a child anymore, Mamá. I don't need a sitter. I can take care of myself."

"Try to understand. I was worried about you," Mamá said. "Please don't be mad. Promise me you'll stop doing these crazy things, Joaquín. It's not enough to cripple the Rangers, anyway. There are other ways of fighting them—better ways."

"Like what?" I asked. "Like sneaking Gerardo's body across the Rio Grande or putting iodine on that girl's face? How is that going to fix anything, Mamá?"

"We are not Sediciosos!" Mamá's lips trembled. I knew she was really upset, because she never raised her voice at me like that. "We don't go around destroying bridges and blowing up railroads. What we do, we do for justice."

"But I don't understand why!" I yelled back, fighting my instinct to be a good son, to back down, to comply. "Why do we just sit around waiting to be attacked? We know who they are. We have the weapons. We should just go after them."

Mamá came forward. She put her hand on my face and stroked my cheek softly before speaking. "We don't want any innocent lives lost," she said. "That's not what we do, not how we solve things. We're not murderers."

"Por favor, Joaquín," Tomás whispered from behind me. "Just promise us you'll stop going out on your own. The Rangers will get what's coming to them, eventually."

"I'm sorry." I lifted my chin. "But I just can't do that.

Eventually is not good enough. They need to be stopped. Now."

The way I saw it, I was on a mission to punish the lawmen in Monteseco now, as often as possible, and nothing Tomás or my mother said was going to deter me.

... brother officer.

The men fought a duel in Anavachi Pass. The colonel was killed in the encounter and the major was wounded.

TEXAS RANCHERS WOULD INVADE MEXICO TO RECOVER STOLEN STOCK

WASHINGTON, D. C., Oct. 24.—Reports from Brownsville, Texas, announce that the border ranchers have appealed to the governor for more protection against the Mexican bandits, who are crossing in small bands and running off cattle and horses and looting ranch houses. The ranchers ask that, in the event of the government not being able to furnish the necessary protection, they be promised immunity from punishment, receiving which they will cross the border themselves and bring back their own stolen stock. They express a willingness to take the law in their own hands if the federal authorities will agree not to interfere with them.

Passage for Carranzistas.

From Laredo it is reported that the federal authorities have given permission for a force of 5000 Carranzistas to cross into American territory at that point and proceed from there to Douglas, Arizona, whence they will return to Mexico.

Vera Cruz despatches say that Carranza has decided not to call for any elections in Mexico until the fighting in the north has been ended. The pre-constitutional period will last for about a year, according to his expectations, at the end of which time he will have Villa and Zapata completely crushed and peace restored. In the meanwhile he assumes personal responsibility for the safety of the lives and property of foreigners in the republic.

Chapter 13

As I lay awake for hours, mulling over the conversation with Tomás and my mother that night, wondering why my father had not been part of it, I realized he couldn't have stayed awake worrying about me. He had a herd of cattle to move out in the morning. More than likely, my mother had not mentioned my disappearance to him to ensure he got plenty of sleep before he left.

How could I have forgotten that? What kind of a son am I? I chastised myself as I tossed and turned in my bed. Too ashamed to sleep, I sat up and wrote in my journal. But my poems felt weak—self-indulgent—so I flipped the journal shut and pushed it under my pillow. Then I blew out the candle on my nightstand, lay back, and closed my eyes.

The sounds of our household stirring at dawn awakened me. Remembering that my father was departing, I tossed the covers aside, jumped out of bed, and scrambled into my clothes.

Pulling my suspenders over my shoulders, I rushed

downstairs. Mamá was coming down the hallway. She put her arms out and motioned her desire for a morning hug. "Slow down. You haven't missed him. He's in the library," she said, hugging me. "He'd never leave without saying good-bye."

I kissed her cheek quickly and rushed to the library. My father was stuffing some papers into his mochila. He looked up at me when I walked in. "Joaquín," he said. "You're awake. Good. Good. Come on in, Son. We need to talk."

"About the horses?" I blurted. A gentle heat flushed over my face. How could I defend my actions in light of his departure? It was one of his many ranching duties. The tedious trail ride was yet one more sacrifice he made for us every year.

My father cleared his throat. "About the horses, yes," he said. "Among other things."

When I hung my head and didn't say anything, my father finished closing his mochila, threw it over his shoulder, and came to me. He put his hands on my shoulders and I lifted my eyes to his.

"I might have been a bit . . . irrational," I began.

"You're a young man, with a young man's passions in a young man's heart," my father said. He squeezed my shoulders with his big hands and I cringed, embarrassed. Did he think me too juvenile now? Had my actions in the last few weeks altered his opinion of me? Was I unworthy of his respect? It occurred to me then that he hadn't asked me to go on the trail with him this year. Was he that upset with me? Did he want to create some distance between us?

Discomfort turned to anger and frustration. "I know you're disappointed." I lifted my chin. "That's why you don't want me on the trail with you. But perhaps it's best I should stay here."

"I need you to stay here," Papá said, dropping his hands to his sides. "It's important to me to leave someone I can trust in a leadership position at Las Moras. Your mother is a good woman, but she can't be expected to do it all. Not with everything else that's going on now."

I nodded. "Things have changed a lot for her," I admitted. "For all of us."

"That's right," my father continued. "As it stands, she and Carlos have all they can handle trying to keep our gente healthy and safe at Las Moras. That means someone else needs to keep up with the work around here. The ranch is not going to tend itself, Joaquín. The campesinos need a patrón, not just to supervise and give orders but to lead by example, to finish clearing that field for next year's sugar-cane crop and to look after the animals."

"That's why you're leaving me here?" I asked, my spirit stirring, soaring, forming a sense of purpose inside me, filling me with pride—and dignity.

My father shook his head and smiled. He put his arms around my shoulders and hugged me tight. Then, releasing me, he backed off a little. "Yes. You are the man of the house now, Son." He pressed his index finger into my chest for emphasis. "In my absence, you are in charge. I expect you to take your responsibilities very seriously."

"Are you sure?" I asked nervously. "I thought you were mad at me—let down—because, well, I haven't necessarily been forthright with you lately. I didn't know you thought I was . . . ready."

My father waved a hand in the air dismissively. "Nonsense. You're ready," he said. "Your passion, your conviction for justice, that all tells me you're ready to take on a man's responsibilities. The question is, can I trust you to act accordingly, Son? Are you willing to focus, to change course and move in this direction? Are you ready to take on full charge of Las Moras?"

"I want to." My voice cracked for a second, and I thought I heard myself croak out the answer, so I cleared my throat a couple of times before I continued. "I need to. Thank you, Papá, for believing in me."

As my father patted my shoulder brusquely, I promised myself I would do everything in my power to keep my word, to honor his trust in me. It would be hard, not letting my dislike for the Rangers get in the way of that promise. But unless they attacked Las Moras directly, I couldn't let anything blindside me. Papá was counting on me. I couldn't—I wouldn't—let him down.

El Sureño

Vol. XXIX | Monteseco, Texas | Friday, September 3, 1915

TELEGRAPH LINES CUT, POLES UNEARTHED! SEDICIOSOS SUSPECT

HIDALGO CO., — Several towns were left without means of communication Wednesday night as rebels pulled out the county's telegraph system. Officials are

RANGERS LEFT ON FOOT! UNKNOWN HORSE THIEVES MAKE OFF WITH THE HERD

—Rebels Strike Again—

MORADO CO., — In an unexpected and unprecedented turn of events the Texas Rangers were left holding

Chapter 14

At first I didn't know what Uncle Carlos wanted when he came to talk to me in the barn. I was cleaning my saddle when he walked in and handed me a folded piece of paper.

"We made the newspaper?" I asked after I unfolded and read the torn-up clipping from *El Sureño*, another article by A. V. Negrados.

Carlos nodded and cleared his throat. "Yes, we did. Unfortunately."

"What do you mean, unfortunately? This isn't necessarily a bad thing, you know," I said. "The Rangers are probably stewing over this one. I bet Munro is making dirt devils with his tail feathers, running around all over town trying to figure out who stole their horses."

"Yeah, but the story's gotten the newspaper man and his daughter into all kinds of trouble." Carlos took the news clipping and folded it before putting it back into his pocket. "Word is Munro is threatening to shut down their whole operation."

"He can't do that!" I said. "Freedom of the press, everybody knows that."

Carlos let out a long, heavy sigh and scratched the side of his neck. "¡Ay, Joaquín! What lawmen get away with these days could fill more than a few of those journals you like to write in. Munro could burn down this whole town if we made him mad enough, and nothing would happen to him."

After hearing from Carlos that our antics had made trouble for Don Rodrigo and Dulceña, I could think of nothing more pressing than going into town and making sure she was all right. It had been too many days since I had set eyes on her, so I rode out of Las Moras with the excuse that I wanted to visit my brother. Because I was in a hurry, I waved at the guards posted at our gate and didn't stop until I got to town.

I tethered my horse in front of a boot shop at the end of Fourth Street, where I knew it could sit for a while. Then I meandered over to Donna's Kitchen to ask Conchita a favor. At my request, Conchita drew Dulceña out of the print shop and away from her father by asking her if she wanted to take a break from work and go for a brief stroll along the boardwalk. Don Rodrigo took no issue with that sort of thing. He encouraged her to go out for a brisk walk, get a bit of fresh of air.

Half an hour later, in the dimness of the old mill, I broke off my kiss with Dulceña to speak to her. Not because I didn't want to keep kissing her, but because we only had a few minutes to talk before she had to get back to the paper.

Clearing my throat, I began, "I have to tell you something."

"What is it? What's wrong?" she asked, cocking her head sideways.

I took her face in my hands and kissed her forehead, worried that by having her meet me here, I might be putting her in danger. "I did it."

"Did what?" she asked.

Taking a deep breath, I said, "I stole the horses. Well, not by myself, of course. But it was my idea. I started it. I'm sorry, mi amor, but I'm the reason Munro's threatening to shut the print shop down. I'm sorry. I had no idea it would cause any kind of trouble for you."

Dulceña stood listening to me without interrupting. When I was done, she shook her head and said, "That's insane! Joaquín! Why would you do something like that?"

"I'm sorry. I really am," I whispered, shame washing over me for the first time since I'd done the deed. Not even my brother's frustration or my mother's anger had the effect Dulceña's disappointed voice was having on me at that moment. She was the one and only person who could make me feel this wretched.

"Do you even understand the magnitude of what you just told me? If they had caught you—if they had arrested you—you could be hanging from a tree right now!" Dulceña put her hands on her hips, like Mamá when she's about to lay down the law. "You still might! Who else knows about this?"

"Just Carlos—and his men," I said, hanging my head. "And my family, of course. I know that sounds like a lot, but it's okay. Nobody's going to say anything. I'm more worried about you and your family."

Dulceña pressed on her forehead with her fingertips, massaging it gently, like she was trying to put off a migraine. "Oh my God, Joaquín!" she cried. "What are we going to do now?"

"Nothing," I said, putting my arms around her and kissing her cheek softly. "You're not going to do anything. You're just going to go back to the paper and pretend I didn't tell you any of this."

"Pretend!" Dulceña said, looking deeply into my eyes. "¡Ay, Joaquín! You have no idea how big this is. There's a lot more to it than that."

"Like what?" I asked.

Dulceña rested her forehead on my chest for a moment, then she reached up to stroke my cheek again. This time, she didn't hesitate. "The reason Munro is threatening to shut us down is not because of the story about the stolen horses. It's because my father won't tell him who wrote it."

"What do you mean?" I asked. "A. V. Negrados wrote it. It was printed in the paper."

Dulceña shook her head. "No," she admitted. "Someone who goes by the name A. V. Negrados wrote it. More often than not, stories like this—wild, outrageous stories—come over the wire. It doesn't matter who wrote them if the writer is not from the area. However, sometimes the stories are written by local reporters, people my father trusts to bring him credible accounts of what is happening out there in the chaparral."

"I don't understand," I said. "Why don't they just do what I did—write anonymously?"

Dulceña lifted her chin. "Well, these people want to get credit, because the stories are important to them, so they take a pseudonym. The story about the stolen horses was written by A. V. Negrados, a reporter who uses the pen name to hide her true identity."

I repeated the name, letting it roll off my tongue for a second longer while I thought about its significance. "A. V. Negrados. I'm familiar with her. My mother loves her stories," I said.

"Everybody does," Dulceña said. "A. V. Negrados took that pen name to echo the voice of A. V. Negra, the reporter who wrote articles for *La Crónica* to call attention to the poor working conditions of the families of campesinos working on this side of the border."

"I can see why your father wouldn't want to turn her over to Munro," I said.

"My father's been publishing A. V. Negrados's stories for months, and now Munro is demanding that we turn her over to the authorities for questioning. It's ridiculous, but he thinks she might be La Estrella."

"No—" I said, shaking my head. "It's not my mother."

"What?" Dulceña asked, her voice going up an octave. "Are you saying your mother is La Estrella? In all my investigations, that's the *one* thing no one would tell me! Now I know why!"

Realizing what I had just done, I covered my eyes and

rubbed my face harshly. I tried to settle my nerves by reminding myself that Dulceña would never say anything to anyone about my mother's secret. She loved me too much to do anything that might hurt me or my family. Of that, I could be sure. "Yes," I finally admitted. "I just found out about it. So much has changed. It's been a crazy week at Las Moras."

"So that's why your father reacted so harshly when my father printed your poem in the paper!" Her eyes grew wide and luminous as she pieced together that mystery in her head. "He wasn't mad at us. He was just protecting your mother. If Munro found out you'd written that poem, it would have meant an investigation into Las Moras. He couldn't afford to take that chance."

I thought about it for a moment. Dulceña might be right. His refusal to have our families associate with each other had never made sense to me until now. "It's a man's job to keep his family safe at whatever the cost," I said, thinking about Don Rodrigo's predicament with regards to the reporter. "So what's your father going to do? Is he going to give in to Munro? I don't think anyone would blame him."

"My father would never do that," Dulceña said, shaking her head. "He would close down the print shop himself and move our family out of town before he would let Munro and his posse have A. V. Negrados."

I couldn't understand that. I would hope Don Rodrigo would think of his family first. "Why not?" I asked. "If it means keeping you and your mother safe. Why should he keep this woman's name a secret? Wait. What did you mean, your *investigations?*"

"Because *I'm* A. V. Negrados." Dulceña's voice was a small whisper, barely audible in the hollowness of the abandoned mill.

"But how?" I stumbled on my words. "When?"

Dulceña took a deep breath. "We all wear masks, Joaquín. No one suspects young girls, especially a waitress, to be smart enough to understand the politics behind the rumor mill around town. Conchita brings me the news she overhears at work and together we listen carefully when we go on our walks."

Of all the things I'd expected her to say, I never thought this was the reason her father might lose his business.

But why had Dulceña kept this from me? Why was I only now hearing about it? Did her father swear her to secrecy? Had she ever intended to tell me?

There were so many questions rushing through my head that I couldn't put any of them into spoken words.

"I can't believe it," I said when I finally spoke. "I can't believe you would keep this from me . . . especially with the way you've been chastising me. Even today, you told me I was insane. And all along, you've been doing crazy things yourself!"

Dulceña shook her head. "This isn't the same—" she began.

"It isn't?" I asked. "This is worse. Why would you keep this a secret from me? I thought we told each other everything!"

"Dulceña lifted her chin and straightened her back. "I'm sorry I didn't tell you before," she said. Her voice was calm, loving, as she took my hand and continued. "You know I have dreams, and sometimes dreams come at a price. As a journalist, I have to get to the truth, even if it means keeping secrets. My father made me promise never to tell anyone I was A. V. Negrados. But I know I can trust you, Joaquín. I know you would never—"

I didn't let her finish her thought because I leaned in and kissed her, a soft, delicate kiss that I hoped let her see how very bad I felt. "I'm sorry I made things worse for you," I said. "Believe me, if I'd known Munro would go after you for printing this story, I would never have done it."

"¡Ay, Joaquín! I'm so sick of this rebellion! What it's done to our families. How it's changed everything. Even you. You would've never stolen those horses if you hadn't seen what you've seen. I just wish we didn't have to live in this nightmare anymore!"

Dulceña turned away from me then. She crossed her arms, as if she was suddenly frightened. I reached for her shoulder, but she didn't open up to me. Instead, she turned and backed into the wall, sliding down to the floor.

After a moment, I hunched down in front of her. "We could run away together." I took her hands in mine and held them tightly.

Dulceña's head snapped up, her eyes haunted. "I can't run away with you," she said.

Her words wounded me, muddled me inside. I took a

long, deep breath and released it slowly before I questioned her. "Why not? Don't you love me anymore?"

"Of course I still love you, but I just can't do that," she continued. "I have responsibilities. Things I must do. Things that have nothing to do with *us*."

"What could possibly be more important than us?" I asked, letting go of her hands.

Dulceña got up then, and so did I. We stood staring at each other for a moment, before she threw her arms around me and pressed her face into my chest. I hugged her back. She felt so small, so fragile in my arms.

She let me go and stepped away, rubbing a spot on the filthy cement floor with the toe of her fancy leather boot before she finally answered. "You have to understand," she whispered. "As a reporter, I have a responsibility to the people of this community. They need me to stay here. I need to be A. V. Negrados—I need to keep writing their stories. If I were to leave, to run away, who would speak for them? Who would voice their fears and document their suffering? No, Joaquín. I'm sorry, but I can't run away with you."

"Dulceña! Hija, where are you?" a deep voice called from outside.

"Shh," Dulceña shushed me by putting a finger against her lips. "It's my father. Hide, quickly, before he finds you here."

She kissed me swiftly on the lips, a quiet whisper of a kiss that said she loved me, despite all that she had or had not shared with me that morning. Then, as her father's voice got nearer, she pushed me away. I ducked behind the old machinery, a bulky piece of rusty metal that concealed my body as I squatted down. I held my breath when the door opened and sunlight crept into the dark warehouse brimming behind the slim frame of Dulceña's father.

"What are you doing here, hija mía?" Don Rodrigo asked. He was frowning at her, a stern, disapproving cleft set deeply into his forehead.

Dulceña walked over to the door. Her back was to me now, so I couldn't see her face. "I was looking for Coquito," she said, sounding worried. "Conchita hasn't seen him all day, and I thought I heard him meowing in here when I called his name."

"He's probably out tomcatting somewhere. You don't need to look for him. He'll be back when he's good and ready," Don Rodrigo said. He put his hand on the small of Dulceña's back and gently guided her out the door. "You should get back to the print shop. Your mother's waiting for you. She wants you to go with her to the dress shop."

Dulceña walked outside, but her father lingered by the door. His eyes, narrow and sharp, swept every corner of the warehouse before he finally disappeared, leaving the heavy wooden door slightly ajar.

I didn't move right away. I waited a good ten minutes behind that bulky piece of equipment before I slipped out of the warehouse, retrieved my horse, and hightailed it all the way back to Las Moras.

—FROM JOAQUÍN, FRIDAY,
SEPTEMBER 3, 1915

D—

Cariño mío,

Since Papá left, I have felt more anxious than ever before. His absence, the threat of attack, not just on Las Moras but on your family's business as well, weighs heavily on my heart. I find myself wishing I could be two places at once, wishing there were more people like La Estrella, citizens willing to protect you and secure the print shop for what it bestows upon them. But freedom of speech comes with a high price these days and there are few willing to risk paying for it.

I know your father wouldn't have it any other way, but I pray for your safety in the dark and think on you every waking hour. At night, I pull off my boots and rest my rifle on the wall beside my bed. It stands upright all night, waiting, listening to me scribbling by candlelight—rants and ruminations—a clumsy poem, this terse note, all of which are surely written in vain. For that is the fate of secret thoughts, quiet fears—nightmares—to dwell in darkness, to dissipate into mists, like fathers led into the chaparral by Rinches or deputies at dawn, their voices muffled, silenced, gone.

Before sleep overtakes me, the rifle slumps sideways,

slides down, until it lies helpless on the floor, its barrel cold, dead against the fingertips of my hand as it dangles from the bed. Forgive the abruptness of this letter, corazón. I can think of nothing else but the weight of this rifle when I place it back upon my shoulder at dawn. I will write more lovingly soon. I promise.

Te amo,

—J

Chapter 15

The sky was burned out, almost blackened, the evening of September fourth when Doña Luz rushed into the dining room looking like she'd seen the Santa Muerte in the kitchen. "I'm sorry to interrupt, señora," she said. "But Manuel needs to see you in the kitchen."

"Manuel?" Mamá asked. Then, realizing what Doña Luz was trying to say, she threw her napkin aside and pushed back her chair. "Is it Acevedo? Is he all right?"

At her words, I put my fork and knife down and got up, scraping the hardwood floor in the process. "Where is he?" I asked. "Where's my father?"

Doña Luz moved aside to let Mamá get past her. "He's all right," Doña Luz said, following us down the hall to the kitchen. "Manuel said he's going to be all right."

"Señora," Manuel said, taking his hat off and toying with it between his hands. "We were robbed. They took all the vacas. The entire herd. All gone. I'm sorry, señora."

Mamá's eyes sparkled, and I could tell she was trying not

to cry. "Where's Acevedo?" she asked. "Where's my husband, Manuel?"

"He's coming, señora," Manuel said, shaking his head. "They're bringing him now."

"What do you mean bringing him?" I asked. "What's wrong with him?"

Mamá gasped. She covered her mouth with a trembling hand, but only for a moment, before she asked, "How bad is it?"

"I don't know," Manuel said, dropping his eyes to the floor. "He won't tell us. But he was riding very slowly, señora, so we unloaded the provisions and put him on the wagon, just to make sure. You understand?"

Mamá took a deep breath and said, "Go into town and get Dr. Hammonds. Tell him this can't wait."

As Manuel rushed out the back door, Doña Luz crossed the kitchen. "I'll boil some water," she said, looking for a pot in the cabinet under the kitchen table.

"Yes. Boil two pots," Mamá said. "And tell Sofia and Laura to get fresh linens and meet me in my recámara."

I didn't wait for instructions. "I'm going to ride out to meet them," I told Mamá as I crossed the kitchen and rushed out the back door.

I didn't have to ride out very far, as the campesinos who had gone with him on the cattle drive were already halfway up the road to the main house.

"Papá!" I called, when I met up with them. "Papá! Are you all right?"

My father didn't try to sit up in the bed of the moving wagon, but he did wave a hand in my direction. "Yes, son." His voice sounded small and weak, and I wished I could see his face in the darkness.

"Are you shot?" I asked, circling the back of the wagon, searching for a better angle from which to see my father. "How bad is it?"

"I'll be all right," my father said, his voice sounding more winded than before. "No need to make a fuss. Just sore from all this jostling around."

From what the campesinos described and the way my father was sounding as we made our way to the main house, he wasn't all right. He had been shot in the stomach the night before, not even a week into their drive. The worst of it was the bullet was still in there because he wouldn't let any of the men touch him.

"I just wanted to get home as soon as possible," he explained when I questioned his sanity. "Doc Hammonds will fix me up when he gets here."

It took four of us—Carlos, Chavito, Pollo, and me—working together using a thick blanket as a harness to lift Papá out of the wagon and into the house. Mamá tried to stay out of the way, but she held his hand the whole time we were hauling him down the hall, past the sala, and into their bedroom, only letting go of it when we were placing my father on the bed.

"It's good to be home," Papá whispered, reaching for my mother. He held her hand against his chest and, with his other hand, stroked her long, lustrous dark hair as if he'd feared he might never see her again.

Mamá touched his face tenderly, but only for a moment. "Let's take a look at this, shall we?" she asked, undoing the buttons down the front of his shirt.

"It's not that bad," Papá said, drawing a hand up to stop my mother.

"You're bleeding!" Mamá cried, and I ran to my father's bedside. A bright crimson liquid was seeping slowly into the brown cotton of his shirt.

Taking my mother's hands in his, my father kissed them. "Please," he said. "Let's just wait for Doc to get here. It'll be okay. I promise."

"¡Por favor, Acevedo!" She pushed my father's hands aside. "Don't be difficult! I have to stop the bleeding!" With trembling hands, Mamá pushed and pulled again at the shirt's buttons and managed to open the garment wide enough to reveal Papá's poorly wrapped torso.

Papá leaned forward to let Mamá undo the makeshift wrap and examine him more closely. "It's not that bad. They weren't trying to kill us, just drive us away from the herd."

"Joaquín," Mamá turned to look at me for the first time since Papá's arrival. "Pour some hot water in that basin and bring it to me."

"Who did this, Papá? Was it Mexican revolutionaries?" I asked as I handed Mamá the porcelain basin, a family heirloom she kept on her dresser.

My father cried out, a short, startled howl. Then he gritted his teeth and said, "I'm not sure, Joaquín. They were wearing masks. We couldn't stop them. There were just too many of them. They took every last head of cattle."

"In broad daylight?" I winced as Mamá cleaned a long, angry laceration that oozed fresh blood from Papá's ribcage. I couldn't tell if the wound was infected, but I prayed that it wasn't.

Mamá put the basin on the floor so she could press on the wound with both hands. I picked it up and put it on the dresser.

"Who would do this?" I asked, turning slightly left to address Carlos directly.

"Insurgents, more than likely." Carlos said. He had been waiting patiently by the door while my mother cleaned Papá's wound. "Tejano rebels or Mexican revolutionaries—there's no way of telling them apart anymore. There's too many bad guys to keep score."

"I can't believe they would hurt an innocent ranchero!" I said. "Papá's just minding his own business."

"It's the way of revolución, Joaquín," Carlos said as he moved to the foot of the bed. "I know it's hard to believe, but not all tejanos are like us. There are some mean rebels out there. Most of them straddle the fence between good and bad—just look at those Sediciosos. Then you have rebel gangs like Los Matadores who don't care whom they kill or steal from. To them, nothing is off-limits. Nothing is sacred."

"But the rebels know Mamá is on their side," I said.

My father shook his head and said, “There are no clear lines anymore, no boundaries, Joaquín. Evil has rooted itself into our lands, dug itself deep into the souls of mejicanos on both sides of the border. While most are out for blood, some just want food or the money to buy it, and a well-maintained herd of cattle is both of those things.”

“The herd is branded,” I said. “They won’t be able to move it. No one’s going to buy stolen cattle—not around these parts. We need to find them before they cross over into Mexico. We can’t let them get away with this!”

“No one moves cattle across the river without the Medina brothers,” Pollo said. “If anyone knows where they’re taking the herd, it’s the Medinas.”

Carlos nodded. “The Medinas do control most of the riverbank on this side of the border,” my uncle said. “They’re not necessarily friendly to our cause, but they might know who took the cattle.”

Mamá dropped her medicine bag onto the floor with such a loud thump that it caught everyone’s attention. “This isn’t the time for this!” she said, standing up and crossing the room to open her bedroom door. “You and your men need to go back to the field house, Hermano. Joaquín has to stay and help me take care of his father for now.”

“But Mamá,” I began. “If we don’t—”

Mamá held her index finger straight up in front of her. “If you don’t stop talking, this night will only get longer. Now, I’m sure there are plenty of things these gentlemen need to take care of out in the field house before they can get some rest. It's not fair to make the campesinos do all the work while we stand around chatting all night, Joaquín."

About an hour after Carlos and his men left, Doña Luz escorted Doc Hammonds into the room. As I sat on a chair on the other side of my parents' bed, Doc Hammonds pulled the bullet out and stitched Papá's wound. I resolved to find out who was responsible for this.

"Go to bed, Joaquín." My mother's hand on my shoulder made me jerk. "Go on. I'll keep an eye on him."

I stood up and patted my father's hand. He opened his eyes and smiled wryly at me, a crooked little smile that told me he was still in a lot of pain. "Hasta mañana, Joaquín," he said, closing his eyes again. "Try not to worry about me. I'll see you in the morning."

Mamá followed me out of their bedroom, closing the door behind herself. She waited until we were down the hall, by the stairs, before she pulled me into a fierce embrace.

"Thank you for listening to me," my mother whispered against my temple after she kissed me. "I'm sorry if I was a bit curt. But I didn't want to upset your father."

I hung my head for a moment. "I didn't want to upset him either," I admitted.

"You're a good boy, Joaquín," Mamá whispered, pushing a stray lock of my hair away from my eyes. "You always have been. That's why I love you so much. ¡Eres mi alma—mi corazón!"

"I know I promised not to take matters into my own hands anymore," I said, letting her caress my face the way she used to when I was a child. "But I need to find out who did this to him."

"I know," Mamá said, then she covered her face with her hands and cried softly. "I just don't —I don't want you to go out and do anything crazy."

"Mamá—" I started.

"No. Please," my mother interrupted me. "Just listen to me, Joaquín. "You're a good son, and you want to take care of us, but this is my battle to fight—my river to cross."

"What are you talking about?" I asked, horrified at the idea that my mother might be thinking of going after the cattle thieves herself. "Mamá—you can't go after them!"

"Promise me you won't do anything rash, cariño," my mother continued. She wiped her tears away and took a deep breath. "Please. Promise me you'll stay put. Promise me you'll let me take care of this."

"Okay," I promised.

But in my heart I was sure that—whatever she did, wherever she went—I was going with her.

Excerpt from Joaquín's journal,
Saturday, September 4, 1915

I KNOW

I know to react is to invite danger.
I know to chase thieves is to hunt coyotes,
to risk stepping into trampas set for them.
I know to approach bandidos is to stand still
and wave a red cape at a raging bull.
I know to roust fugitives is to tackle a rabid dog
and bite into its wounded ear.
I know to confront renegades is to test the scythe,
to snicker at La Muerte.
But I also know I have to do this.

I know pride has a temper
because it beats angrily against my temples.
I know honor has corazón
because it hammers furiously against my ribcage.
I know integrity has an appetite for vengeance
because I hear it gnashing its teeth.
I know coraje has sharp talons
because they dig into my flesh when I make a fist.
I have to make things right.

Chapter 16

"There's no doubt about it. Slater and Davis are behind this," Carlos said as he stood in the sala talking to us the minute he got back from meeting with the Medina brothers, two Mexican brothers turned revolutionaries when their families where killed in their presence by soldados in Matamoros. "The brothers wouldn't do business with them. They don't deal with lawmen, especially dishonorably discharged lawmen. So Slater and Davis are moving the cattle across the border themselves. Word is they hired some thugs from up north, some out-of-work foreigners, vagrants, too hungry to ask questions."

Pollo confirmed his story, saying, "Slater and Davis were bound to do something like this. The rumor mill says they blame Joaquín for having their badges taken and being run out of town by that new sheriff, Caceres."

"I don't know why," I said. "They had to know they had it coming."

Mamá didn't hesitate. She lifted her chin and said, "We have to go after them. We have to get our herd back."

"I was afraid you'd say that," Papá said, resting his shoulder against the frame of the door and clutching at his side.

"What are you doing out of bed?" Mamá rushed over to push her shoulder under his arm and help him regain his balance. With her assistance, my father walked all the way into the room and sat down on the nearest chair.

"Please don't do this," my father implored, taking my mother's hand and kissing it. "Let it go, Jovita. We have so much to be thankful for. We can afford to lose the herd. We'll have this year's sugarcane harvested soon. And if we can ever finish clearing out the new field, we'll have a bigger crop next year. With everything that's been happening, we've delayed the expansion too long as it is."

Mamá pulled her hand away and shook her head. "It's not about the cattle," she said. "This is about justice. We have to catch them in the act and bring them in and demand that they be put in jail."

"Mamá's right," I said. "We can't let them get away with this. We have to go after them. If we don't, they'll never leave us alone. They'll come back over and over again, como tlacuaches enmañados, taking whatever they want whenever they want because they can."

My words had not inspired my father. He was still very upset a few hours later when Mamá and I left Las Moras and set out with Carlos and his men in search of Slater and Davis. With our herd in tow, they couldn't move very fast, so it wasn't likely that they had crossed the border yet.

The moon was a drawn silver sliver in the sky, providing us little light as we moved quietly through the brush. It took us the better part of the night to track down the cattle thieves. They were almost at the nose of the Eagle's Nest when we first spotted them.

We lay low in the brush and watched them over the ridge of a hill, resting on the bank of the Rio Grande. No doubt they were settling in for the night, celebrating their good fortune by sharing a bottle of tequila with their new partners in crime.

Pollo came out of the brush, squatted down next to me and my mother, and said, "It's your herd for sure. Chavito checked, and they've got the LM brand on 'em."

"Good," Carlos said. "Let's go."

We mounted our horses again, quietly. Carlos hooted softly and lifted his arm in the air. Our men moved quickly, efficiently in both directions, keeping to the brush while at the same time encircling the herd of cattle, their rifles at the ready. Then Mamá, Carlos, Pollo, and I rode right up the center, making no effort to be quiet or disguise our intentions to have a word with them.

"Who's there?" one of them yelled.

"That's Slater," I said, nodding to Carlos. "I recognize his voice."

Carlos reined in his mount and stopped. Mamá, Pollo, and I stopped too, keeping our eyes on the group of men before us. Slater and Davis were standing around talking to each other, but there were at least twelve more cattle rustlers milling around my father's herd. I had counted them when they'd first come into view.

"Morning, boys!" Carlos said, loud enough for everyone to hear. "Nice herd you have here."

"Who's there?" Davis asked, putting his hand over his holstered gun.

I lifted my rifle, aiming at him. "I wouldn't do that if I were you. We have you surrounded."

"Joaquín?" Davis called out without moving his hand off his sidearm.

Slater grinned at Davis. They whispered to each other, and then Slater shook his head at him and stepped toward us. "You should take your mother home, Joaquín. The brush's no place for a woman."

"My mother knows how to take care of herself," I said. I'd made up my mind—I wasn't going to hesitate. One false move, and I would be forced to shoot him.

Slater considered my words for a moment. Then he turned to speak directly at my mother. "What are you doing out here, señora?"

"This is our herd." Mamá's voice came out so assured, so clear, I hardly recognized it as my mother's. "We'll be taking it back to Las Moras with us now."

"Is that so?" Davis asked. "And what makes you think you can have 'em?"

Without warning, my mother lifted her rifle, aimed, and fired a quick progression of shots that bounced off the ground around Davis and Slater's feet.

"Now hold on!" Slater lifted his hands palms up and walked over to speak to us up close.

Carlos pointed his rifle at him. "No. You hold on. In fact, why don't you just stop right there, and tell me why you felt compelled to steal this herd. It's obvious you have no connections out here. What made you think you and your friends here were going to get away with it?"

"I wasn't—" Slater didn't get to finish because, one by one, Carlos's men emerged from the brush, circling their mounts around the other cattle thieves, who were quick to raise their hands and back away from Slater and Davis.

"We don't want any trouble," one of the cattle thieves said from behind Davis. "We just needed the money, and these two paid us in advance."

Carlos spoke to the men gathered together behind Slater and Davis. "Then I'm sure you'll want to make amends," he said. "Joaquín's brother is a priest. His parish serves the families of our people. They could use a donation."

The men standing directly behind Slater squirmed in place, sliding their feet back and forth nervously. They murmured to each other before coming to a consensus. "The money's in that satchel," the speaker for the group said. "By the fire. We hadn't split it yet. You can take it all. We don't want anything more to do with this. We just want to go home to our wives and children."

"And you will go home," Mamá said, sliding off her mount and walking over to Slater and Davis. "As soon as we have your weapons."

She stood before them, fearless. I dismounted and joined my mother, aiming my own rifle at Slater's chest while she walked around them, pulling their pistols out of their gun belts. She threw their weapons off to the side, where Pollo and Chavito could collect them after they dismounted.

In the end, Mamá decided to let the rest of the cattle thieves go. Once they were out of sight, Slater dug into the saddlebag by the fire and handed Mamá a roll of bills thicker than my fist. My mother threw it at me and I caught it, ramming it into the pocket of my saddlebag. I kept my eyes on Slater the whole time. I didn't trust him not to pull a hidden gun on me, even with Carlos and his men watching over the exchange.

"Well, you have your herd back," Carlos said, dismounting and approaching Slater and Davis. "You should head back now, Jovita," he told my mother. "I don't think you want to stick around for what's coming, but we can't waste any time. We have to take care of these pelados before the sun comes up."

"What are you going to do to them?" I asked.

"String 'em up." Pollo coughed, then spat in the general

direction of Slater and Davis without actually hitting them. "That's what they would do if the shoe was on the other foot."

"There's no doubt they deserve to die," Carlos said. "But I'd rather just work a confession out of them . . . the old-fashioned way."

"Yeah, give them a taste of their own medicine," Chavito said, laughing at the two men sitting on the ground, glaring at us.

"Señora," Davis called out from behind me. "Help us! Please."

"Come on, Joaquín. Help us get these cattle home." Mamá remounted her horse and joined the rest of Carlos's men, where they were starting to round the cattle up in the direction of Las Moras.

"Move it!" Carlos hollered, pulling rope out of his saddlebag.

"They're going to kill us," Davis said, his voice warbling. "Please, don't let them do this to us. We don't deserve to die." Carlos pushed Davis face-first to the ground, kneeling on his back as if he were going to hogtie him.

"Shut up!" Carlos yelled, tying Davis's hands behind his back. Chavito was doing the same to Slater. "You'll get what's coming to you if you don't cooperate—traitors deserve la cuerda. Come on, Pollo! Get these guys taken care of. I'm tired of listening to their whining."

At that very moment, the sun broke through the horizon, illuminating Carlos's top two men as they yanked on the riatas knotted over Davis and Slater's wrists. They stood up, reluctantly being led away from the herd in the direction of the chaparral, where their horses were tied.

Dragging his feet, como mula, Slater pulled away from Chavito long enough to get in my face and mumble something, but I couldn't understand him.

Suddenly, Slater turned and rushed at me. I stepped aside, and he went flying by. Pollo tugged on Slater's rope, and he fell over, unable to catch himself with his arms tied behind his back. Grimacing, Pollo jerked on the cord again, heaving Slater back onto his feet and leading him away. The wind whirled dust around us and Slater cursed, stringing together a slew of maldiciones.

After a bit of a struggle, Carlos, Chavito, and I managed to get the two men up on their horses. My mother waited patiently for us to join her on the moonlit hillside. "Time to head home," he said. "Manuel and I can take these two into town and deliver them to the new sheriff on your father's behalf."

U. S. TROOPS IN A BORDER BATTLE

Mexican Bandits Eleven Miles North of Brownsville, Texas, Set Fire to Bridge.

Brownsville, Texas, Sept. 2.—A detachment of troop C, Third United States cavalry, and a band of Mexican bandits were reported engaged in a battle this afternoon, eleven miles orth of Brownsville.

Brownsville, Texas, Sept. 2.—Uni- States troops today were trailing nd of Mexican raiders who set o, and partly burned, a railroad fourteen miles north of ville, shortly after midnight. troop trains from Browns- rlingen and San Benito were to the scene about 2 o'clock g. Reports at 10 o'clock xicans had not been over-

of Americans traveling to San Benito in an passed the trestle re it was set on had been fired etween 25 and 30

ed shortly after passenger train . officers be- ad no desire to sengers mpose xas s

Chapter 17

The next morning, Mamá practically beamed with pride when she opened the newspaper and read how Slater and Davis had been taken into town tied and gagged and strapped to their saddles. There was no doubt in anybody's mind that they were responsible for the assault on Papá and the stolen cattle because after a long interrogation, they had confessed everything to Sheriff Caceres down at the jailhouse.

Unlike my mother, I couldn't take comfort in reading the headlines of *El Sureño*. The word Disgraced! ran across the whole front page of Don Rodrigo's paper. The single word screamed at me, and I couldn't help but worry. Was this it? Would Munro shut down the print shop for good? What would become of Dulceña's family if her father couldn't print any more papers?

Setting the newspaper aside, my mother put her hand over mine and squeezed it. "You should take it easy today. Your body needs to recover from that long ride. Here, have something to drink before you eat." She picked up the coffee pot and poured, filling my cup to the brim.

I speared a piece of ham with my fork off the platter at the center of the table and dropped it onto my plate. "I can't," I said. "Manuel and his men are going to start clearing out the north field and building that new fence to separate it from the orchard. I don't have time to take it easy. Some of the younger campesinos have never done this kind of work before, and with Papá laid up, I'm going to have to supervise their workload. Manuel can't be everywhere at once."

"Just try not to overdo it," Mamá said. "Come in and sit down with your father during the heat of the day. You can eat and rest while you update him on the men's progress."

"I'll do that." My head was swimming, either from Mamá's medicinal teas or my fitful sleep.

"He's ready," Mamá said as we watched Manuel and the twins through the dining room window pull up in a wagon full of wood.

My mother and I left the table and walked outside. "How are things in town? Did you have any trouble getting Papá's lumber?" I asked Manuel as I strode up to the wagon and inspected the load.

Manuel stepped off the wagon and took off his hat before he spoke. "No. Everything was ready," he began. "We have some bad news, though."

Mateo and Fito scrambled out of the wagon. Mateo stood quietly beside his father, his eyes hooded. Then, exhaling, he said, "The print shop burned down, Joaquín."

"What?" My chest suddenly hurt, like someone had reached in, taken hold of my heart, squeezed it, made it stop.

"Is everyone all right?" Mamá asked. "When did this happen?"

"Did anybody get hurt?" My father came out of the house and stood listening just outside the door.

Mamá ran up the porch steps and rushed up to my father. "What are you doing out of bed? You shouldn't be out here, not yet. You don't want those stitches to pop." She lifted my father's left arm and put her shoulder under him.

"I'm fine. Doña Luz dug up this old stick for me to lean on," Papá said, tapping my grandfather Tomasito's red wooden cane against the porch floorboards. "How are the Villas doing, Manuel?"

Manuel put his hat back on. "I don't really know, Patrón," Manuel admitted. "They weren't around when I went by. But there's nothing left. The print shop's gone."

"What about Dulceña? Did any of you see her?" I asked.

Manuel nodded. "Everyone's all right. The print shop caught fire in the middle of the night, so no one was there when it happened. But the whole place burned to the ground within minutes, with all that paper in there. There was no stopping the destruction. The Villas lost their business. There's nothing left to salvage. I'm sorry, Joaquín."

"How did it start?" my mother asked.

"Munro and his men are blaming the rebels." Manuel shook his head slightly as he spoke. "But you know how it is. There are rumores everywhere—nobody's buying their story."

Rebels—*right*! I didn't believe that for a minute. *El Sureño* may not have treated the rebels with complete adoration, but rebels were glad to have the paper around. It was getting their story out to the public. They would never burn it down.

"I have to go," I said, pushing my way past Mateo and Fito and running down the road to the barn. When I reached the barn doors, I was so disoriented. I stood in the sunlight for a moment not knowing where to turn. *Go!* my mind screamed. *Get on a horse! Go check on her!*

"Joaquín! Please don't go. It's not safe," my mother called after me.

Mateo came inside the barn as I was saddling up. He put his hand on the nose of my horse and asked, "You want me to go with you?"

"Joaquín." Mamá entered the barn and came to stand behind me. "M'ijo, please don't go."

"Don't be mad at me, Mamá," I said, taking the reins and mounting my horse. "I have to make sure Dulceña's all right. I can't help it. I love her."

Without waiting to hear what either of them had to say, I trotted out of the barn and raced through the gate toward Monteseco at a full gallop. I rode right through the woods, up and down hills, past the creek, through bramble-ridden paths, until I got to town.

The last thing I expected to see when I got there was my father's Packard parked across the street from the print shop. My mother and father were standing outside the car next to Manuel, in front of what was left of the Villas' newspaper.

I should have known they would come after me. I promised myself as I dismounted that I wouldn't let them deter me. I would speak to Dulceña. I refused to leave town without seeing her.

A shiver ran through my body and my heart ached as I stood staring at the blackened remains of the building that used to house the Villas' business. The walls were burned down to stubs, and in the center, a huge, thick, hulking mass of blackness exhaled thin slivers of smoke.

As I stood there staring at the molten mess, Mamá came over and wrapped her arms around me. We weren't the only ones standing in front of the burn site. Other citizens of Monteseco had left their shops and businesses and were milling on the boardwalk and along the street, watching from afar, shaking their heads and speaking in low whispers.

"Where are they?" I asked my mother. "Have you seen her?"

"No," Mamá said, rubbing my back and then reaching up to push a lock of my hair behind my ear. "We just got here a few minutes ago."

Beyond the boardwalk, past Fourth Street, where the Villas lived, Rangers sauntered up and down Main Street in small, conspiring groups. Rage, like a fuse, suddenly lit up inside me. Several of them stood around, casually leaning against the posts outside Nina's shop and Donna's Kitchen, laughing as they visited with each other without a care in the world, and I wanted to shoot every one of them for the horror and destruction they continued to bring on us.

Of course, taking them on, even saying anything to them at that moment, would have been dangerous, and I had better things to do than get myself in trouble. I had to make sure Dulceña was safe. I had an image of her in my mind, a miserable image. She would be devastated. I had to be there for her, to hold her, comfort her.

"Come on, Son. It's time to go home," my father said. He turned away, leaning on my grandfather's cane for support. "You should ride with us. Manuel will take your horse home."

At his words, Manuel came over and extended his hand to me. I handed over the reins to Manuel, but I didn't get in the car as my father expected. "Not yet," I said. "I have to see her. I can't go home until I see her."

After a long pause wherein my mother used the toe of her shoe to toss pebbles aside, my father cleared his throat and handed me the keys to the Packard. "Then let's go."

When I drove us up to the Villas' house, Don Rodrigo was locking the front gate with a wide padlock while Dulceña and her mother stood watching me from inside the tall iron fence. I drove right up to the gate and jumped out of the car to get to him, but Don Rodrigo was already waving me away as I began to ask him what was going on.

"It's better if we don't talk," he said, gripping the keys so tightly the knuckles on his left hand stretched and paled.

"But I don't understand." Childish, embarrassing tears pricked my eyes as I stole furtive, nervous glances at Dulceña being led quietly into her parents' house by her mother.

"I'm sorry, Joaquín," Don Rodrigo said as he started to walk away. "But I have to protect my family. Please, go home. It's what's best for all of us."

Then, to my astonishment, Don Rodrigo turned around, walked into his house, and shut the door behind him, leaving me paralyzed. I was still standing there a few minutes later, staring at that closed door, when a hand landed on my right shoulder.

I jumped away, wiping at my tearstained eyes. My father put his arm around my shoulder, pulling me away from Dulceña's gate. Worry came over his eyes as he said, "I'm sorry, Son."

I hung my head. Suddenly I couldn't hold my emotions in anymore. I didn't make a sound, but my body shook, and I did the only thing I could do to make the pain go away. I wiped my angry tears away and tore away from my father.

"Son!" my father called out as I walked over to the right side of the gate and started to climb the Villas' iron fence. "Joaquín! Por favor—don't do this!"

I jumped over and ran around to the back of the house to climb up the jacaranda tree. It was the fastest I'd ever climbed a tree. I didn't care if my shirt got torn or if my hands got cut in the thorns. I jumped onto Dulceña's balcony and tapped on the glass frantically.

Dulceña opened the balcony door and threw her arms around me. She hugged me tight, sobbing earnestly and kissing my face like she was never going to see me again.

"Are you okay?" I asked.

"No! I'm not. Everything's ruined, Joaquín. Everything we ever dreamed, everything we ever talked about. Our future, it's all gone," she cried. She clung to my arm and pressed her forehead into my shoulder.

"It's not ruined," I said. "Your father can rebuild the shop. You'll see."

Dulceña lifted her head and pointed at the corner of her room. I saw her bags sitting open, halfway packed with toiletries. Her shoes were neatly stacked on top of her clothes in a medium-sized chest. "What's going on?" I asked. "Where are you going?"

"I don't know," Dulceña whispered. "Somewhere up north, I think. Mamá says she has family in Seattle. Oh, Joaquín. This is the worst day of my life! I don't want to go! I don't even know those people!"

"Get your hands off my daughter!" Don Rodrigo said, removing his key from the keyhole and opening the door all the way to let Doña Serafina through.

"This is not appropriate!" Doña Serafina said, pulling at Dulceña's arm and stepping between us. "You have to go. Right now!"

"You don't have to do this," I said, talking directly to Don Rodrigo. "You don't have to go."

"That's not for you to say, son. Leave, please. I don't want to use force." Don Rodrigo put the key in his pocket and opened the door widely for me. "Now, son."

"You can't leave town, Don Rodrigo." I walked over to stand in front of the door. "You can't let them win. If you stay, if you rebuild, you would be sending a message. They can't keep the news from running. Stories like the ones in *El Sureño* are being printed all over the state. He can't stop that. He can't send his posse to burn down every print shop out there. What are they going to do? Pick up torches and run along the border, all the way to California? Because that's what it's going to take to suppress our voice."

"Listen to him, Father!" Dulceña said, pulling away from her mother and coming to engulf her father in her arms. "It's nothing *you* haven't said before. The truth must be printed. Evil must be exposed. We can't run away from this. We have to stay and see this through."

"Okay, Joaquín," Don Rodrigo said, pointing toward the hall. "You've said your piece. It's time to go home, son."

I hugged Dulceña one last time and started out the door. Then, turning around, I said, "Whether Munro likes it or not, the world is ready to hear our stories. Munro can't stop progress. It's not his call."

"NEVERS" FOR CHILDREN

ever cross the tracks by night or by day,
Without stopping to listen and look each way.
Never walk along the railroad ties—
You can't always trust your ears and eyes.
Never hop a freight, for nothing quite heals
The wounds received under grinding wheels.
Never, on a hot sunny day,
Sit beneath a box car to rest or play.
Never crawl under a car of frieght,
When the crossings blocked—play safe and wait.
Never board, or alight from, a train that is moving,
Accidents daily its dangers are proving.
Never play games 'round the tracks at the station,
There are much safer places to seek recreation.
Never leave on the rail any spikes or bars,
Because, in this way, you may wreck the cars.
Never a railroad bridge should you cross,
A train may come and result in your loss.
Never pick up coal 'round the railroad yard,
A train may catch you off your guard.

Edw. L. Tinker, in Leslies.

HUNTERS TAKE NOTICE

At a meeting of the township board ...Heman township, it was unani...ly carried that hunters be forbid... to hunt on any lands in Heman ...ship.

...der of the Board.

F. J. BIGNALL, Clerk.

...OF IN-
...ORTH DAKOTA

...rth Dako-
...in crop

Raiding by Mexican Bandits Threatens Peaceful Relations

WHEN NOT TO USE VIRUS

Grand Forks, Sept. 1.—Never use virus in vaccinating an unthrifty herd of hogs. If cholera breaks out in such a herd, the department of animal pathology at the Grand Forks farm recommends the use of serum alone. Two or three weeks later when the hogs have improved in condition, give the simultaneous treatment. If the unthrifty condition is due to worms, give some well-known worm remedy.

Where there is no cholera in the vicinity, it is not advisable to vaccinate on account of the possibility of starting a center of infection. The exception to this is the breeder of pure bred hogs. Where virus is used in such cases the owner should use every precaution against infecting the premises.

FORWARD TO THE HOME TOWN.

That town that has no life is a dead town but YOU can put town spirit into your home town. You cannot bring "back to the land" the many who have gone, but you can bring "forward to the home town" (if it is a live town) the right kind of people; men and women of energy and ambition and enthusiasm—the kind of men and women who like to live in a town because it is a live town. By doing this, you not only increase the value of your business and enlarge the opportunity of success for your store, but you make your home town the kind of place which the young folks who are growing up, will be glad to stay in —and that is the best kind of town building.

INTEREST—A JOKER IN FARMING

Grand Forks, Sept. 1.—It is a com... ...ke to consider the difference ...ceipts and farm ex-

Washington, Sept. 4.—Border raids by Mexicans, in the view of American officials, have become a menace to the already strained relations between the United States and Mexico.

Although Major General Funston, in charge of the troops at the border, has practically all of the mobile forces in the United States under his command, today's report of firing across the frontier and encounters with the raiders, led to discussion among ...ministration officials as to whethe... some more positive measures should not be taken.

Battle Lasts All Day

Brownsville, Tex., Sept. 4.—With atleast 10 known Mexicans dead and probably as many more bodies lying dead in the brush, the battle between Mexicans and 80 United States cavalrymen, aided by a force of Texas rangers and armed citizens, ended at 4 o'clock this afternoon. One American trooper was wounded.

At 4 o'clock the Mexicans withdrew from the south bank of the Rio Grande and hid in the brush. The battle was waged practically the entire day, the two forces firing at each other across the Rio Grande at a point four miles west of Old Hiedalgo, Tex.

The participants were stretched out in the brush on a battle line two miles long. The injured American was John Salvini, private in troop "D", Third cavalry, who sustained a serious wound in the left hip. He was taken to Mission, Tex. Captain J. C. Mccoy, who accompanied the American forces, returned to Mission tonight. He reported that 10 dead Mexicans could be seen from the Texas side and that probably as many more had been killed in the brush by shots fired from the Texas side.

The number of Mexicans engaged was placed at 40. When the fight ended, the Americans were in possession of three crossings between Mexico and Texas in the vicinity of Mission. The Mexicans made no attempt to cross the river.

The battle started early today when a party of Mexicans, said to be Carzana soldiers, appeared at the river near Old Hildalgo and fired on an American ranchman named Drew.

All the United States soldiers w... ...dered to arms at Fort Brown ...official reason was give... ...the American soldie...

Chapter 18

I WAS OUT PATROLLING THE GATE THE next night when Tomás showed up at Las Moras. He rode up on his horse at about two A.M. like the devil was chasing him. "What is it?" I asked as I closed the gate behind him.

"Please tell me you had nothing to do with this," he said, breathing heavily. "Tell me no one left Las Moras tonight."

"No one's left," I assured him. "Why?"

Tomás took a deep breath and crossed himself. The dark skies above us grumbled. "Thank you, Jesus."

"What is it?" Carlos asked, jumping off his horse and stepping up to us. "What's going on?"

My brother waved in the direction of town. "The Ranger station was attacked," he began. "It happened so fast, nobody really saw anything. But two Rangers are dead. I just finished giving them last rites. Someone threw a stick of dynamite into the building through a back window. Five others were injured. They're being taken to Austin, to the hospital up there. It's a mess, Joaquín. Munro's out for blood, pulling in all kinds of sospechosos, trying to figure out who did this."

"Well it's nobody from here," I said. "Nobody's been out the gate tonight, right, Carlos?"

"No, none of my men were involved," Carlos said. "That's not what we're here for. That sounds like something the Sediciosos would do."

Tomás nodded, relief softening the lines of his tired face. "Good," he said. "Let's go up to the house. I need to tell Papá what's going on."

When my father heard about the explosion, he cursed under his breath and shook his head regretfully. "We have to double up on security," he said. "Munro will be on high alert. We can't take any chances in case he decides to raid Las Moras."

"This is a nightmare," Mamá said. "Things are getting more and more out of hand."

Papá put his hand on Carlos's shoulder. "Who's taking care of the gate?" he asked.

"Pollo and Chavito are on the two towers," Carlos said.

"We need more men out there," my father insisted. "Please go. Take care of that. Go with him, Manuel. Pull every campesino out of bed and tell them what's going on. I want everyone on security detail. I don't want any man, woman, or child to be caught off guard."

As Mamá and I walked Tomás to the door, she turned to him and said, "Those Rangers didn't deserve to die, but Munro had to see this coming. He and his vigilantes have pushed the people too far."

"There's no denying that," my brother said. "I just hope he doesn't retaliate by going after any more women and children at Calaveras. They don't need any more bloodshed."

"I don't know why Munro can't see that this is his own doing!" I said. "He has to know, deep down inside, he has to have taken notice. This madness, this tragedy, is of his own design."

"Munro's not the type to blame himself for anything," my brother said, taking my mother's hand and stroking it. "He can't backpedal now. He's gone too far for that. If I know him, he's going to see this through even if it kills him."

"I should get back to town." Tomás put his hat on his head and opened the door.

"I wish you would wait to go back in the morning." My mother took my brother by the arm. "You need to rest. You can leave after breakfast. Please. I won't be able to go to sleep if you leave tonight."

Tomás leaned down and kissed her forehead. "I have to go," he said. "I can't wait to leave in the morning. I might be needed tonight. I'll be all right. I have a cot at the rectory."

My father came down the hall toward us. He took his automobile keys out of his pocket and shook them. "You want to take the vehicle?" he asked. "It's easier than riding that old horse back. I'll get Manuel to put him up for the night. He can take him to you in the morning."

"I wish you would listen to me," Mamá said, hugging my brother and resting her forehead on his chest. "I hate knowing you're out there in that parish all alone at night without your familia to keep you company."

"Maybe I should take him," I said. "I'm a better driver, and I can stay and keep him company. That way I can bring Manuel back in the morning when he delivers the horse."

Mamá lifted her head. Her eyes shone brightly, and she bit the side of her lip nervously.

"What do you think?" Tomás asked, holding Mamá's arms.

My father tossed me the keys. "I think it's a fine idea," he said.

I caught the keys in midair and weighed them in the palm of my hand, grinning. I loved driving the Packard, although I hardly ever got to. There's just not a lot of opportunity for such things when your life revolves around ranching. "Let's go!" I said. I pulled my hat off the nail on the wall and pushed it down onto my head. "The road waits for no man."

Papá grumbled under his breath. Mamá hugged and kissed me and my brother at the door.

We walked with my father—slowly, to his pace—to the small barn he had built when he first bought the car. "I know I don't say it enough," he said. "But I love you boys. Be careful out there. With everything that's going on, it's best not to stop until you get to the parish. You never know who's lurking in the chaparral."

The town was quiet, the streets barren of citizens, but the silhouettes of Munro's lawmen could be seen throwing shadows in the dark. Some stood on corners, their rifles in hand, while others walked up and down on rooftops, looking down onto every street. There was an atmosphere of danger and threat in the night air. Mal aire, my mind whispered as I walked from the street into the parish courtyard and followed my brother down the alley to the back.

I couldn't help but breathe a sigh of relief when I finally entered the softly lit haven of my brother's room.

"What time do you want to get up?" he asked.

"I don't know," I said, plopping down onto the extra cot my brother kept for me for occasions such as this, when I needed to stay in town for the night. Tomás picked up the small metal clock that sat on his mantle and started cranking it.

I was about to take off my boots and set them aside when there was a quiet rap on the door. Tomás stopped cranking the clock and looked at me. "Did you hear that?" he asked.

"Yeah. Someone's at the door. You expecting anyone?"

"No, of course not," Tomás said, putting the clock back on the mantle.

I went over to the window to pull the curtains slightly to the right and nearly jumped when I saw the silhouette of a person move quickly past the window. Whoever it was tapped at the door, quietly, but urgently enough to get my heart racing.

"¡Cucui!" I said, when I saw my brother standing frozen in place by his cot. "Relax, Hermano. It's not La Calaca."

"Stop it!" he said, crossing himself against the thought of having La Calaca, the skeletal embodiment of death, at his door. "You shouldn't joke like that."

"Oh, you shouldn't be afraid of the Santa Muerte," I said. "Mamá says she is not evil. La Santísima protects us against violence and assaults. She is merciful and offers us safe passage to the afterlife."

"Remind me to have a long talk with Mamá about this," Tomás said, coming over to peek out the window. "Can you see who it is?"

"No," I said.

I was about to call out to the visitor outside when Tomás turned the doorknob and opened the door slightly. "Conchita," he said. "What are you doing here?"

"Conchita?" I pulled the door the rest of the way open to see her clutching the frayed edges of her black shawl as she peeked in and looked at me.

"Forgive me, Padrecito," she said, throwing her shawl over her shoulder and crossing herself. "But I have an urgent message for your brother."

Tomás stepped aside. "A message?" he asked as he ushered her inside.

"Sí, una carta," Conchita whispered. "From Dulceña."

Quickly, Conchita searched between the folds of her white shirt and her dark skirt and took out a small pink envelope. She offered it to me. I took it and tore into it, making short work of pulling the note out and unfolding it.

The pink paper trembled delicately in my hand. I read halfway through Dulceña's letter before looking up to meet my brother's gaze. "She's very upset," I said.

"About what?" Tomás asked.

After reading the rest of the letter, I took a moment to process it before I finally let my brother know what was going on. "Apparently my words made an impact on Don Rodrigo," I said, tapping the letter against the palm of my hand, thinking. "He's decided not to leave town."

"That's good news," Tomás said.

"No. It's not," I said. "Her parents are staying, but they're still sending Dulceña away. They're putting her on a train tomorrow morning."

"Alone?" Tomás raised his eyebrows. "That can't be right. Surely you have that wrong."

"Here." I handed my brother the note. "I have to do something. She doesn't want to go."

Tomás read the letter, then snapping his head up, he asked, "You asked her to run away with you?"

"Yes," I said. "A few days ago. She didn't want to do it then, but apparently, she's changed her mind."

"You can't do that, Hermanito," Tomás said. "You would be doing her a great disservice. Think of her reputation. Think of her future here in Monteseco, or anywhere else for that matter."

I took the note back from my brother, folded it, and tucked it back into the envelope. "I can't—I won't—let them send her away," I said. "If she wanted to go, I might be able to live with this. But you read the letter. She's desperate. She needs me. I have to go to her."

Excerpt from Joaquín's journal,
Tuesday, September 7, 1915

BLESS ME BROTHER

Bless me, brother,
for I have sinned.
Como Adán, I crawled out
of the primordial pond
and kept secrets—told lies—
carefully cloaked deceptions
delivered in the dark.

I remember the morning
a crimson cloud crept
across the sky
and overwhelmed the sun,
how it opened its mouth,
howled at the wind,
and poured Hell upon us.

I stood on the edge
of the creek, testing
the slippery mud
with the toe of my boot

before falling into darkness.
Roaring, gurgling muck
clogged my lungs.

You ran down the ravine,
reached in, and pulled me out
of Arroyo Morado.
I shivered and shook,
a sliver of a boy,
scared, ashamed,
but safe within your arms.

I was twelve to your twenty,
and you were about
to leave Las Moras
to become a Father,
a healer of hearts.
You asked me then,
as you ask me now
"How could you risk
such a fall?
How could you plunge
into those murky waters
without regard for your life?"

I stand before you
now as I stood then,
shivering, confused,
a sliver of a soul,
soaked in fear,
begging forgiveness
for forging my own
commandments—
acquiescing to Love.

Chapter 19

THE NEXT MORNING AS TOMÁS DROVE me and Dulceña back to Las Moras before dawn, I couldn't help but feel apprehensive. It had taken Conchita, my brother, and I only a few minutes to devise a plan, but within the hour, Dulceña was safely out of her house and back to my brother's parish without her parents finding out she was gone.

Beside me in the backseat of my father's Packard, Dulceña fidgeted with her dress. She smoothed down her skirt half a dozen times and then fussed with her collar. She kept a calm demeanor, but she twisted the pearl buttons on her sleeves too many times to be as composed as she pretended.

"Relax," I whispered. "It'll be all right."

"I know," she said. When we got to Las Moras, Carlos opened the gate and let us through.

Carlos peered into the backseat of the car, took a deep breath, and said, "Miss, just so you know, your parents are here."

"My parents?" Dulceña leaned forward and grabbed the window frame with both hands.

"Yes, and they're not happy," Carlos said. He tried to smile at Dulceña, but his cheek started to twitch, pulling his lips to the side into a crooked little grin that fizzled out almost as soon as it started to form on his face.

"Well," Tomás said, making eye contact with me in the mirror as he pulled away from the gate. "You knew this moment would come. Best to get it over with all at once. Two birds, one piedra."

When we drove up and parked, I couldn't help but notice every window of the bottom floor of the main house was full of light. Doña Luz must have used every gas lamp and candle at her disposal because I hadn't seen Las Moras all lit up like that since La Noche Buena, when we traditionally invited every campesino at Las Moras to celebrate the birth of Jesus with us.

By the time we walked through the front door, the entire household was abuzz with activity. Pepita, our new laundress, stood in the hallway gawking at us. Mamá, coming down the hall, sent her back to her room in a rush. However, Doña Luz had to fuss at Sofia and Laura because they had crept under the stairway and were lingering there, trying to eavesdrop as my parents ushered us into the library and closed the door.

Dulceña's parents were waiting there for us. They stood in front of the leather couch as if they had just risen when they heard we had arrived. Don Rodrigo's lips were pressed tightly together, his nostrils flared out and his hands balled up at his sides.

Doña Serafina's eyes were rimmed with a slight reddish tinge, and her voice faltered and trembled a little when she turned to Dulceña. "Why would you do this to us? Do you know what we've been through? We called the sheriff's office, Dulceña! Sheriff Caceres and every deputy in the county is out there looking for you right now."

"I'm sorry," Dulceña said.

"You two have a lot of explaining to do, Joaquín," Mamá said. She was frowning at us, holding the folds of her robe close against her nightgown with one hand. "This is highly inappropriate!"

"Let me just say that I understand how upset all of you are," Tomás said. "But Joaquín and Dulceña have been with me this whole time. So while these are certainly unusual circumstances, they have been under my constant supervision."

"I don't care if you were with the Pope," Don Rodrigo said, raising his voice. "Sneaking out of the house in the middle of the night to run away with your boyfriend is still unacceptable!"

My brother closed his mouth tight. I cleared my throat. "Well, it's not completely inappropriate. Not anymore, it isn't," I said.

"What do you mean *not anymore?*" Papá asked Tomás directly.

I put my arm around Dulceña's shoulders and pulled

her in. Shaking, Dulceña leaned into me, anchoring herself against my side. "Mamá, Papá," I said, holding my head up high. "I would like you to welcome the newest addition to our family, my wife, Dulceña del Toro."

"Del Toro!" My father took a step back, like something wild and poisonous had just struck at him.

My mother's eyes widened and she opened her mouth, but nothing came out of it. She froze for a second before she closed her mouth and turned back to my father who was standing directly behind her.

Then, pale and a little unbalanced, Doña Serafina said, "Oh my God!"

"You got *married?*" Don Rodrigo asked, staring down at Dulceña, his eyes dark, murderous.

"Yes, married." I tried to sound calm, but my nerves betrayed me and my voice quivered just a tiny bit. "In the parish, about an hour ago. Conchita was our witness. It's been recorded in the church registry, so it's official."

"And I suppose you were behind this little scheme?" My father asked, turning to my brother.

Tomás nodded once, a very small nod. "My hands were tied. They love each other. They always have. I couldn't let them run off together."

"You were going to run away together?" Doña Serafina asked, her eyes narrowing as she looked at me. "Why would you do this? Oh my God! You're not—"

Dulceña and I waited for her mother to finish her question.

"Not what?" Mamá asked, genuinely confused at the direction the conversation was taking.

"You're not"—Doña Serafina began again—"*with child*, are you?"

At her question, every person in the room tensed. Their eyes shifted, focused on Dulceña, who gasped as if she didn't know how to answer the question.

"With child?" I asked then, because it suddenly hit me what they were all thinking. I pulled Dulceña in tighter, close to me. "No. Of course not. *We would never!* No. No."

Papá leaned over, put a hand on his desk, and let out a loud, exhausted breath. "Then why would you do this if it wasn't absolutely necessary?"

"With the attack on the Ranger station and the threat of more violence against us, my parents decided Monteseco isn't safe anymore," Dulceña told him. "So they were going to send me away. I was scheduled to get on a train in a few hours, but I can't leave here. I have a job to do, a very important job. My whole life is in Monteseco. Everything I need, everyone I care about, is here. But more importantly, Joaquín and I love each other more than anything else in the world. So how can I go, when my heart is here?"

Dulceña's words, her passionate declaration, made both Mamá and Doña Serafina soften. Our mothers became misty-eyed.

"But this is not the way we do things," Papá said, interrupting the tender moment to speak his mind. "A suitor's parents are supposed to visit the young lady's house and ask for her hand in marriage. We are not unreasonable parents, Joaquín. You should have come to me—to us—and declared your intentions."

"And have you question it?" My remark must have hurt my father, because he winced. "We asked Tomás to marry us because we needed to do something that showed everyone just how serious we are about each other, Papá. We had to do something no one could undo."

"What God joins . . ." Tomás said, letting the phrase speak for itself.

Papá rubbed his forehead. "I need a drink." He walked over to the liquor cabinet and poured himself some brandy. "How about you, compadre? Do you need something to drink?"

"No," Don Rodrigo said. His furrowed brow said he was still upset. "What I need is a justice of the peace. We need to have this marriage legalized. You two will have to repeat your wedding vows in court. I won't have my daughter move out of my house and into Las Moras without a signed marriage certificate."

Dulceña nodded, blushing.

"You have every right to request this, Rodrigo," Papá said. "I assume you have no objections, Joaquín?"

"No, Papá," I said, putting my arm around Dulceña's shoulder and then taking her hand and kissing it. "I want to do this right."

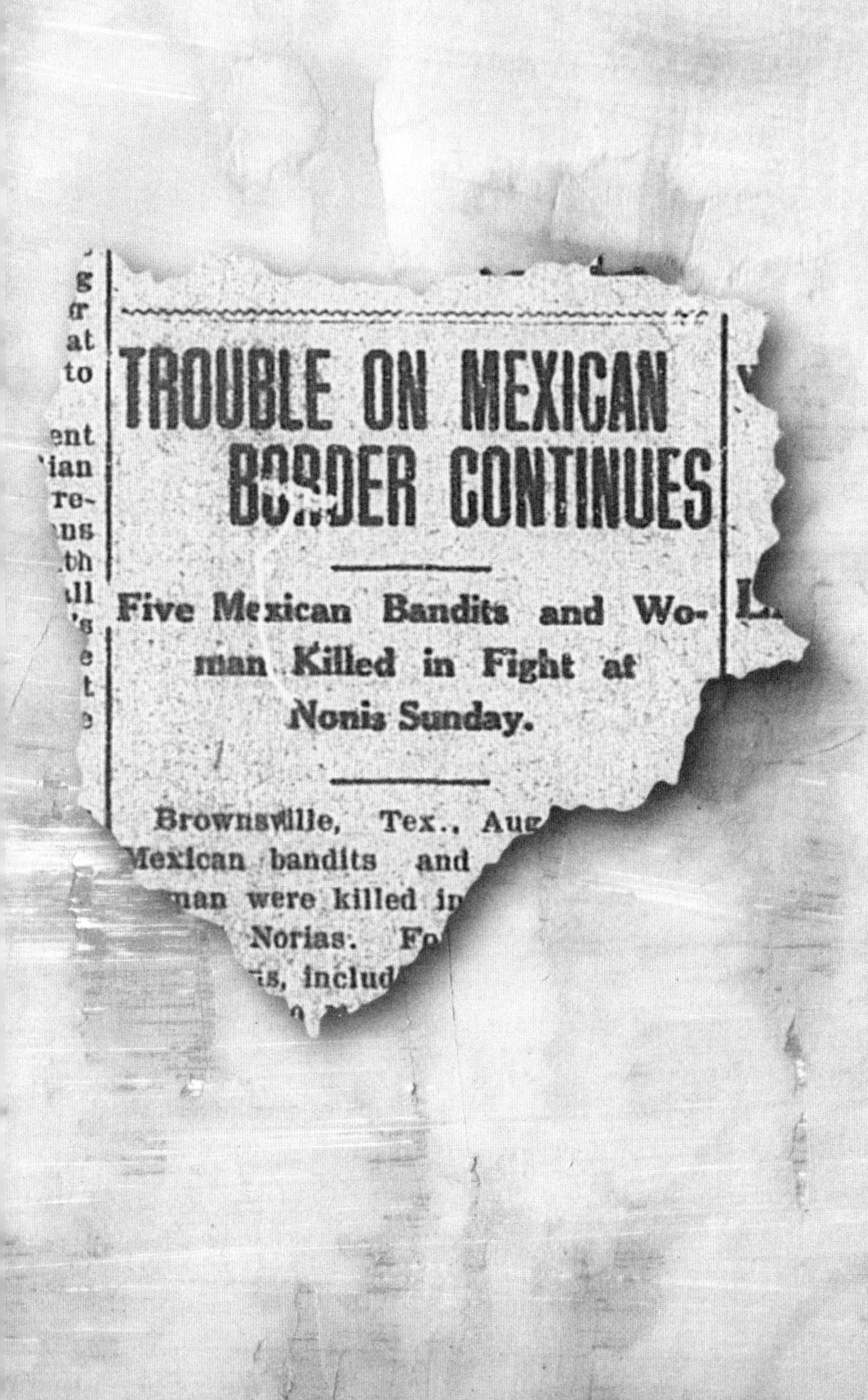

TROUBLE ON MEXICAN BORDER CONTINUES

Five Mexican Bandits and Woman Killed in Fight at Nonis Sunday.

Brownsville, Tex., Aug
Mexican bandits and
man were killed in
Norias. Fo
is, includ

Chapter 20

It happened so fast. At dawn, Papá and Don Rodrigo went into town to let Caceres know everything was okay with Dulceña. After that, they paid a visit to Judge Thompson at his home. Like Munro, Judge Thompson didn't have our people's best interest at heart, but he was the only judge for fifty miles, and he didn't hassle us too much before he agreed to meet us at the courthouse and marry us that very morning.

No sooner had the courthouse opened than we were inside, standing side by side, Dulceña and I, saying our vows. We signed our names on a marriage certificate, were pronounced husband and wife, and kissed for the first time in front of our parents. I can honestly say, there is nothing stranger and more uncomfortable than that first kiss in front of the in-laws.

Papá hugged me, put his hand on my shoulder, and said, "You're a man now, Joaquín, with more responsibilities than ever before in your life. Make sure you take care of your wife. You are to protect her and respect her and never, ever, forget that she honors you with her love. You understand?"

"Sí, Papá," I said, trying not to grin, but finding it very hard because it felt so good to have our families reunited again.

Mamá cried, happy tears, of course, and so did Doña Serafina. Then they hugged us and kissed us and whispered blessings in Spanish against our temples and cheeks. "Oh, how I wish there had been time to give you a reception," Mamá said. "I'm so happy, I could dance all night!"

"Dance all night?" Papá asked. "Oh, I don't know about that."

"Why not?" Mamá asked, turning to my father and putting her hand under the crook of his arm. "You and I are not past our dancing days. There's still life in these old bones."

Papá grinned and leaned down to kiss my mother. "You are much too young and beautiful to be talking about old bones. I was referring to this miserable cane," he said, tapping my grandfather's wooden walking stick against the floor.

Dulceña squeezed my arm and smiled up at me as we watched my parents act like a young couple in love. In that moment of euphoria, I put aside everything else that was going on. I pushed aside the rebellion and Munro, and the Rangers outside the walls of the courthouse, and I allowed myself to drift back to that sunlit morning, our last Easter Sunday together at Las Moras. Full of hope and joy, I envisioned so many more family gatherings to come, so many more sunlit mornings with a bright future ahead of us.

The cool morning air hit my face and filled my lungs

as I stepped out of the courthouse. Squinting, I smiled at Dulceña as she clung to my arm. She smiled too, and leaned in and pressed her nose against the sleeve of my shirt and took a deep breath.

We were standing in the square, in front of the courthouse, talking about having breakfast at Donna's Kitchen, when Munro and his posse came down the street toward us. They were armed, holding their rifles, picking up speed as we turned to face them. Other people noticed them too and came out of their businesses to watch as the captain and his lawmen stepped off the boardwalk and came right up to us.

"Hold on, there!" Munro called out.

"¿Qué pasa?" Papá asked, stepping in front of me and Dulceña. Don Rodrigo took Doña Serafina's hand and they huddled to the right of Dulceña while Mamá stood on my left. We had no idea what Munro wanted, but it couldn't be good. I put my arm around Dulceña and pulled her in tight.

"I'm here for your daughter, Rodrigo," Munro said. "She is a person of interest in an ongoing investigation."

Beside me, Dulceña gasped and squeezed my hand. I looked at the lawmen, one face at a time, as they stood clustered together, and that's when I noticed it. *Mateo was with them.* He wasn't armed, but he was standing right there, in the middle of Munro's posse. Our eyes met, and he blinked and hung his head.

"Mateo," I whispered to Dulceña. She scanned the crowd and found him, standing to the left of Munro. Her eyes widened.

"What are you talking about, Munro?" Papá asked. "What could you possibly want with my daughter-in-law?"

Munro nodded to his men and they moved. Like coyotes, keenly attuned to us, some of his men went to the left while others went right, until they were surrounding us. Mateo didn't move. He just stood beside Munro. He was unarmed, but I could tell something inside him had shifted since we last spoke a few days before at Las Moras. The sternness of his gaze and the tightness of his lips told me he was just as dangerous as the rest of Munro's men.

"Mateo," I called out to him. "What happened? What's going on?"

Mateo took a deep breath before answering me. "They have Conchita," he said. "They won't let her go. They won't even let me see her."

"Conchita!" Dulceña cried out. "Why?"

Don Rodrigo came around us and spoke to Munro directly. "What is Conchita being charged with?" he asked.

"Conchita Olivares was the last person to be seen with your daughter," Sheriff Caceres said, answering Don Rodrigo. "We picked her up in connection with Dulceña's disappearance."

"But I met with you this morning and told you that my daughter had been found," Don Rodrigo said. "Why is her friend still in custody? She should have been released immediately."

"That's what I told them!" Mateo blinked nervously.

Munro spoke to Don Rodrigo. "Conchita has come

forward with information that is of utmost importance to us," he said. "Her testimony last night revealed that Dulceña Villa is A. V. Negrados."

"What?" Doña Serafina cried out. "That's ridiculous!"

Munro closed in on our tightly clustered family. He looked right at Dulceña's mother as he said, "Understand this, señora. I am very serious. As a reporter—as A. V. Negrados—your daughter has had direct access to La Estrella for months, maybe even years, and I intend to find out just how closely associated they have become, what her role is in the rebellion."

"That's a long leap! You're chasing squirrels, Munro," Don Rodrigo said, waving his hand as if to dismiss the accusation. "My daughter has nothing to do with La Estrella. A reporter simply reports the news. Have you never read the Constitution?"

"Oh, but she does," Munro said, pushing Mateo out of his way to come stand in front of Don Rodrigo. "I have to admit, it was clever of her, having that negrita, Conchita, running up and down on her behalf the whole time. She really had me going around in circles for the last few months trying to figure out who was who and what was what, but I finally put it all together. With a little help from her accomplice, I know that love letters to Romeo here were not all that was being delivered for her. Your daughter was also communicating with rebels at Calaveras. She had a whole system of correspondences coming in and out of your print shop."

"Are you mad?" Papá asked. "How could you possibly

think this girl is a renegade? Look at her! She's nowhere near being a fugitive. Get out of our way, Munro. We have no time for bogus accusations."

Munro didn't get out of my father's way. He pulled his pistol out of its holster and said, "I'm afraid I can't do that. Dulceña Villa, you are under arrest for conspiring to commit treason."

At his words, Munro's posse rushed in and pulled Dulceña out of my arms.

Mamá cried out, "You can't do this!"

"Let her go!" Doña Serafina cried. She reached for her daughter, but two deputies blocked her way.

"Say something, Joaquín!" Mateo said, breaking through the crowd of lawmen separating our families. "They're going to kill them both! Please! Say something!"

"I don't . . . know," I stuttered. I wanted to say something to stop them, but my mind was blank. I couldn't think. I couldn't even breathe at the sight of the deputies manhandling my Dulceña.

Mateo, unable to hold his emotions in check, pointed at Mamá and yelled, "Stop! She's the one you want! She's La Estrella!"

"What?" Munro asked Mateo. "You mean Doña Jovita?"

"Yes!" Mateo nodded vigorously. "Yes. I'm sure. Dulceña and Conchita have nothing to do with it. They didn't even know about her. I swear. They're innocent!"

"Mateo, don't—" I said, grabbing at his sleeve.

"Shut up!" Mateo said, shrugging himself loose from

my grip. "Munro was right about you. You're nothing but a spoiled brat—both of you are spoiled brats, you and Dulceña! You don't deserve our friendship. We're nothing but slaves to you. Well, I'm tired of being at your beck and call. I'm done keeping secrets for you and your Mamá!"

Spit glistened on Mateo's lips as he hurled insults at me. Before I knew what I was doing, I was throwing punches at him.

As two deputies pulled me and Mateo apart, Mamá fought her way past Munro. Lawmen pulled at her, trying to restrain her, but she kept fighting them. Papá pushed at lawmen too, screaming for them to let her go.

That's when it happened.

A deputy stood no more than ten feet away from us, aiming his rifle in my mother's direction. I blinked.

Then I saw him pull the trigger.

"Mamá!"

Shot after shot whistled through the air.

Everything slowed down. My mother put her hand on her chest as a quiet, slow stain formed right below her neckline, darkening as it expanded until bright red overpowered azure blue.

I dived for my Mamá. There was a brief hissing sound. A hot, burning pain rushed down my arm. My mother's face went pale, and we fell to the ground together.

Dazed, I leaned over her and pushed aside her hand to see how badly she'd been hurt. Blood—her crimson lifeline—stained my hand a dark, mournful red.

"I'm sorry, Acevedo," Mamá said. My father broke through the throng and quickly knelt at her side.

"Don't move, mi amor," he said. He put his arm around my mother and held her against his chest.

At the sight of our mother, bleeding in my father's arms, Tomás let out a scream that sounded more like a wounded beast than a human being. "No!"

He turned to the deputy who had shot my mother and pulled the rifle out of his hands. Raising the lawman's weapon over his right shoulder, he hit the deputy on the head with the butt of it. When the deputy fell to his knees, Munro and his men rushed in to arrest Tomás, pulling him aside and cuffing him.

"Take him away," Munro ordered, and a group of deputies walked off with my brother as I fought to keep myself from passing out from the fevered pain that blazoned across my torso and pierced through my left shoulder blade.

"Joaquín! Joaquín! Are you all right?" Dulceña screamed.

I wanted to reassure her, but my head was spinning. My eyes blurred and focused and blurred again.

"Yes. I'm okay," I said, fighting through the pain to sit up and take my mother's hand in mine. She was pale and weak and her breathing was ragged. She was dying, but I didn't want to accept it. I clung to the hope that she might pull through.

"Jovita, please don't leave me, mi amor," my father begged, kissing my mother's forehead. He buried his face in her neck, swallowing his sobs as he cried like a child.

"Joaquín, listen to me, corazón." Mamá squeezed my hand. "M'ijo, you have to help your father take care of our family. Please don't let Munro punish Tomás and Dulceña for my part in the rebellion. They're innocent. You know they're innocent."

"Sí, Mamá, I promise," I said, kissing her hand and feeling the tears that had welled in my eyes start to fall down my face.

Like a vulture, Munro cast a long, dark shadow over my mother as he swooped down on us. "Is it true, then?" he asked her. "Are you La Estrella?"

"Sí," Mamá said, a small smile lifting the corners of her full lips as she glared at the Ranger. "Sí . . . I am La Estrella. . . . I'm the ghost you've been chasing. . . . Let my son and Dulceña go, Munro. They're innocent."

Munro took his hat off and ran his hand across his forehead, back over his bald head. "So this is all your doing, then? ¿Es tu culpa?" he asked, shaking his head. "Tell me something, Jovita, was it worth it? Are you happy with the chaos you brought to your family?"

"¡Hijo de Satanás!" Papá cried. "This is all *your* doing! Leave her alone. Can't you see she's dying? Get away from us, canalla!"

"I regret nothing," Mamá whispered. The shallowness of her breath as she spoke to the Ranger belied her defiance. "What I did . . . I did for my people . . . my love . . . my devotion . . . that's something you can never take away from them."

As the last words left her mouth, Mamá closed her eyes and sighed peacefully. Her hand slackened inside my grip and I cried out to her, "Mamá! Mamá!"

"Jovita! Talk to me, cariño," my father begged, crying and shaking my mother lightly at first and then more forcefully. "Stay with me, mi amor! Stay with me!"

Excerpt from Joaquín's journal,
Wednesday, September 8, 1915

THIS WOMAN, MI MADRE

Because this woman won't be there
to smuggle supplies to rebel troops,
into darkness—tejanos will reach out,
hands outstretched, fingers splayed out,
groping, grappling empty weapons, empty shells.
Because this woman won't be there
to deliver kerosene,
into the darkness—rebels will stumble
and fall, skin their knees, scrape their elbows,
split their lips, and trudge along unaided.
Because this woman was La Estrella,
their Morning Star, their sky will be darker,
denser, disillusioned, now that she is gone.

Because this woman won't be there
to dispense food and medicine,
into despair—mujeres tejanas will wander,
creep through the chaparral, search in vain,
and go back to their empty hearths
to watch little ones unravel.
Tiny hands outstretched,
stomachs groaning, children will sleepwalk,

stumble over to empty pots,
peer into empty kettles, and cry.
Because this woman won't be there
to tend their wounds, into despair—they will fall
to bed and dream feverish nightmares.

Because this woman won't be here
to hold me tight, kiss my forehead,
and whisper tenderly at my temple,
"Eres mi alma—mi corazón,"
my life will be darker, denser, disillusioned,
now that she is gone.
Because this woman was mi madre,
the one who brought me to light,
into darkness—into despair—I stumble and fall.

Chapter 21

MUNRO CONDUCTED HIS INVESTIGATION IN THE presence of Gregorio Luna, a lawyer Papá and the Villas had hired jointly to defend everyone arrested the day of our wedding. Luna had made a name for himself as a great defense attorney in Brownsville. He knew what he was doing, so Caceres and Munro had no other choice than to let Dulceña and Conchita go free.

Whereas the deputy who shot my mother was not being brought up on charges, my brother, Tomás, was being charged with attempted capital murder for beating him up. Despite Luna's best efforts to have the charges dismissed, or at least reduced, Tomás was quickly indicted by Judge Thompson.

"Don't worry about it," the lawyer told us, as I sat across from him and my father in our living room back at Las Moras. "I'll get this all sorted out."

Luna tried interviewing members of the captain's posse, but Munro told them they would hang for treason if they talked to him. He sat in on all interrogations and verbally intimidated Sheriff Caceres every time Caceres agreed with anything Luna said, reminding him that as an officer of the law it was his duty to remain neutral. He was not to side with defendants or their attorneys.

I went with Dulceña's parents to pick her up the morning she was released from jail. When she saw me, she put her arms around me, hugging me gently because Doc Hammonds had immobilized my arm with a sling after he'd pulled a bullet out of my shoulder.

"I knew you'd come for me," she whispered, kissing me softly.

"Of course," I whispered against her cheek. "I love you. You are my wife now. There was no way I wasn't going to be here."

After releasing me, Dulceña threw herself upon her parents. "Thank you," she said, her voice trembling as she hugged them. "I'm sorry I've been such a burden to you."

"You're not a burden," Doña Serafina said. "Never, ever, think that."

We returned to Las Moras together. Don Rodrigo drove us in his Ford so that we could all get there as fast and as safely as possible. Dulceña sat beside me in the backseat, completely exhausted. She leaned into me, weeping into my shirt as we headed home to my mother's velorio.

Doña Luz informed us that Conchita was set free a few hours after we left town. Her parents picked her up and took her straight home. According to Doña Luz, Conchita was keeping her distance from Mateo. He was staying in a boarding house, hoping to get a chance to see her, but like many people in Calaveras and Monteseco, Conchita blamed Mateo for my mother's death. Doña Luz was sad, but also relieved that, soon after Conchita's release, Mateo had decided to leave town to go live with Luz's in-laws in Mexico.

"We'll be leaving too," Carlos said when Doña Luz finished telling us all about Mateo's departure. "After the funeral."

"Leaving?" I asked, looking up at my uncle. "Why?"

"This isn't over, Joaquín," Carlos said. "La Estrella may be gone, but her mission must be kept alive. We have to go back to the brush; we have to keep fighting. It's what she would want us to do."

Because Tomás was still in jail, we had to bring in a priest from Hidalgo County to give my mother last rites at Las Moras. We prayed for her throughout the night of her velorio as was customary, and then we buried her right beside my paternal grandparents in the family cemetery at Las Moras. Because my mother's obituary was printed in several small papers in Hidalgo and Cameron Counties, a huge procession of people from all walks of life came to pay their respects. At the velorio, Mr. Simmons came up to talk to me. He'd heard from his friends in town that it was La Estrella who had sent men to stop rebels from blowing up his mill.

"The people of Morado County owe your mother an enormous debt," he said solemnly. "She saved more than our livelihoods. She saved our families from starvation and ruin. I'm just sorry I never got to thank her."

Las Moras never felt as populated or as desolate as it did during the days leading up to my mother's funeral. My father was inconsolable and stood by my mother's coffin the whole time we prayed for her. Because he was emotionally distant and overwhelmed by his loss, it fell to me and Dulceña to see to the comfort of the people who came in and out of Las Moras for the funeral.

Admittedly, Don Rodrigo and Doña Serafina carried a lot of the burden of providing for the people in attendance. They made sure tarps, tables, and chairs were brought in from town and set up at the gravesite to facilitate the service. With the help of my brother's congregation, there was enough food to keep everyone well nourished during the long visitation. Because they were so helpful, even offering to stay and clean up after the funeral, I had newfound respect for my in-laws.

"Thank you so much for taking care of all this," I said as Don Rodrigo and Doña Serafina were leaving after the funeral. "I am sure my father is very grateful. I hope you understand he is not quite himself right now. He would be seeing you out personally if he weren't so grief-stricken."

"Of course," Doña Serafina said. "But please, you don't have to apologize for anything. You are family now. We would be most honored if you looked upon us as parents."

The day after the funeral, I read all about the death of Jovita del Toro, otherwise known as La Estrella, in several newspapers. I couldn't help but notice that the stories were written in both Spanish and English. Whatever else might have gone by the wayside, my mother's death had created a shift in perspective. More and more newspapers written in English were willing to take a chance on covering her story.

La Estrella was no longer a legend told for and by tejanos. The death of Jovita del Toro, an American woman of Mexican descent, killed by a deputy sheriff on American soil, outside a courthouse no less, drew a lot of attention in our area. Her face was plastered over every front page in our newspapers.

For the first time since I was a small child, I started to have nightmares again. I woke up that second night after the funeral in a cold sweat, a silent sob strangling me, suffocating me, because I was drowning in sorrow. Because Dulceña was just as devastated by my mother's death as I was, she was especially attentive to me. It grieved me to see her go to such trouble to comfort me. But no matter how much I tried not to be a burden to her, she was always ready to soothe me with one of her herbal teas.

My father suffered too, more than the rest of us. Not long after the funeral, he took to sleepwalking. The first time, Dulceña woke me up in the middle of the night from a deep sleep to say that my father was walking around in the garden.

"He went outside?" I asked, pulling a shirt on and pushing my feet into my boots before rushing out ahead of Dulceña. She followed me down the stairs and out the back door to the courtyard, where we found my father standing by the fountain, crying out loud with his eyes half-closed, like a wolf howling at the moonlight.

"Papá," I called out softly as I touched his shoulder. "Papá, what are you doing out here? Did you need something?"

"Joaquín," Papá whispered. Then he opened his eyes and stared at the fountain. I leaned in to get his attention, but I could tell by the way he looked right past me that he was still asleep. "Come weep with me; past hope, past cure, past help!"

Dulceña came around the other side and wrapped her arm around my father's elbow like she was about to go on a moonlit stroll with him. "Don Acevedo," she whispered. "Let's go inside. It's too cold to walk barefoot out here."

"No," my father said, pulling his arm away and lifting his face to the sky. "I can't go inside. She's not there. She's here with the crickets and the chicharras. I heard her singing to them."

It took us a while, but with gentle coaxing and a lot of patience, we managed to get my father to come back into the house. Dulceña refused to come back to our bedroom. She took a chair from the sala and sat in the hallway downstairs, afraid he would get up and do it all over again.

"God only knows what would have happened if I hadn't heard him," she said.

I stayed up too, sitting across from her on the stairway. Doña Luz found us at dawn, curled up together, half-asleep on the three bottom steps. She chastised us for not waking her up to help keep watch over my father.

"I could have put Sofia and Laura on a schedule," she said. "A couple of hours between the three of us and you two wouldn't have had to stay up all night."

However, my father's wanderings, his growing mental instability, was the least of our problems. We still had to worry about Tomás. While my father refused to eat, wandering off to my mother's gravesite like a ghostly apparition, our lawyer worked diligently to obtain my brother's release.

TWENTY-FOURTH YEAR.

A MEXICAN TO HANG

NO MERCY SHOWN RODRIGUEZ; DEATH PENALTY TO BE VISITED

Chavez County Jury Deliberates Briefly and Returns Verdict of Guilty of Murder in First Degree. Story of Prisoner Not Given Credence.

Roswell, N. M., Nov. 21.—Juan Rodriguez, charged with the killing of Marion Cartwright, a sheepman, was found guilty of murder in the first degree, the jury returning a verdict at an early hour this morning. In New Mexico this verdict carries with it the death penalty. The attorneys completed their arguments about midnight and the deliberation of the jury was not long.

In many respects the case was the most remarkable ever tried in this county. District Attorney K. K. Scott was assisted by L. O. Fullen, formerly county prosecutor, while C. O. Thompson and R. B. Bowers were appointed by the court to defend Rodriguez. Although it was a charity case Rodriguez' attorneys made a hard fight, putting every effort at all stages of the trial to save the Mexican's life.

The [illegible] night were [illegible] an[illegible] rebuttal late this afternoon and the argument began at a night session. It was thought the jury would get the case by midnight.

Evidence of Escape.

Much time was lost this morning when the attorneys argued at length as to whether testimony relating to Rodriguez' flight was admissable as evidence. The tilt started when Sheriff Young was called to the stand and asked if Rodriguez had been in his possession ever since last August. The attorneys for the defense cited a ruling of the appellate court, which held that evidence of flight in a particular case was not admissable. However, the attorneys could not show to the satisfaction of Judge McClure that the cases were alike, and Sheriff Young was allowed to tell of the flight and the capture. However the state's attorneys on cross-examination this afternoon were not allowed to ask Rodriguez about his escape.

Following Mrs. Havens on the witness stand her two young sons testified. They were with their [illegible] on the night of the murder [illegible] and corroborated the [illegible] Havens. [illegible] Havens' [illegible]

The [illegible] this even[illegible] Guardia[illegible] Oma[illegible] pr[illegible] Gi[illegible] Respo[illegible] Mana[illegible] Solo[illegible] Pi[illegible] EAKI[illegible]

Chapter 22

"I'm just worried about you, Joaquín," Tomás told me when Señor Luna, the lawyer we'd hired, and I went to visit him in jail a few days after the funeral. "You're looking a little worse for wear."

"I'm all right," I said. "I just wish we could find a way of getting you out of this place." I glanced over at Luna, but he was too busy reading through a stack of papers related to Tomás's case to pay attention to our conversation.

"Don't lose faith, little brother," Tomás said. "I haven't. Everything will be all right."

"But how can you keep believing when your life is in jeopardy?" I asked, fighting the urge to scream at him. "I mean, doesn't *He* care?"

Tomás reached around my neck and pulled my head to his. He pressed our foreheads together and whispered, "I understand. These are difficult times. You were bound to question Him. But you'll find answers in prayer. Even Jesus had to do that. He went to the Garden of Gethsemane, remember? Sometimes, a man needs to be alone with the Lord, to talk to Him, to be reminded of who's really in charge."

"Amen," Luna said, his face buried in the book in front of him.

"Do you really believe that?" I asked Tomás, resentment crawling up inside of me, welling up in my eyes in the form of hot unshed tears. "Because I can honestly tell you I'm beginning to worry about His plans for us."

"I'd like to think there's a purpose for everything," Tomás concluded, and then he pulled at the back of my thick blond hair and kissed my forehead. "My purpose here will be revealed soon enough."

That was the last time I saw my brother before Munro and Judge Thompson held a private hearing and sentenced him to hang in one week's time without even the benefit of a trial.

"They can't do that!" I cried, when Luna came by Las Moras to tell us of Tomás's death sentence. "That has to be illegal! Isn't it illegal?"

"Yes," Luna said. "It is. Unfortunately, it happens all too often, especially in small towns like this one. I'm sorry, Joaquín."

"So that's it?" I asked, horrified at the thought of giving up and letting my brother hang. "Isn't there something you could do? Can't we get Governor Ferguson involved? Do you know anyone in the capitol?"

Dulceña, who had been standing behind me as I sat at

the table with Luna, came around and sat down on the chair beside me. "What about a petition?" she asked.

"That could take days to put together, and it probably wouldn't help," Luna said. "We don't have time to waste. What we need here is immediate action. We need to call this to the attention of the world, not just the capitol. We need to do something drastic. Give me till tomorrow morning. I'll think of something."

After Tomás was sentenced to hang, fear, dark and menacing, started seeping into my dreams. I couldn't close my eyes without having nightmares. Sometimes I dreamed that Munro came after me, dragged me out of bed, and shot me in the forehead in front of Dulceña. Other times, I dreamed the Rangers ransacked my room before they burned me alive as I lay hogtied on my bed at Las Moras.

My father was suffering too. He moved from innocent sleepwalking sessions straight into nightmares that grew more and more dangerous. He lost all sense of reality as he walked through the house, acting out his anxieties in delusional episodes.

"Never leave a loaded weapon where your enemy can get to it," a voice snarled in the darkness. The cold metal barrel of my own rifle was pressed savagely against my face as I lay trapped in my bed next to Dulceña. "Don't worry, Son. I'm not mad at you. Just trying to teach you a lesson."

"Papá!" I hollered, relief rushing through every pore of my body. "You scared me. What are you doing in here? You should be sleeping."

"Sleeping?" Papá asked, pushing himself off me, leaving the rifle lying on my chest. "You don't have time to be asleep when you're under attack. You don't have time to think either. You need to learn to react when you hear something, Joaquín. A sharp mind is your best weapon!"

"Why are you doing this, Papá?" I asked, picking up the rifle and sitting up in bed. "Do you know how crazy this is?"

"Keep your voice down," Papá said, putting a hand over my mouth. "You don't want to wake up your wife."

"I'm awake, Don Acevedo," Dulceña said, sitting up in bed and taking my rifle away from me to set it down on the opposite wall, away from my father.

Papá glanced around the room for a second, "Just making sure no one was listening," he said. "Come with me, Son. I need to tell you something."

"What is it? What's going on?" I asked, but my father didn't answer me. He turned away and wandered out of my room. "Where are you going?" I asked, following him as he scuffled down the stairs.

He weaved in and out of the shadows through the house like a specter, until he got to the kitchen. "Are you hungry, Don Acevedo?" Dulceña asked from behind me. But my father didn't answer her either. He walked over to the pantry, picked food off the shelves, piled it in his arms, and hugged it to himself like he'd just found a treasure trove.

"No time to eat, no time to sleep either," Papá said, ripping into a box of crackers. Crumbs fell out of his mouth as he ate standing up.

"I'm sorry," I said, taking the crackers out of his arms and gently guiding him to the table. "What's happening? Why don't you have time to eat or sleep?"

"I'm going to need to borrow some of this food, Joaquín. I need to take it back to the men in the brush. We're starving, m'ijo!" He struggled to open a can of sardines. His hands were trembling so much that I took it and opened it for him.

"You don't borrow food," Dulceña said, getting up to light the wood stove. "Food is nourishment. You don't need to borrow your own food, much less offer to pay it back."

"What are you doing?" I whispered so that only Dulceña would hear. "He's sleepwalking. He doesn't understand what you're trying to tell him."

"Yes, I know," she whispered back. "But you have to be careful what you say to him. You can't startle him awake. That could hurt him—mentally. It's best to just go along with the delusion. He won't remember any of this when he wakes up anyway."

"Money can't buy you food when you're holed up in the brush," Papá said. "We haven't been able to get our hands on any provisions for over a week now."

"Want the rest of this?" I asked, handing the open can of sardines back to my father. He contemplated it like he wanted to cry. Then he pulled the tiny, delicate fish out of the container one by one and ate them slowly, silently. Then, as if he'd just remembered something of great importance, he reached over and grabbed me by the collar. Leaning over and pulling me in, he whispered, "We have to help him, Joaquín. We have to help your brother."

"I know," I said, trying to ignore the dementia reflected in my father's eyes.

"We have to talk to your mother," Papá whispered, as he let me go and got back to eating sardines. "She'll know what to do. She always knows what to do."

"Mamá?" I asked. "Mamá's dead."

"She's dead!" Papá's voice boomed across the room. His body trembled, and his balled fists whitened. Then he reached across the table again and grabbed my shirt, twisting it in his hands, choking me. "Your mother's dead, Joaquín. You hear me? Dead! We can never be a family again. Do you understand?"

Dulceña came over and tried to pull my father off me. "Please, don't hurt him," she begged. Her hands shook as she pried my father's fingers off one at a time until I could breathe again.

"¡Venganza!" Papá said. "Bloodthirsty, cold, calculating revenge is what we need here. I know men who will do it, men of honor and integrity. They can help us, Joaquín. We'll go in there with guns blazing and take out every one of those demonios! We'll string them up—lynch the lot of them. Give them a taste of their own medicine."

"You're tired," I said, getting up and going around the table to help my father out of his chair. "You should go back to bed."

"¡Desgraciados!" My father slammed the table with both

fists. He swept his arm, and the can of sardines went flying across the kitchen. Then he did the same thing with the pots and pans on the counter. "I won't stand for this! Do you hear me? I won't stand for this!"

"¡Cálmate, Papá!" I cried. I put my arms around my father's waist and pulled him back across the room, guiding him back to his chair. He sat down, panting and crying, his body quivering with emotion.

Dulceña picked up the can of sardines and tossed it in the trash, then came to stand on the other side of my father. "You need your rest, Don Acevedo," she said, trying to calm him down.

"Aztec blood runs hot and fierce through our veins, Joaquín," Papá said, a murderous spark glinting in his tear-stained eyes. "Our ancestors were warriors! They plunged their knives into the chests of their enemies, carved out their hearts, and ate their flesh. Join us, Joaquín. Join the rebellion! We'll make pozole out of lawmen!"

"Papá, listen to me," I said as I pulled my chair to sit directly in front of him. My father's hands were cold, clammy, as I held them fiercely in mine. "Can you hear me? Are you somewhere in there? Please, look at me."

"Here," my father whispered, touching his temple as he sank down in his chair again. "I must endure a living hell. Here. In here."

"Yes," I said, putting my hand on his shoulder. "Do you understand what's going on?"

"Going?" Papá's eyes were luminous as he stared through me at the wall.

"You're delusional, Papá," I said. "Please stop this nonsense and look at me."

"He can't see you," Dulceña whispered, rubbing my back gently.

Hot tears started to pour down my face. "Why can't you see me, Papá? Why can't you let me in? Don't you know how much I love you? How much I need you right now? You're the only parent I have left. Please, please, come back to me. I love you."

"Love is a curse." Papá got up and started to walk out of the kitchen. "Love is infernal. Love is a white banderita."

Excerpt from Joaquín's journal,
Thursday, September 16, 1915

ANTI-ODE TO DEATH

Ladrona de alientos—what do you want with breath?
Your empty lungs cannot sustain it, yet you claim it
from every creature you climb upon. A dog snarls,
growls, and barks before it whimpers and shivers
and scratches at the door, begging to get inside.
Then a black bird cries and takes flight, and we,
afeared, lock doors and slam windows shut.
Too late, we come back to the deathbed to find
our loved one's breath has been sucked out.
Estafadora de amores—what do you want with our beloved?
They cannot with their closed eyes behold you,
in their crossed arms enfold you! Deny yourself this
malevolent indulgence and from our humble homes
be gone. Let us dwell peacefully in this, our earthly
heaven, without your treacherous, malignant touch.

Chapter 23

"He'll be all right," Doc Hammonds said, handing me a small brown bottle of tincture of opium. "I gave him a bit to knock him out for a few hours, just so he can start resting properly. Don't give him too much. A small teaspoon before bed every night ought to do the trick. Once he regains his normal sleeping pattern, you'll start seeing a change in him."

I gave the bottle to Dulceña and she put it in the cabinet. "So he's not too far gone?" I asked, feeling apprehensive at the idea that my father might need to be committed. After the night before, I was afraid we might need to take him to a sanitarium.

"No, no," Doc Hammonds said. "Let's see how he reacts to restored sleep and medication first. I suspect that's all that's wrong with him. Your wife said she hasn't seen him sleep all the way through the night since your Mamá's funeral. That's all that's wrong with him. His nerves are wide awake up in his brain. We need to shut them down. The opium will take care of that. You'll see."

"Thank you, Doctor." Dulceña stepped aside to let Doc

Hammonds through. We walked the doctor down the hall.

As I opened the front door, Señor Luna was standing there. "I have an idea," he said, squeezing past me and the doctor.

I saw the doctor out, closed the door, and escorted the lawyer into the library. "What is it?" I asked, when he'd settled onto the leather couch. "Did you find a way to save my brother?"

Luna waved his hand in the air. "No, no," he said. "That's not the way it works. We don't have enough time to get the sentence overturned."

"Then what's all the fuss about?" I asked, sitting on a high-backed wing chair in front of the attorney. Dulceña sat on the armrest of the wing chair.

"Your wife," Luna said, pointing at Dulceña. "Your wife is the answer to our prayers."

"My wife?" I asked, looking at Dulceña. "How?"

The lawyer grinned for second. Then he looked straight at Dulceña and said, "She can write a long, scathing editorial letter addressed to the governor himself. An exquisite ballad, a corrido in English condemning the Rangers and glorifying your brother."

"That's it?" I said, sitting forward in my chair. "That's your big idea? How's that going to help anything?"

"Now, wait a minute, Joaquín," Dulceña said, putting her hand on my shoulder to get my attention. "Señor Luna might have something here. Words are important, and passion lends them power. I truly believe that. If we do this right, if we get the public's attention, we could very well force the governor's hand."

"There's no way of knowing until you try," Luna said. "Just think of everything you could say here. You could finally unmask Munro. You could chronicle this whole town's journey. You could really make a difference."

Suddenly, I knew exactly what needed to be done, what needed to be said. "You're absolutely right! We've been fighting the wrong kind of fight. Going the legal route has gotten us nowhere. It's time we went public."

"Exactly," Luna said. "Munro's biggest fear is exposure. So I say you expose him. I say you put your talents to work here. Your wife's father is a printer. He has to have some connections. Someone must owe him a favor somewhere. Getting an important editorial in circulation shouldn't be a problem for him."

My hope was so great that once our lawyer left, I sat at my father's desk and pulled out some pages from a journal in the side drawer and started writing. The words that had been jumbled up inside me finally fit together, like a puzzle fully formed in my mind, and I knew what I had to say in this letter.

"Do you need my help?" Dulceña asked as she stood behind me, reading over my shoulder as I scribbled away frantically.

"No," I said. The words were coming so quickly, in such a wave of emotion, that I couldn't stop to ask her what she thought of any of it. "Not yet. I have all these ideas swirling around my head. I want to get them all down first; then you can revise it. You can help me with the details, put it all together for me."

Dulceña leaned down and kissed my temple. "Sounds good to me," she whispered. Then she left me to it, only talking to me when she brought in coffee and pan dulce to keep me nourished.

Feverishly, I wrote out our story, the story of a family trying to love and protect each other during difficult, treacherous times. The story of the firstborn, a man of faith, a man of honor and integrity, a man of God. I dubbed my brother the Martyr of Las Moras, Monteseco's forsaken son, un Jesucristo moreno, about to be crucified, hung by the neck until dead, to feed Munro's pride.

I wrote about my mother too, about her support of our people, which was the reason Tomás was in jail. He had come to our defense against her murderer, a man who had never been brought up on charges because the law was blind and mute in Morado County.

Dulceña offered advice several times as I put pen to paper. It was she who added flare to the letter. Her words sparkled like diamonds and burned like fiery brands through the paper as I wrote them out. It was her ardent voice that said, "Don't forget, you're not just speaking for your brother. You are speaking for the people! You are their voice—you are their archangel."

I understood what she had been trying to tell me. In order to get the attention of great men, of politicians and lawyers, men of power, I had to be brutally honest. I had to be clear, but truthful. It was the best chance, the last chance I had to save my brother.

As I scribbled furiously, passionately, I thought about what A. V. Negra and all those other fearless journalists would say at a time like this. How would they *address* the problem? What angle would they take? What angle would my own beautiful wife, the brilliant A. V. Negrados, take? Mimicking her style, I started by quoting the laws of man and the laws of God. I referenced history both recent and past, from both sides of the border.

I condemned Captain Munro and Judge Thompson for fashioning nooses out of laws, wrapping them around our necks, and twisting them just tight enough to suppress our voices, forgetting little things like our right to a trial by jury and the necessity of evidence. I likened the lawmen to pharaohs, denying us our God-given right to prosper in the promised land, the land of our ancestors, the land they bought from under our feet without our permission. I alluded to unwritten laws—the laws of nature, the laws of humanity, the laws of brotherly love.

It was the longest piece I'd ever written, an emotional piece—a story of faith and courage in the face of social injustice, subjugation, and prejudice. One which I hoped would make politicians and common men nod over in unison and clamor for answers. When we were done and Dulceña was satisfied with our efforts, I folded the pages, put them in my pocket, and we headed into town to see the one person we knew had the courage to help us publish our masterpiece.

El Sureño

Vol. XXXVII | Monteseco, Texas | Friday, September 17, 1915

MARTYR OF LAS MORAS TO HANG!

—Justice Is Blind and Mute in Morado County!—

Chapter 24

"IT'S THE BEST PIECE OF WRITING I've read in a long time," Don Rodrigo proclaimed, taking his glasses off and putting them next to the lamp on the coffee table beside us.

"Can you help me get it circulated?" I asked. "Do you know anyone with a printing press nearby? Someone who's not afraid to put this in the hands of the people? Time's running out, so I can't go too far."

"You won't have to," Don Rodrigo said. "Come with me."

Using a lantern to light our way, my father-in-law led us through the darkened hallway until we were at the back of his house. He opened the back door and led us down a path. Past the secluded garden walls we went, until we were standing in front of a small shed. He unlocked the door of the shed and led us inside. Once there, he handed the lantern to Dulceña and moved furniture around until he cleared the area surrounding a bulky object covered by a dark tarp.

"This was my first machine. I cranked out the first issue of *El Sureño* with this old thing," he said as he removed the heavy cloth to reveal an ancient printing press, a relic compared to the one he'd had in his shop. "I bought it off a widow who was short on cash. It was old *then*, so it's worn out and decrepit now, but it still works, if we baby it. I think it's got enough life left in it to get the job done."

"Thank you, Papi!" Dulceña threw her arms around her father and kissed him.

"Don't thank me, cariño," Don Rodrigo said. "The truth is I should have thought about this myself. But with Jovita's funeral taking all of our attention, we were too distracted to consider resurrecting the paper. I'm sorry, Joaquín. I'm sorry I didn't get the word out sooner."

I put a hand on Don Rodrigo's shoulder and patted him gently. "There's no need to apologize," I said. "You've been a great help to me and my family."

"Well, we should get started then. Do you want me to print this anonymously or did you want to use a pseudonym?" Don Rodrigo asked. "A. V. Negrados has a huge following. It would get the people's immediate attention if we used that name. Or we could make one up for you, if you prefer."

"No," I said. "This is *my* battle, *my* fight, and I want *my* name on it. The people may know and recognize A. V. Negrados, but they know Las Moras too. They'll recognize our family name and sympathize more. I want them to see I'm not afraid to speak up and they shouldn't be either."

It took us the rest of the night to get five thousand copies of my article printed before dawn. In the end, we settled on a two-page spread, an exclusive, just long enough to get the story out in both Spanish and English. Its enormous headline screamed out in bold letters the word **Rebellion**, and I couldn't be prouder.

Don Rodrigo got the local paperboys running from one end of town to the other. When the patrons of *El Sureño* woke up to the appalling news of Tomás's secret sentencing, they offered to help distribute it to nearby towns. Hard metal and strong flesh drove the news out of town as men in vehicles and boys on horseback took to the roads in every direction to get the news of my brother's impending demise out to the rest of South Texas.

Don Rodrigo and Dulceña drove the paper up north as far as Agua Dulce, and I personally drove around Morado County and distributed the paper to every local merchant who would take it. By the time we all got back to Monteseco, there was a huge crowd outside the old print shop asking questions and looking for answers.

"There he is!" Panchito, the boy who shined shoes in the streets on the weekends, screamed when I stepped out of my father's automobile and into the street. "Joaquín!" they screamed. "Joaquín! Tell us what to do! What can we do to help Tomás?"

I was at a loss for words. What could they do, other than stand behind me? "I don't know what you can do," I said. "I just know that I can't let my brother hang."

"Free Tomás!" someone screamed, and suddenly, they were all chanting it, together, in unison. "Free Tomás! Free

Tomás!" They kept screaming and chanting, getting louder and louder as more and more people joined us.

"To the courthouse!" someone else screamed, and before I knew what was going on, the people were leading me. Toward the center of town we all walked, chanting and screaming and picking up more and more people along the way, until it became very apparent to me that we had become bigger and more powerful than any posse Munro could muster. When we were standing before the courthouse, the people stopped screaming and stood together, looking at me, waiting.

"Go on, son! Get up there!" Don Rodrigo said as he shouldered his way through the crowd. "Bring that thing over here. This boy has something to say. He needs something to stand on." He pointed to a rickety trunk sitting on the porch of the dress shop.

When I was finally standing steady over the crowd, I said, "I am Joaquín del Toro. Tomás is my brother. We are the sons of Jovita and Acevedo del Toro. My mother is dead now. Some might say she died for her beliefs, for the cause, but I think she died for *us*, for me and Tomás, so that we might have a future in this world. So that we might have the freedom to live and love and speak our minds here, en los Estados Unidos."

"That's right, son! Speak your mind," Donna Sabrett said, pumping her fist in the air, at which everyone whistled and cheered.

"Speak your mind! Speak your mind!" the mob chanted, and then the doors of the courthouse opened, and Munro, Sheriff Caceres, and their men stepped outside. They stood on the front steps of the courthouse on the other side of the street, talking, shaking their heads, watching us.

"My brother is not a murderer," I said. "He's good and kind. My mother raised him that way. She raised him to love his fellow man, to honor and protect them. She raised me that way too. Only I haven't been as good as Tomás. Up until today, I've been fighting back, but as you well know violence only begets violence. It took me a long time to realize that. But it's time we learned how to fight the intelligent war. It's time to speak up. It's time to raise our voices together. What we need here is a revolution evolution, a peaceful resolution, a new way of life."

"What should we do?"

"How can we help Tomás?"

"We're all here because my brother needs us. He's a good man, a good priest, a brother to everyone in Monteseco, and now the law wants to hang him. They say he tried to kill that deputy, but we all know that's not true. We all know he's not a killer. He only did that because that man murdered our mother. He shouldn't hang for that."

"That's right!" a man in the front row yelled. He turned his back on me and spoke to the crowd directly, "We need to free Tomás! We need to free our brother!"

"We need to speak up for him!" I raised my hands high again and again as I spoke. "We need justice! We need freedom! We need to put pressure on the governor! He needs to know we're tired of his crooked lawmen. We're tired of his bigoted politics!"

"Free Tomás! Free our brother!"

"Free Tomás! Free our brother!" The crowd had worked itself into a frenzy, and to show her support, Dulceña ran to her father's automobile and brought out another batch of the papers we'd been distributing all morning. Holding the papers in one arm, she lifted an issue into the air and waved it, saying, "*El Sureño* lives. It speaks *our* truth!"

Her words set the place on fire. Munro walked toward us, his steps deliberate, purposeful. Sheriff Caceres and his men flanked Munro. Without saying a word to any of us, the captain tore the papers out of Dulceña's hands. And when she fought him and called him a "desgraciado," he backhanded her across the face, sending her sprawling sideways into the dirt.

It happened so fast I didn't have time to react. I was barely off the trunk when Dulceña stood up and spit in Munro's face, an act that had him reaching for his gun. But he didn't get to it because Caceres drew his own pistol.

"Don't!" The sheriff's voice was high-pitched, nervous. It was clear to everyone he wasn't quite at ease as he pointed his gun at the Ranger.

The crowd was mute in the face of what had just transpired. Nobody dared to take a breath. Not even the wind moved as we all stood silently still, waiting for the captain to react.

"How dare you!" Munro said to the sheriff. "Who do you think you are, pulling your gun on me?"

"Elliot!" The name coming out of Caceres's mouth was

a nervous warning, a quiet, jittery rattle lost in the density of the thicket. "Please. Don't do this, sir. You can't lawfully tell the press they can't operate here."

"Shut up!" Munro said. "And put that thing away before you hurt yourself."

"Don't make me do this," Caceres said, pulling back the hammer and placing the barrel of his weapon inches from the Ranger's chest. "For weeks now, I've watched you tear this family apart one member at a time because I was afraid to say anything. But that's over now. I'm not afraid anymore. Enough is enough. This girl's upset, but she's not hurting anyone."

"She's an insurgent—just like the rest of them," Munro said. "She has no respect for the law. But I'll take care of that, as soon as I'm done with you."

Then Munro took a swing at the sheriff, knocking the gun out of Caceres's hand. The sheriff stepped back and righted himself, but his gun landed behind him.

Caceres was younger and thicker, and he punched Munro so hard the Ranger went sprawling and landed on his back. His own pistol flew out of his hand and landed a few feet away from him. The captain didn't have a chance to stand up because the sheriff threw himself on top of the Ranger and reached back for his handcuffs.

But Munro wasn't going to let himself get arrested. He wrapped his arms around Caceres and rolled the sheriff onto his back. Then Munro sat on Caceres's chest and pounded at his head, one punch after another, until the sheriff's blood covered the Ranger's fist. And when Munro saw that the sheriff was too weak to fight back, he did the unthinkable. He picked up his sidearm. Bringing it up, he pulled back the hammer, aimed, and then—

I jumped him.

I jumped out of the crowd and went straight for Captain Munro. We slammed so hard onto the ground that the impact knocked the wind out of me. But I managed to rip the pistol out of Munro's grasp, and I sent it flying away from us into the dirt. Munro twisted under me, tried flipping me, but I pressed my hands at his throat, choking him. The images of my mother, dead in my father's arms, her body lying prone in her coffin, the mournful prayers, the painful funeral, all of it came flooding back as I held the Ranger's life in my hands. And then suddenly someone was pulling me off Munro.

"Let him go, son," Don Rodrigo said as he and several other men pried me and the captain apart.

"Arrest him," Caceres said breathlessly. He lifted his head and started to get up, wiping blood from his face.

"Which one?"

The crowd stopped moving, everyone stood still, watching, waiting. Caceres glared first at Munro, then back at me, before he finally said, "Both of them."

among a knife into Jo

MOB TRIES TO FREE MEXICAN PRIESTS

Two Thousand Storm National Palace in Effort to Rescue Imprisoned Men of the Cloth.

HIEF OF POLICE IS STABBED

BULLETIN.

EW YORK, March 12.—Th case went to the jury at 5:2 today. The jury went to din at 6:30 p. The indication from

Chapter 25

A SHOCKED SILENCE SETTLED OVER THE CROWD when Sheriff Caceres ordered our arrests. Then quietly, like a puma, a great murmur moved over the throng. It raised its head and broke into a roar, an angry, outraged cacophony of voices: quiet and loud, meek and boisterous, old and young, weak and strong, all mixed together, all speaking up for themselves.

"Gente, por favor," Caceres said, holding his hand up with his palm out in front of the crowd of enraged citizens. "Listen, I know you're angry, but like this young man said, violence is *not* the answer. I need you to calm down and give me an opportunity to make this right."

"Then let Joaquín go!" Dulceña said. "He saved your life."

"I know, I know," Caceres said, nodding in agreement. "But the law's the law—"

"You're fresh out of grammar school," a man in the back yelled. "What do you know about upholding the law?"

"You're in over your head, son. I have whiskers older than you!" Roy, the town barber, said.

"He's learning, give him a chance!" Don Rodrigo said.

"Listen!" Caceres yelled as his deputies handcuffed me and Munro, being careful to keep us at least ten feet apart from each other. "I know I'm just an acting sheriff, but in light of everything that's happened, everything you've lost, it's my duty to make sure things get done properly. Now, I'm young, I admit that. That's why I'm going to make some telephone calls, seek advice. I'll talk to the governor himself if that's what it takes to make sure justice is finally served in Monteseco."

"Yeah, call the governor! See what that gets you! What a joke!" the barber yelled.

"Get him down here! Tell him I want to talk to him!" Donna said, pointing at the ground at her feet.

Sheriff Caceres took a deep breath and addressed the crowd again. "I'm with you on that. This has to end. Too much pain has come from this conflict. We don't need any more violence in this town. That's why you have to listen to me. Go home, please. Go home to your loved ones and give me a chance to do my job."

As it turned out, the people of Monteseco weren't ready to let the matter go. They stood outside the jailhouse the rest of the day and the whole night through. The first rays of dawn found them still standing there, chanting slogans, picketing, and singing hymns, waiting for Caceres to make good on his word. There were so many of them, and they were so riled up, the governor was forced to grant a stay of execution for Tomás until they could *clear things up*.

I sat in my corner cell and listened to Tomás hum along with the picketers, off and on. I was grateful to the sheriff for one thing: he had put me in the cell immediately across from my brother and had Munro put in a cell on the opposite side of the building. We all waited for him to get the call down in his office on the first floor.

We caught up, Tomás and I, talking, but mostly we listened to the ever-growing crowd. And when the sun went down, we lay awake, letting the day's events settle into our consciousness and lull us into a disquieting sleep that had us both tossing and turning all night.

Dulceña and her mother visited us three times a day. They kept me abreast of how things were going with Papá at Las Moras. He was recovering slowly, although he wasn't altogether himself yet. So Dulceña thought it best to keep my imprisonment from him until he was recovered.

Doña Serafina insisted on bringing us food from her own kitchen because she and Dulceña didn't trust the deputies who might still be loyal to Munro not to poison us in our cells. The first time they came, as soon as they were allowed to visit, a few hours after my incarceration, Dulceña also brought me and Tomás new leather-bound journals and black fountain pens. Her hand lingered on mine when she passed me my journal through the iron bars, saying, "For your thoughts, mi amor. May they bring you comfort."

"I'm sorry I've made such a mess of things," I said, hanging my head.

"Don't," Dulceña said, squeezing my fingers in her hands. "This isn't your fault."

"It's that demonio, Munro," Doña Serafina said, cursing under her breath. "This is all his fault. He's always thought he owned this town, but the people are tired of him and his bullies. Listen to them out there, they're not going to let him get away with this. They're all behind you, m'ijo. You spoke to them from your heart, and they heard the message in your words. You're their hero."

"Don't give me too much credit," I said. "I'm not a hero, I'm a terrible role model, and I hope nobody follows my example and starts something out there. And as far as my words are concerned, I wouldn't say I'm very good at that either. I'm in jail for attacking an officer of the law. I'm as stupid as they come. There I was, standing in front of our people, telling them it's time we stopped using violence to solve our problems, and then what do I do? I jump in and try to choke Munro."

"You saved the new sheriff's life," Dulceña reminded me.

"It's useless. I failed," I whispered. "I wanted to save Tomás, to make things right, for Mamá's sake, because I promised her I'd keep him safe, but I failed. I'm sorry, Dulceña. I'm sorry for not taking my own counsel and for letting everybody down."

"You're being too hard on yourself, Joaquín," Tomás said from the confines of his own cell. "I read what you wrote in the paper about me. You're a great writer, a great poet, and from what's come of it so far, you're a great orator too."

Dulceña reached up and caressed my cheek. "Tomás is right, Joaquín," she said. "The people are united now, and it's all because of you. You did this. Your words brought them together."

After Dulceña and her mother left, Tomás lay in his bed writing sermons, and I wrote a few poems while we waited for the wheels of justice to turn. A week later, after an exhausting series of long-distance telephone calls from the sheriff and our lawyer to their *new* friends at the capitol, Judge Thompson had no other choice than to have Tomás released. After all, the governor himself had read the papers, studied the case, and granted my brother a full pardon. As for me, my charges were dismissed after it was determined I had acted in defense of Sheriff Caceres.

When we were released, Tomás dropped to his knees and thanked the Lord out loud and crossed himself before he stood up and hugged me. The smile on his lips, the tears on his cheeks, the love in his eyes, these are the things I will never forget. Nor will I ever forget how hard Dulceña hugged me when she met us in front of the jailhouse. Her wet cheeks cooled my burning face as she clung to me and cried with happiness.

Excerpt from Joaquín's journal,
Saturday, September 18, 1915

EVOLUTION REVOLUTION

Let's start a revolution
evolution of the mind.
Put away your rifles,
wrap your riatas,
wind them tight.
Gather up your courage
don't let justice pass you by.
Let's start a revolution,
evolution's on its way.

Shake their trees, disturb
their nests. Don't be afraid
—rattle that cage.
It's time to start a revolution
evolution on the page.

Write your words in crimson,
brush them up
with beads of sweat.
Fly your words against
the clouds, let them rage,
let them age.

Drape them over streams
and rivers, toss them
quietly into springs.

Throw them up into the air,
make them spread
their brand-new wings.

Stand up. Speak up.
It's the only way to start
an evolution revolution—
thinking with your hearts.

Chapter 26

After we dropped Tomás off at the parish, Dulceña and I went back to Las Moras, where we set about the job of nursing Papá back to health. I won't say he made a full recovery. Sometimes, he would wake up crying because he'd dreamed of Mamá again. But those days were few and far between. Mostly, he concentrated on Las Moras and our new family. The sugarcane was finally harvested, more land was cleared for next year's crop, and the fence we'd once meant to put in the pasture finally got built.

Tomás and the Villas came to visit often. In the spring they started making noise about our future. "This house is too empty!" Papá said, as if he'd suddenly awakened from a foggy dream.

"Yes it is!" Doña Serafina said, reaching over and patting Dulceña's hand. "Perhaps someday soon, we might hear news of grandchildren."

"Grandchildren?" Dulceña blushed. Then, giggling, she added, "Why not. How many would you like?"

Don Rodrigo's eyes gleamed as he considered Dulceña's

question. “Lots of them. Lots and lots of them!” he said, lifting his coffee cup high up in the air in salute to the grand idea.

“Oh my!” Dulceña said, blushing brighter than before.

“I think you’re embarrassing our daughter,” Doña Serafina said, leaning over and kissing Dulceña’s temple affectionately.

Dulceña’s eyes glittered for a moment and then she said, “I think it’s time to go inside.”

“Yes, grandchildren will be forthcoming,” I said. “But Dulceña and I have decided to take care of our studies first. We hope you understand we have dreams to chase, careers to build, when things settle down.” Dulceña gave me a small hug and a chaste kiss on the cheek before she picked up her coffee cup, and we all went back into the main house for a quiet family dinner.

For months to come, Sheriff Caceres and other county officials went knocking on almost every door in Monteseco. They probed and prodded, shook our hands and nodded, and eventually things started to change. Some lawmen, mostly Rangers, were reprimanded. Judge Thompson was removed from office and run out of town, and vigilantism of any kind was no longer tolerated in Morado County.

Munro was investigated, prosecuted, and ultimately sent to prison in Huntsville. Some say he met up with inmates he’d helped put behind bars and finally got his comeuppance. I didn’t care to listen to los rumores, because, to be honest, I didn’t think too much about him after that. I was just glad he was out of our lives for good.

When election time came around, Miguel Caceres ran for office and officially became our sheriff. He might have been young, but his word was gold as far as the people of Morado County were concerned. Even though by the middle of 1916 the "uprising" in South Texas had begun to fade into history, the practices of the Rangers continued to come into question. Over the course of the next three years, more and more reports of their cruelty and abuse of power came to light, and the government saw it necessary to intervene and protect its citizens.

In 1919, the state legislature finally launched a full investigation. As a result, a handful of leaders were dismissed, several companies were disbanded, and the remaining members were held to much higher standards.

However, the matanza left in its wake a great amount of uncertainty for Mexicans and tejanos alike, as most of them worried that the racial tensions and prejudices brought about by the rebellion might forever mar the future for their children. They foresaw a long and difficult road before them and wondered if it was even possible to ever triumph over the challenges yet to come.

As for me, I couldn't help but feel blessed in those days. With the exception of my mother, I had everything I'd ever wanted. When I wasn't busy running the ranch, when I was alone with my thoughts, I wrote articles for *El Sureño*. It sustained my soul to see my words in print next to Dulceña's, clipped and pasted into Mamá's old scrapbook, adding to my mother's legacy.

It brought everything full circle for me to see that Mamá's living document now included my own words. Her death had devastated our lives for a time, but the ordeal had not killed our spirits. The loss of my mother had not erased the memories of her courage and love from our hearts, and *that* was the most important thing of all.

Excerpt from Joaquín's journal,
Wednesday, September 6, 1918

LEGACY

In the end, the sun rose,
and began its long march
across the cerulean sky.

Flowers opened their buds,
bloomed, and blossomed.
Baby goats bleated and stood
on wobbly new legs.

Golondrinas built nests
under sunny porch roofs.
La Gente woke up, worked,
ate and smiled again.

Merchants opened
their chiming doors.
Paperboys delivered
the daily news.

El Río Bravo surged
forth, moving along
the border—its song
a low, soft sob—its ebb
slow, moribund.

Author's Note

A few years ago, my eldest son, James, was taking a college history course. He was in his room one night, studying, when he suddenly burst into our living room holding a book and asking, "Mom! Do you know what happened to our people?"

I was sitting on the couch with my husband at the time. His family are Scotch-Irish American, so I looked at my husband, then back at my son, and asked, "Which people?" Well, he was talking about us, me and him and our side of the family. He held in his hands a copy of Benjamin Heber Johnson's book, *Revolution in Texas: How a Forgotten Rebellion and Its Bloody Suppression Turned Mexicans into Americans.* He sat on the couch that evening and showed me horrible pictures and shared terrible details while I flipped through the pages appalled by what happened to tejanos (Mexican Americans) and Mexicans in Southern Texas in 1915, at the time of the Mexican Revolution. These were things my father had talked about, but which had meant very little to me as a child, as I had never heard of them anywhere else other than at home when my father was "storytelling."

That day on the couch, I became the student as my son explained the discovery of the Plan de San Diego, a manifesto written in 1915 by Mexican radicals calling for the uprising of a "Liberating Army of Races and Peoples." The manifesto was brought into the United States through South Texas territory in January by Basilio Ramos and urged US-born Mexicans, immigrants, indigenous people, and Blacks to join the Mexican Revolution and help reclaim Texas, New Mexico, Arizona, California, and Colorado. The plan outlined a process in which Texas would become its own republic and later would seek annexation from Mexico. In February, less than a month later, a second copy of the manifesto would be discovered, and the lives of tejanos and Mexicans in South Texas would change forever.

The discovery of the Plan de San Diego came with many conflicts, most of which were fueled by political agendas. However, the human factor had much to do with the horrific crimes that were committed against tejanos and Mexicans in South Texas at that time. The racial tensions that had long existed in the region were heightened by local politics, misappropriated lands, and acts of rebellion, as more and more tejanos became disenfranchised. Losing their properties, farmlands, and ranches to the increasing number of Anglo immigrants, tejanos became field hands and peons in the very land their parents and grandparents had owned and cultivated for generations in the United States.

As tensions rose between tejanos and Anglos, more political and social issues came into play, and soon shoot-outs, explosions, and other, more violent, acts of insurgence from tejanos and Mexicans became the norm. The Texas Rangers, along with local authorities, tore through the territory enforcing vigilantism, their own brand of swift and lethal justice, in an attempt to enforce the law in South Texas. The lynchings, executions, fusillades, round-ups, and draggings of tejanos and Mexicans in South Texas only served to fuel the rebellion. The insurgence and its punishment became a vicious cycle that was too horrific to be spoken of, much less documented. Many of the crimes committed against tejanos and Mexicans in South Texas went unreported. Most have been forgotten.

No one can ever do justice to the retelling of the extent of the horrific atrocities committed during that time with complete accuracy and authenticity because so much of it was concealed, poorly recorded, or swept under the proverbial rug. Back then, nobody up above in the US justice system really cared what happened to tejanos and Mexicans on the borderlands. Nobody in Washington worried about us or our plight at the hands of the Texas Rangers. There were those of us who would speak for our people, tell of our woes. Reporters like Jovita Ituarte, aka A. V. Negra, who wrote for her father's paper, *La Cronica*, tried to illuminate the plight of tejanos and Mexicans in those times. However, her father's small paper, written in Spanish, at a time when only tejanos and Mexicans read Spanish-text circulars, went unread by those who might have made a difference, those whose jobs it was to protect us, those who chose to turn a blind eye to us in our small, ever-darkening corner of the world.

Suffice it to say, I went to my room that night, after listening to my son go on and on about the Plan de San Diego and what it means in the scope of American history, unable to get those pictures out of my mind. I wanted to inform myself, so I took Johnson's book with me to read in bed, but time and time again I kept turning back to the picture of Rangers dragging the bodies of alleged Mexican bandits through the brush. That such a picture would become a postcard that people bought and mailed to their loved ones is incomprehensible to me. All I can think when I see that picture is that those men and boys had mothers, and as a mother of three boys, my heart aches for the loss of them. I thought about the Texas Rangers' motto to shoot first and ask questions later if the person of interest was a Mexican, and I wept for all the mothers whose innocent sons were killed in the name of justice. I wept for all the brothers and sisters, all the tios and tias, the padrinos, the primos, the novias, the amigos, the vecinos . . . all the gente, the people, who suffered because of the discrimination and abuse of tejanos and Mexicans at the hands of the Texas Rangers and the lawmen who joined them and formed posses, killing indiscriminately, summarily, because the color of our skin dictated they could.

So why didn't I know this part of my culture's history? Well, a long, long time ago I was a small child, and like many a small child in America, I read textbooks that did not include these horrific events in American history. Why don't I know much more now after doing all this research? History books being published and printed for American schools today still make no mention of this part of our history. Perhaps textbook publishers find this topic too controversial. Or maybe they are just worried about what might happen if we educate ourselves with truthfulness. I can't begin to answer that question.

What I can do, I have done. I've included in this book a small ofrenda, a different point of view—a rebellious, contentious voice—along with a small sampling of source materials, both fiction and nonfiction, so that American students might be able to cull through them and better educate themselves. My hope is that students of any and all ethnicities and cultures will begin to understand the difference between primary and secondary sources, valid and unreliable sources, all of whose distinction they must learn to assess and categorize as they venture to study, appraise, and discover their ancestral identity and presence in historical documents in the minefield that is the Internet. May this book open up important and truthful conversations with teachers, family, and friends. May this book give them something to consider, something to research, something to push against when they encounter injustice. May this book help them pave the way to a better tomorrow.

SOME BOOK RECOMMENDATIONS FOR TEACHERS AND MENTORS

Anglos and Mexicans in the Making of Texas, 1836–1986 by David Montejano, University of Texas Press, 1987

From Out of the Shadows: Mexican Women in Twentieth-Century America by Vicki L. Ruiz, Oxford University Press, 2008

Revolution in Texas: How a Forgotten Rebellion and Its Bloody Suppression Turned Mexicans into Americans by Benjamin Heber Johnson, Yale University Press, 2005

River of Hope: Forging Identity and Nation in the Rio Grande Borderlands by Omar S. Valerio-Jiménez, Duke University Press Books, 2013

NEWSPAPER CLIPPING SOURCES

Chapter 1: **Nonfiction**: Excerpt from a handbill, "Plan de San Diego," 1915

Chapter 3: **Nonfiction**: "People of Southern Texas Fear Race War; Sleep Under Arms: Wild Scheme Backed by Ignorant Mexicans, Escaped Convicts and American Fugitives from Justice to Turn Texas Back to Mexican Control Responsible for Hostilities," *Burlington Weekly Free Press* (Burlington, VT), August 12, 1915, Page 1

Chapter 4: **Fictional news article**: "One Dead, Two Arrested at Morado Creek Sugar Mill," *El Sureño* (Monteseco, TX), August 20, 1915

Chapter 5: **Nonfiction**: *True Politeness: A Hand-Book of Etiquette for Ladies,* An American Lady, Leavitt and Allen, New York, NY 1847-1915

Chapter 8: **Nonfiction**: "Mexicans Killed by Texas Rangers: Several Outlaws Reported Slain in Fight Near Norias, Texas: Americans Are Reinforced," *The Ronan Pioneer* (Ronan, MT), August 13, 1915, Vol. VI, No. 16

Chapter 10: **Nonfiction**: "Modern Amazons of Mexico Keep

Armies Alive: Soldaderas Rustle the Grub for Fighters and Thereby Effect Gigantic Saving for Leaders," *The Sun* (New York, NY), March 14, 1915, Fourth Section Pictorial Magazine, Page 12

Chapter 13: **Nonfiction**: "Texas Rangers Would Invade Mexico to Recover Stolen Stock," *Honolulu Star-Bulletin* (Honolulu/Oahu, HI), October 25, 1915

Chapter 14: **Fictional news article**: "Rangers Left on Foot! Unknown Horse Thieves Make Off with the Herd," *El Sureño* (Monteseco, TX), September 3, 1915

Chapter 17: **Nonfiction**: "U.S. Troops in a Border Battle: Mexican Bandits Eleven Miles North of Brownsville, Texas Set Fire to Bridge," *The Ogden Standard* (Ogden, UT), September 2, 1915

Chapter 18: **Nonfiction**: "Raiding by Mexican Bandits Threatens," *Weekly Times-Record* (Valley City, ND), September 9, 1915, Page 11

Chapter 20: **Nonfiction**: "Trouble on Mexican Border Continues: Five Mexican Bandits and Woman Killed in Fight at Nonis Sunday," *The Intelligencer* (Anderson, SC), August 10, 1915, Page 1

Chapter 22: **Nonfiction**: "A Mexican to Hang: No Mercy

Shown Rodriguez, Death Penalty to Be Visited," *The Carlsbad Current* (Carlsbad, NM), November 26, 1915, Page 1

Chapter 24: **Fictional news article**: "Martyr of Las Moras to Hang!" *El Sureño* (Monteseco, TX), September 17, 1915

Chapter 25: **Nonfiction**: "Mob Tries to Free Mexican Priests: Two Thousand Storm National Palace in Effort to Rescue Imprisoned Men of the Cloth; Chief of Police Is Stabbed," *Omaha Daily Bee* (Omaha, NE), March 13, 1915, Page 1

Acknowledgments

FIRST, I WOULD LIKE TO ACKNOWLEDGE my family: my husband, Jim, and our children, James, Carelyn (our new daughter-in-law), Steven, and Jason, for being so very good to me. Their love and support of my art feeds my creative soul.

Thank you, Jim, for helping me research the "little things" on your phone and reading the many, many revisions this novel has undergone. You are so much more than a driver and escort on my writer's journey, you are the windmaster, the torchwielder, the shieldbearer in this adventure, always protecting me and keeping me strong, and I love you all the more for it. Thank you, James, for sharing your studies with me, for opening your heart and teaching me so much that evening on the couch. You are a great tutor and a light in my life. I am very proud of *your* accomplishments! Thank you, Carelyn, for loving us, all of us, the McCall clan, and for cooking Thanksgiving and Christmas dinners and putting up with our antics during the holidays. Your smiles bring joy to our hearts. Welcome to the family, cariño. Thank you, Steven and Jason, for being so supportive and enthusiastic and letting me go on and on about my work-in-progress. Your sweet, tender hearts inspire me to continue rowing this boat! I am very honored to be your mother.

Next, I have to absolutely thank Stacy Whitman, my editor and friend at Tu Books. Your patience and diligent care during the evolution of this manuscript as we moved toward publication has been so very kind and generous. I thank the heavens every day for the gift of you. Thank you for listening and questioning and reading and discussing and rereading and championing my beloved Joaquín! You are a blessing in my life, a bright star in my universe.

I would also like to thank my Southwest family, Dr. Verstuyft, Jan Perry, Michelle Guajardo, Antoinette Richardson, Cynthia Trejo, Miquela Ovalle, and the rest of the energetic, fabulous teachers at SWHS who are my secondary support system, as well as the rest of my readers and fans, those who continue to cheer me on from far and wide. Thank you for always believing in me and for extending your friendship beyond the classroom. I carry you in my heart! Special thanks to Dr. David Bowles at the University of Texas Rio Grande Valley for reading the first draft of this novel when it was young and innocent and quiet, and for giving me constructive feedback on it. Your attention to detail, specifically historical detail, saved me a few embarrassing moments. I owe you a solid. I'll have to get you a brand new gaucho hat for Christmas!

Glossary

abuelito (ah-bweh-LEE-to): grandfather

A dónde (ah-DON-deh): where or where to

almuerzo (ahl-moo-EHR-so): midmorning meal or lunch

atole (ah-TO-leh): porridge

atrevido (ah-treh-VEE-do): a very daring person

ay (aye): oh

¡Ay, Dios mío! (aye dee-OS MEE-o): Oh my God!

baile (BAH-ee-leh): dance

banderita (bahn-deh-REE-tah): little flag

calaca (kah-LAH-kah): skull

cálmate (KAHL-mah-teh): calm down

campesino (kahm-peh-SEE-no): field worker

campo (KAHM-po): woods or woodland

canalla (kah-NAH-yah): riffraff, bum, traitor

Capilla del Sagrado Corazón (kah-PEE-yah dehl sah-GRAH-do ko-rah-SON): temple of the sacred heart

capirotada (kah-pee-ro-TAH-dah): Mexican bread pudding made with nuts, sugar, spices, and cheeses

cariño (kah-REE-nyo): sweetheart, beloved

cascarón (kahs-kah-RON): confetti-filled Easter egg

chaparral (chah-pah-RRAHL): thicket

chicharras (chee-CHAH-rrahs): cicadas

chiquita (chee-KEE-tah): little one, female

chongo (CHON-go): chignon, twist, bun

cochinilla (ko-chee-NEE-yah): pill bug

Colonia Calaveras (ko-LO-nee-ah kah-lah-VEH-rahs): a fictitious impoverished neighborhood on the outskirts of fictitious Monteseco

comadre (ko-MAH-dreh): female friend

como Adán (ko-mo ah-DAHN): like Adam, Biblical allusion

como halcón (ko-mo ahl-CON): like a hawk

como mula (ko-mo MOO-lah): like a mule

como prostitutas (ko-mo pros-tee-TOO-tah): like prostitutes

como salvajes (ko-mo sahl-VAH-jehs): like savages

¡Cómo te extraño! (KO-mo teh ehx-TRAH-gno): How I miss you!

como tlacuaches enmañados (ko-mo tlah-KWAH-chehs ehn-man-NYA-dos): like nefarious possums

compadre (kom-PAH-dreh): male friend

compañeros (kom-pah-NYEH-ros): friends

compórtate (kom-POR-tah-teh): behave

conjunto (kon-HOON-toh): a small musical ensemble of usually four members who play traditional norteño or tejano music

corazón (ko-rah-SON): sweetheart

corrido (ko-REE-do): ballad

¡Cucui! (koo-KOO-ee): Boo!

cuetes (koo-EH-tehs): fireworks

demonios (deh-MO-nee-os): devils

demonios tejanos (deh-MO-nee-os te-HAH-nos): Texas Devils, derogatory term for Texas Rangers

desayuno (deh-sah-YOO-no): breakfast

¡Desgraciados! (dehs-grah-see-AH-dos): Miserable wretches!

El Sureño (ehl soo-REH-nyo): fictitious newspaper printed in fictitious Monteseco, translates to "The Southerner"

en los Estados Unidos (ehn los ehs-TAH-dos oo-NEE-dos): in the United States

¡Eres mi alma—mi corazón! (EH-rehs mee AHL-ma, mee ko-rah-SON): You are my soul—my heart!

estamos enlazados (ehs-TAH-mos ehn-lah-SAH-dos): our hearts are tethered

estafadora de amores (ehs-tah-fah-DO-rah deh ah-MO-rehs): swindler of loves

estrella/estrellita (ehs-TREH-yah/ehs-treh-YEE-tah): star/little star

¿Es tu culpa? (ehs too COOL-pah): Is this your fault?

familia (fah-MEE-lee-ah): family

favorcito (fah-vor-SEE-to): little favor

gente (JEHN-teh): people

gracias a Dios (GRAH-see-ahs ah dee-OS): thank God

guelito (weh-LEE-to): grandfather

hasta mañana (AHS-tah mah-NYA-nah): see you tomorrow

hermano/hermanito (ehr-MAH-no/ehr-mah-NEE-to): brother/little brother

hija (EE-hah): daughter

hija mía (EE-hah MEE-ah): my daughter

¡Hijo de Satanás! (EE-ho deh sah-tah-NAHS): Son of Satan!

hola (O-lah): hello

jacalitos (hah-kah-LEE-tos): huts

jefe (HEH-feh): boss

Kineño (kee-NEH-nyo): the King men, field hands working at the King Ranch in South Texas in the early 1900s

La Calaca (lah kah-LAH-kah): feminine form of the Angel of Death, also known as La Santa Muerte (Saint Death) and La Santísima (the Most Saint)

la cuerda (lah coo-EHR-dah): the rope

ladrona de alientos (lah-DRO-nah deh ah-lee-EHN-tos): breath thief

La Nochebuena (lah no-cheh-boo-EH-nah): Christmas Eve

lechuzas (leh-CHOO-sahs): barn owls, folktale witches

lentejuelas (lehn-teh-hoo-EH-lahs): sequins

Los Matadores (los mah-tah-DO-rehs): fictitious tejano rebel gang

Los Sediciosos (los seh-dee-see-O-sos): infamous Texas gang of bandits led by Aniceto Pizaña and Luis de la Rosa during the rebellion of 1915

mal aire (mahl AY-reh): evil air

maldiciones (mahl-dee-see-O-nehs): curse words

máscaras (MAHS-kah-rahs): masks

matanza (mah-TAHN-sah): slaughter

mejicano (meh-hee-KAH-no): Mexican

mi amor (mee ah-MOR): my beloved

m'ija/m'ijo (MEE-hah/MEE-ho): contractions of my daughter/my son

mochila (mo-CHEE-lah): saddlebag, bag

monte (MON-teh): woodland

muchacho (moo-CHAH-cho): young man

mujer/mujeres (moo-JEHR/moo-JEH-rehs): woman/women

músicos (MOO-see-kos): musicians

negrita (neh-GREE-tah): young black girl

niños (NEE-nyos): little boys

ojitos (o-HEE-tos): making eye contact, flirting

padrecito (pah-dreh-SEE-to): priest (the *-ito* denotes a loving tone)

pan dulce (pahn DOOL-seh): Mexican sweet bread

pásenle a lo recogido (PAH-sehn-leh ah lo reh-ko-HEE-do): come in, to the clean part of the house

patrón (pah-TRON): boss

pañuelo (pah-nyoo-EH-lo): handkerchief

pelados (peh-LAH-dos): scoundrels, rogues

piedra (pee-EH-drah): stone

plumas (PLOO-mahs): feathers

políticos (po-LEE-tee-kos): politicians

por favor (por fah-VOR): please

¡Por favor, no te olvides de mí! (por fah-VOR no teh ol-VEE-dehs deh mee): Please, don't forget me!

potrillos (po-TREE-yos): colts

pozole (po-SO-leh): a soup made with pork, hominy, red chiles, and spices

pulque (POOL-keh): a fermented alcoholic drink made from the maguey cactus

¿Qué pasa? (keh PAH-sah): What's going on?

quinceañera (keen-seh-ah-NYEH-rah): a coming-out party for a girl's fifteenth birthday celebrating her transition from girl to young lady

rancho (RAHN-cho): ranch

ranchero (rahn-CHEH-ro): rancher

recámara (reh-KAH-mah-rah): bedroom

remuda (reh-MOO-dah): slang for herd of horses

revolución (reh-vo-loo-see-ON): revolution

rumores (roo-MO-rehs): rumors

sala (SAH-lah): living room

sediciosos (seh-dee-see-O-sos): seditious men, rebels; Los Sediciosos was the name of a prominent, well-known rebel gang in South Texas at the time of the Mexican Revolution

señorita (seh-nyo-REE-tah): young lady

sí (see): yes

siéntense (see-EHN-tehn-seh): sit down

sirena (see-REH-nah): siren, seductress

socorro (so-KO-rro): help

soldadera (sol-dah-DEH-rah): female soldier

soldados (sol-DAH-dos): soldiers

sospechosos (sos-peh-CHO-sos): suspicious men

también (tahm-bee-EHN): also

te amo (teh AH-mo): I love you

tejano (teh-HAH-no): Texan

Tejas (TEH-hahs): Texas

¡Tengo miedo de perderte! (tehn-go mee-EH-do deh pehr-DEHR-teh): I'm afraid to lose you!

Tierra y libertad (tee-EH-rah ee lee-bear-TAHD): Land and liberty

tlacuache (tlah-KWAH-cheh): possum

trenzas (TREHN-sahs): braids

trueno (throo-EH-no): thunder

una carta (OO-nah KAHR-tah): a letter

una señorita de familia decente (OO-nah seh-nyo-REE-tah deh fah-MEE-lee-ah deh-SEHN-teh): a young lady from a decent family

un Jesucristo moreno (OON heh-soo-KREES-toh mo-REH-no): a brown Jesus Christ

vacas (VAH-kahs): cows

vámonos (VAH-mo-nos): let's go

velorio (veh-LO-ree-o): viewing

¡Venganza! (ven-GAN-sa): Vengeance!

verdad (vehr-DAHD): true

¡Viva la Independencia! (VEE-vah la in-deh-pen-DEN-see-ah): Long live Independence!

zarape (sah-RAH-peh): serape, a colorful shawl worn especially by men

zopilotes (so-pee-LO-tehs): buzzards